ALL THE MAJOR CONSTELLATIONS

ALL THE MAJOR
CONSTELLATIONS

A NOVEL

PRATIMA CRANSE

VIKING

VIKING
An imprint of Penguin Random House LLC
375 Hudson Street
New York, New York 10014

First published in the United States of America by Viking,
an imprint of Penguin Random House LLC, 2015

LIBRARY OF CONGRESS CATALOGING-IN-PUBLICATION DATA
Cranse, Pratima, date–
All the major constellations / Pratima Cranse.
pages cm
ISBN 978-0-670-01645-7 (hardcover)
[1. Coma—Fiction. 2. Friendship—Fiction. 3. Christian life—Fiction.] I. Title.
PZ7.1.C73Al 2015
[Fic]—dc23
2014044806

Printed in the USA

10   9   8   7   6   5   4   3   2   1

For My Parents

eden

two or three times i've stood under

you

this window of yours is so

incredibly

painfully

blue

and you never come out or show

me

(past this infinite garden of regrets)

your face

—WALEAD ESMAIL

ALL THE MAJOR CONSTELLATIONS

1

HE STOOD AT THE TOP of the stairs and listened.

A single note.

A vibrational pull.

A silk string.

Laura.

"Jeeeesus, Jesus saves. He saves . . . *me*," she sang. And then the single note returned, a wordless *mmmm*. Like the sound you make when you're kissing someone, or pretending to kiss someone when you're actually just pressing your face into your pillow.

Laura.

Their eyes had met in the hallway that morning. She had blinked at him, slowly, like a cat. Hadn't she? What did it mean? Maybe she'd merely been blinking because people constantly blink, and time had slowed down when their eyes met. Laura's almond-shaped eyes were dark blue and beautiful, but it was their expression that most intrigued him: unreadable. Her long hair was the lightest shade of amber, like custard under burnt brown sugar. She looked like a doll, a Disney princess, a Greek statue, a goddess.

"They shouldn't be doing that. Church and state, right?"

"Who cares?"

Andrew glanced toward the voices and saw two girls from the junior class. They looked like preppie high-achievers. One of them smiled up at him and tossed her hair over her shoulders. He returned her smile but then looked away. The sound of their retreating giggles echoed down the hall. A piece of paper slipped from the wall and drifted down to his feet. He picked it up and studied it. An Uncle Sam–like caricature pointed at him with a stern accusation: *Class of '95! Have YOU ordered your GRADUATION gown?* His graduation. Then summer, then college. This was it.

"Fuck it," Andrew said, and he squared his shoulders and marched in the direction of the singing.

The hallway was quiet, except for the low hum of voices coming from the girls' bathroom. It was ridiculous, church and state aside, to sing about Jesus in a high school bathroom. And yet that was exactly what Laura and her friends—the girls, anyway—did almost every afternoon. Their free periods must have lined up. Or maybe some of them snuck out of class or got passes just to join in a song or two. Everyone knew about it, including the teachers. But they were harmless, and the singing was nice, so no one bothered much about it. It was Vermont, after all. People were pretty laid-back about stuff.

Laura was deeply religious, some fundamentalist something or other. Andrew wasn't quite sure. She kept to herself and her crowd of Christian fellows. They were a mild and nice bunch of kids who went to church together, hung out together, and sometimes, he suspected, quietly dated one another. They had an after-school club with an open invitation for new members. How many times had Andrew walked past the door of their gatherings, eyes fixed on the ground, headphones jammed in his ears, hands shaking in his pockets? More times than he liked to recall.

Her devotion to her faith made her practically inaccessible. Infatuated as he was, Andrew was smart enough to understand that Laura's untouchable quality was part of her appeal, her mass appeal. He was well aware that he was one among the many boys who loved her. At best, a lovesick army; at worst, a horny horde. There were boys who bulked up their muscles because of her, became better students because of her, cultivated sexy sneers and reckless rebellion in case that was her thing. *It's not, obviously,* Andrew thought with contempt for his rivals.

The singing grew louder, more impassioned. Andrew wondered, *Why the bathroom? Privacy? Refuge?* Or perhaps it was just because the acoustics of the tiled walls made their voices sound better.

"Hey, you," Sara said.

"What's up?" Andrew said, taken aback. "I thought you had gym."

"Class canceled. Mrs. Calin went home sick."

"No sub?"

"What can I say? End-of-the-year madness. Marcia scurried off to the library before I could stop her."

"Poor Mar," he said.

"Are you coming over today? She wants to practice her valedictory speech on us."

"Nah. I got work."

"Avella already?" Sara said.

"Busy this year. We're making a pond or some shit."

"*Making* a pond? What are you, God?"

"And on Thursday, He made a pond for the pharmaceutical company," he said in a deep, portentous voice.

"And it was good," Sara said with equal solemnity.

They laughed.

"Speaking of which, you here for the show?" Sara said as she glanced at the bathroom. She gave him a sly smile.

"Uh, no. Just wandering around," Andrew said. He could feel himself blushing.

"I love to go in there to get tampons when they're at it. I wish there was a condom machine. *That* would be hilarious."

"Indeed."

They started walking in the opposite direction, toward the lockers, and Andrew glanced behind him. The bathroom door swung open as someone went in, and Andrew thought perhaps he caught a glimpse . . . but he turned away. *Don't be a perv,* he thought.

"Are they weird?" he asked.

"Who?"

"The Christians."

"That's a loaded question," Sara said. "No, they're fine. They'll even stop singing if you ask. And hardly anyone uses that bathroom because the one on the second floor is nicer."

"But you use it."

"Well, yeah, but I like to mess with people."

"Please," Andrew said.

"You sure you're not checking out Laura? Hell, even I think she's a piece of ass," Sara said, and nudged his shoulder.

"Cute, sure," Andrew said. He tried to look disinterested. He did not want to be teased about his pathetic unrequited crush. It just seemed so typical, so high school. He had tried hard to hide his obsession from Sara and Marcia, his two best, and only, friends.

"Come on, you can tell me anything," she said.

"Okay, you have something in your teeth," he said.

"Bullshit!" she said. But she started rubbing her teeth vigorously with her finger.

"And you have something right there," he said, tickling her stomach. "And there," he said, aiming for her armpit but accidentally grazing her breast. He started to apologize, but she dissolved into laughter as she grabbed his hands.

They were still wrestling around when Kyle Donovitch walked up to them and said loudly, "Hey, Sara. 'Sup?"

"Nothing," Sara said. Andrew and Kyle nodded to each other. Sara started sifting through one of her notebooks, not looking up. Kyle watched her for a moment, tossing a baseball back and forth in his hands. Kyle was team captain of everything, it seemed, and was good-looking and popular. Andrew didn't know him that well. Sara had become engrossed with her history notes, so Kyle turned his attention to Andrew.

"How's Brian?" he asked.

"Fine," Andrew said.

"Hell of a season for him."

"Sure, yeah."

"Been down there at all?"

"Nope."

"Oh."

An awkward silence followed this exchange. Sara continued to flip through her notes. Kyle cleared his throat.

"Busy this weekend, Sara?"

"Yup," Sara said, and snapped her notebook shut. "Sorry." She slipped her arm through Andrew's, and they walked away.

"What was that about?" Andrew asked.

"What's it ever about? Old news."

Andrew looked at her sharply, but she seemed, as usual, careless and carefree.

"Besides," she said, "who gives a shit about shitty Brian?"

"Only everyone."

"Except *us*," she said, and squeezed his arm tightly to her side.

2

"I'M STARVED," ANDREW SAID.

"So let's get Marcia and go to lunch."

They went to the library and threw things at Marcia, little bits of fluff and crumpled-up pieces of paper, until the librarian shooed all three of them out.

"Thanks a lot," Marcia griped as they walked to the cafeteria.

"You're going to ace all your exams anyway," Sara said. "Like always."

"Seriously, you study too much," Andrew said.

"I do not," Marcia said.

"You make yourself sick with anxiety," he said.

"Chance favors the prepared mind," Marcia said.

"Chance is just 'chance' by definition," he said.

"That's a facile argument," Marcia said.

"Whatever," he said.

They got in line at the cafeteria. Andrew got a cold deli sandwich, Sara a burger and fries, and Marcia a salad.

"And you always say 'whatever' when you know I'm right. I *hate* that comeback. It's not even a real response," Marcia said once they were seated.

"It's the perfect response. It dismisses the speaker. It dismisses the whole argument. If you don't care, you can't lose."

"It's mean and sarcastic. It's a cheap way to step back and refuse to engage."

Marcia half stood up as she spoke, closing her little hands into fists as if readying herself to pound on the cafeteria table. A few kids sitting near them giggled. Andrew glared at them before he continued. "But isn't that what being a teenager is all about? The privilege of not giving a shit?"

"So that's victory? To *not* care, to *not* be invested?"

"A pyrrhic victory, for sure, but still a win."

"Now you're just screwing around, which is a lesser form of sarcasm."

"Or a higher form."

"Come on, knock it off," Sara said.

Sara disliked it when Andrew and Marcia argued, especially when they threw around words like *facile* and *pyrrhic*. Marcia was the valedictorian, Andrew an effortless and lazy B student, but Sara had to work hard to maintain her own B average.

"Can I have some of your fries?" Andrew said.

"Go ahead," Sara said.

"Do you have any salt?"

Sara dug around her tray and found a mini salt packet. She tossed it to him.

"So, how's the speech coming?" Sara asked.

Marcia waved her hand in response.

"Don't ask," Andrew said.

"Don't you have to turn that thing in, like, tomorrow?" Sara said.

"Technically. But graduation is still two—no, shit, a little over a week away," Marcia said. She began chewing on her fingernails.

"Marcia, chill," Andrew said. He placed his hand over her torn cuticles.

"Easy for you to say. You're not the one—"

"Just thank everyone ever and get out of there," Sara said.

"Or pass out kazoos and lead the audience in a round of 'Pomp and Circumstance,'" Andrew said.

"Or flash your bra—"

"Or your panties—"

"Or give the speech in Korean with, like, no explanation."

"Or declare your undying allegiance to some obscure band."

"And then drop the mic."

"The possibilities are endless!"

Marcia finally laughed. "I'll run it by Mr. Gonzalez tomorrow," she said.

"Good plan. He's cool," said Sara.

Marcia frowned as she pulled the sprouts off her salad. Then she left to get some milk. Andrew made a stick figure out of Sara's fries. He drew a face with ketchup and decorated it with curly sprout hair.

"That your girlfriend?" Sara asked.

"My dream girl."

Sara smirked at this, then took the fry girl's torso and popped it into her mouth. Marcia returned with three chocolate milks and three straws.

"Thank you," Andrew said as he reached for one of the milks. Marcia liked surprising them with little treats every once in a while. Chocolate milk never failed to delight.

"Oh, Marcia. You're a peach," said Sara. She tore the wrapping off the straw with her teeth and blew it gently. The headless tube drifted down across the table and out of sight. "Andrew's making a pond at Avella. We should break in and go night swimming," she said.

"Break in to Avella? We'll get shot," Marcia said.

"I'm sure Andrew has an in," Sara said.

"I have no in," Andrew said.

"No big jangling set of keys?" Sara asked.

"Why would you want to go swimming in a man-made pond anyway?" Marcia asked.

"Even if it is nighttime," Andrew added.

"Oh, I don't know. I just thought it would be something silly and fun to do during our last summer together."

"Oh," Marcia said. They finished their lunch in silence. The din in the cafeteria grew quieter as kids left for their classes. Marcia began packing up her bag.

"Wait for me, okay?" Sara said.

Marcia liked arriving early to her classes. She had a little routine of setting up her desk, sharpening her pencils, and even checking her pens for ink. Sara preferred drifting in just under the wire.

"She likes making an entrance," Marcia had once complained to Andrew, but Andrew knew better. Sara, with her curly blonde hair and phenomenal body, was one of the prettier girls in their school. She generally made an entrance whether she intended to or not. Her wanting to go in late was actually an attempt to break Marcia away from her spastic little habits.

"Sara, let's go. I don't want to be late," Marcia said.

"All right, all right." Sara put their leftover food and wrappers on her tray and grabbed her bag.

"I got that," Andrew said, reaching for the tray.

"Thanks," the girls murmured as they got up.

Andrew watched them as they left for class. Marcia had a focused walk. Her steps were brittle and nervous compared to Sara's loose and graceful stride. He and Marcia were smarty bookworm types with fucked-up families. They found solace in each other's loneliness and awkwardness. Sara was different; there was nothing awkward about her. She was vivacious and confident. Her mom was working-class and single, so Sara never quite fit in with the popular crowd, which tended to be preppie and sporty and well-to-do. She took great pleasure in the fact that the guys who used to make fun of her secondhand clothes now pined after her first-rate looks. She dated a lot, fooled around a little, but her heart was untouched.

Sara had befriended Marcia freshman year after defending her against the type of people that bullies harmless nerds, and then the three of them became almost inseparable. Their little triad was disturbingly like a family, Andrew mused. He and Sara hovered protectively over Marcia, who was practically parentless, Andrew was like a brother figure to both, and Sara was instinctually mothering. Andrew had never sought friendships beyond the trio, nor had they. They were a self-contained unit, the only members of a gang of three, and they needed no one else. In a few short months they'd go in separate directions. It was hard to comprehend the idea of life without them always near. At the same time, a small part of him was looking forward to something new.

He turned his attention back to the tray of trash. It was his free period, which meant he could do one of three things. He could report to the library, aimlessly wander the halls, or continue to stare at the garbage in front of him.

Or he could go ahead and keep stalking Laura Lettel.

3

A WALL OF WATER APPROACHED him, a vertical ocean that threatened to engulf and crush him beneath waves and waves of moving weight. He was in such a panic that when he woke up, he knocked his bedside lamp to the floor. Becky bolted up and started barking.

"Shh," he said.

Becky quieted down, but she remained alert, standing at the foot of his bed. He listened to her pant. Or was that him? Yes, *he* was panting like a dog and quivering like a child. Her bark had oriented him, at least.

I'm in my bedroom.

It's nighttime.

I just had that fucking ocean dream again.

He glanced at his alarm clock. It was two in the morning.

He thought again of that moving wall of water. The dream had felt apocalyptic and inevitable. Those feelings lingered with him now, even as he calmed down and steadied his breathing. He listened for his parents. He heard nothing.

A little moonlight came in through his window. The lamp, a sturdy plastic thing, was unbroken. He placed it back on the table and turned it on. Becky blinked at him. He'd had some kind of night terror, he realized, because his sheets and blanket were half across the room. How had Becky stayed on the bed? He reached over to pet her. She stretched and yawned beneath his hands. Then she jumped up and started wagging her tail.

"Two in the morning, Becks, not time for a walk."

Becky whined.

Andrew sighed and got out of bed. His back ached from digging at Avella for three hours after school. All twenty men on the maintenance crew, the regulars and the summer hires like him, had been tasked with shoveling dirt for the pond. They couldn't use the excavator because the suits complained that the noise disrupted their meetings. He groaned as he bent over to put on his sneakers.

He opened his bedroom door. There was only silence and darkness in the hallway. Apparently his parents had not been awoken by the lamp falling to the floor or his thrashing around in bed. Or more likely, he had woken them up, his mother at least, but she'd probably just turned over and gone back to sleep.

He and Becky slipped out the back door and walked up the street. It was colder than he'd expected. Late May in Vermont could still be frigid at night.

He wondered if he shouted during these nightmares, which had been with him since he was a kid. He was almost eighteen, and he still had dreams that were bad enough to wake him up. It made him feel foolish. When he sheepishly admitted his problem to his friends, Marcia had suggested he keep a dream journal, and Sara had told him to jerk off before going to sleep. That, or get a girlfriend.

The first two were easy, but the last was impossible. There was only one girl Andrew really wanted.

Laura lived in his neighborhood, which was a source of both pleasure and pain for him, as he frequently walked his dog past her house. It was nice to be near her, however remote the possibility of an actual connection.

He gazed at her house as he stamped his feet and rubbed his arms to ward off the chill.

Laura.

Andrew's proposed dream journal had quickly become a Laura journal. It was filled with pictures of her, poems about her, but mostly unsent letters to her.

> *Laura,*
> *I feel like I can smell your hair around the*
> *school, around our neighborhood. It's like I'm*

*always just missing you. I never know where you
are, but I know where you've been. I love you, but
you haunt me like a nightmare. When I'm an old
man, I know that I'll still dream about you.*

He knew the memory of her would haunt him, because he didn't really believe he'd ever get to have her in the first place. But the knowledge of his inevitable doom didn't stop him from obsessing over her. He entertained himself daily with dozens of scorching, crazy, lurid fantasies, imagining a Laura who most certainly did not exist. Other times he daydreamed about some idyllic future together. He knew she was going to college somewhere out West. They'd get together this summer, fall in love, he'd transfer to whatever school she was attending, maybe even study the same stuff, take the same classes. They'd live in each other's dorm rooms, or get an apartment together. They'd probably have to get married first because of her religion. That was all right; he'd marry her tomorrow if he could. Their life together would be wonderful. Would he have to convert to whatever sect of Christianity she belonged to? That was the only question mark in his fleeting fantasies.

Sometimes he wondered why he loved her so much. After all, he barely knew her. But she was kind, that much he knew, because she did volunteer work and was nice to everyone, even the most decrepit and socially outcast misfits at their school. And she had some self-contained confidence, some inner glow unrelated to her beauty that made her mysterious and compelling. Was it her faith?

Laura.

She was asleep inside that little house. Andrew felt attuned to her every toss and turn. He thought that he might wake her with the force of his will or summon her to him with the strength of his love. He stared hard at her house and at the window that he imagined to be hers.

"What the hell am I doing?" he asked himself out loud.

A light came on. Andrew felt a painful rush in his heart.

There was a slight movement. A shadow flickered across the window frame, and the curtains fluttered. He did not blink.

The coherent part of him knew that in a moment the light would go out. The other him, the one whispering to himself in the dark, held out for better things. *She'll come to the door. She'll open the door. Our eyes will meet, and it will be like the movies where neither of us has to say anything, but whole histories and lifetimes will pass between us. It'll be like that but better. . . .*

The light went out.

With fury, he wiped at the tears that ran down his cheeks. He felt romantic despair, but also he just felt fucking cold. He was dying of cold. He was ashamed of not being a stronger person who could somehow withstand cold and disappointment. He turned around and walked home, jogging and then sprinting the last few blocks to his house. Becky followed, fast on his heels.

When he got inside, he sank to the kitchen floor. He buried his hands deep inside Becky's fur while she licked his face. They stayed that way for a while. Becky was a big dog, a black Lab mixed with some other large breed. She stood strong and solid and still as Andrew leaned against her.

"Where were you?"

Andrew looked up at his mother. She wore her old purple robe and a pair of tiny slippers, small and pink like those of a ballerina. Under her slippers she had on a pair of gray wool socks. The seams of the slippers were permanently overstretched from this arrangement. She was thin and tall like him, her younger son. They shared the same coloring too, a sort of peachy paleness and hazel gray eyes.

"Going for a walk. Becky had to pee," Andrew said.

"It's two thirty in the morning."

"I know, I know," he said. He looked away from her.

"You're not . . . You're not on drugs or something, right?"

"What? No."

"Well, then, where were you?"

"I just told you," he said. "What, were you actually worried?" he added.

She crossed her arms over her chest and glared at the floor. He regretted his words, but just barely. His mom had chosen sides a long time ago. He stood up and headed for the stairs.

"Your brother's home in two weeks," she said.

He stopped. "So?" he asked, without turning around.

"He's coming home, that's all," she said. Her voice was vague and soft, as though she had spoken through a pillow.

"Whatever," Andrew said.

When he reached his room, Becky leaped around, grabbed one of his socks in her mouth, and curled into a tight ball. Andrew felt himself deflate. Two weeks. Two weeks before Brian came home and took over. Andrew and Brian barely spoke at this point, but Brian's presence was like a poisonous fog: suffocating and unavoidable.

Andrew got into bed and pulled the covers around him tightly. As he warmed up, his body hurt all over with tingly, prickly sensations. Were these his nerves coming back to life? Had they been frozen? *Marcia will know*, he thought. *Marcia knows everything*.

4

"IT'S YOUR BLOOD."

"Really?"

"Yeah. Your blood rushes back to your extremities once you're in a warmer environment."

"Where's it been? What's it rushing back from?"

"From protecting your vital organs. Once you're safe, back under shelter, so to speak, your blood redistributes and causes that painful tingling."

"Cool."

Marcia was editing her valedictory speech and talking to him at the same time. First drafts, second drafts, index cards, pencils, pens, and highlighters were strewn across the desk—Sara's desk actually, but at this point it belonged to Marcia. Marcia and Sara more or less lived at each other's houses. They had been holing up in Sara's room together every day after school for years, with Andrew frequently dropping by to join them or smoke pot or watch TV. It was Friday night, one week from graduation, and Marcia had yet to complete her speech.

"Why were you wandering around in the middle of the night, anyway?" Marcia asked.

"I'm a vampire, baby," he said. She snorted in response.

"Someone come hang out with me. I'm bored!" Sara shouted from the bathroom, where she had just showered and was shaving her legs. Andrew and Marcia rolled their eyes at each other before Andrew got up and walked down the hallway. He knocked on the half-open bathroom door.

"You decent?" he asked.

"Oh, please," Sara said. He walked inside.

Sara was messy with a razor. Her right leg was propped on top of the bathroom sink and covered with uneven globs of strawberry-scented shaving cream. She shaved her legs carelessly and fast. If her shapely limbs suffered only one or two nicks, she considered herself lucky.

"Careful," he said. He closed the toilet seat and sat down.

"Got something for you," she said, gesturing toward a magazine that lay on the counter. Andrew picked it up and flipped through it. It was a porn magazine and looked to be about twenty years old.

"Chicks were hairy back then," he said.

"Still are," Sara said. "The fucking upkeep is brutal."

"Where did you get this thing?" Andrew asked.

"Attic. It was in a box labeled DIRK'S STUFF." Sara ran the razor under the water and readjusted the towel that was wrapped around her chest. Sara had never met Dirk, her father, so in a way it made sense that she didn't get upset when the subject was brought up.

"I wouldn't think your mom was the type to keep an old boyfriend's back issues of *Barely Legal*," Andrew said.

"You never really know your parents."

"Or anyone else."

"So true," she said. With a washcloth she wiped down one leg and proceeded on to the next. The shaving cream made a horrid squishy sound as Sara sprayed it on her legs. She frowned, shook the can vigorously, and sprayed again. Andrew grimaced. He sometimes resented how casual Sara could be in front of him. *We may be friends,* he thought, *but I'm still a dude.*

"This is kind of grossing me out," Andrew said.

"That's why I brought the magazine for you," she said.

"Give me a break," he said.

Sara laughed. He watched as she ran the blade up her leg. The white of her thighs flashed beneath her towel. She followed his gaze.

"What's up?" she said softly.

He thought of Laura. "Nothing." He looked at the floor when he spoke, then looked back up at her and smiled. She nodded.

"So, UVM?" she said. Both he and Sara had been accepted to

the University of Vermont. Marcia would be attending Stanford and was already enrolled in the premed program.

"Yeah, yeah," he said. With a sigh, he folded up the magazine and slapped it against his knee.

"At least we'll be close," she said. "After my trip," she added. Sara had vague plans to take a year off before college and bum around abroad on a Europass.

"I know. I just—"

"Didn't want to be so close to home," she said, finishing his thought.

"I could join Brian in Georgia. You know, be a superfan, go to all his games," Andrew said with a forced laugh. Sara reached down and pushed back the flop of bangs that fell over his eyes.

"You need a haircut," she said. She tucked the hair behind his ear and turned back to the sink.

"I'll be in the living room." He stood up.

"*Alone* in the living room with a dirty magazine?" she said with an impish grin that Andrew knew drove other boys mad. Him, too, a little bit.

"Don't worry. I'm leaving the porn here. It's not my thing anyway," he said. Andrew thought about Brian's collection of porn under the floorboards of his old bedroom, which Andrew occasionally pilfered. But he wasn't lying to Sara; porn made him excited in a nauseated kind of way, and the satisfaction it provided was empty.

"Come on, hang out with me. I'm almost finished," Sara said.

She began to hurry even more. Andrew flinched, thinking about the little micro cuts she was giving herself. Sara liked constant company. She became quite petulant when left alone for too long.

"I'm going to check on Marcia."

"Leave her alone," Sara singsonged back to him.

"She's going to make herself crazy," Andrew said. He put his hand on the doorknob.

"I'm telling you: don't bother her," Sara said. She examined a trickle of blood as it slid down her shin.

"You need a Band-Aid?"

"Nah," she said.

From the bedroom they heard Marcia curse in German, a habit from her childhood abroad.

"Uh-oh, she's speaking in tongues. Maybe you *should* go check on her." She stood up straight, and her brow wrinkled with concern.

Andrew walked out the door, careful to close it behind him. He felt a sudden chill out in the hallway. It *had* been stuffy in the bathroom, but also warm and cozy, with the steam of the shower and his pretty, half-naked friend perched like a bird of paradise on the sink. A bleeding bird of paradise.

Sometimes he thought Sara was challenging him to get an erection when she pranced and chatted, half naked, in front of him. Would she do anything about it? Did he want that? Of course he wanted it—sort of. Sara could sometimes be a little *too* flirty. Or confusingly flirty.

He walked down the hallway and opened the bedroom door a crack. Marcia still sat at the desk with her back to him. She was scribbling and muttering at the same time. Andrew crept up close to her, peered over her shoulder, and read what she had written.

When my father was killed

After my father died

My father was a surgeon, and I've always felt a strong desire to follow in his footsteps. My best friends, Andrew and Sara, as well as Ms. Devaux, have been so supportive. . . .

"Andrew!" Marcia stood up and spun around to face him.

"It's good!" he said. He laughed and tried to get at the speech.

"You were reading it?" Marcia shouted, and stamped her feet like a child. In response, Andrew grabbed Marcia around the waist and slung her over his shoulder. With his free hand he took the papers on the desk and tossed them up in the air. For a moment the papers and index cards rained around them like white flakes in a snow globe. He spun her amidst the paper storm while she alternately shouted in rage and laughed hysterically, pounding her fists on his back.

"You . . . are going . . . to help . . . me," she said between gasps, "put . . . all . . . my shit . . . back . . . together." Her voice trailed off in a half sob. Andrew stopped spinning her and loosened his grip. She slid from his shoulder.

"Sorry," he said. He breathed hard, unsure what had come over him.

Together they gathered up her speech. Sara swept into the room. She looked strangely magnificent, Andrew thought, with her gleaming legs and her hair wrapped up in a pink towel like a turban on her head.

"Are you two fighting *again*?" Sara asked.

Andrew flopped onto the bed. The ceiling was painted dark green, like the walls, and gave the room the feel of a mossy cave. He'd spent half his adolescence in this room, sometimes a little buzzed, staring at the walls and wondering what inspired Sara and her mother to paint them such an unusual color.

"When's the movie start?" he asked.

Marcia reached for the newspaper and began searching for the movie section. Sara unwrapped the towel turban and shook her head. Andrew watched her. Sara was pretty, no doubt about it, and her curly blonde hair was especially beautiful: exuberant, sexy, unrestrained—always on the verge of falling apart or coming undone. He started to reconsider his actions, or rather non-actions, in the bathroom a few moments earlier. She caught him looking at her and gave him a slight smile. He smiled back, then shifted his gaze toward Marcia, whose brows were furrowed in concentration.

"How's the speech?" Sara asked. She slipped behind her closet door to change. Marcia tossed the newspaper at Andrew. It fluttered through the air and landed, disassembled, at his feet.

"I can't find it," Marcia said to Andrew. She turned toward the closet, adding, "And it's terrible. Terrible. The speech is crap. I don't want to do this."

"We're proud of you. You're doing this!" Sara shouted from the closet. She emerged in a tight blue dress. "And you're not letting that douche-bag Jason take your place," she said with her hands on her hips.

"Who cares? What's the point? I don't give a shit about anyone from school except you two. Everyone else can kiss my ass," Marcia said. Marcia wasn't exactly disliked by her classmates, but people thought she was nerdy, weird, and way too into school. But they were wrong about her, thought Andrew. It wasn't school that she was into; it was knowledge. Marcia actually cared about things like Spanish poetry and physics and the Crimean War. A guy like Jason just pretended to.

"It's not about that. It's about celebrating how hard you've worked and how brilliant you are." As she spoke, Sara walked toward Marcia and put her arms around her shoulders. She shook her lightly and said, "Marcia, don't be ashamed or embarrassed." Sara was a close talker, and her face was inches from Marcia's. Marcia laughed nervously and stepped back.

"I'm not embarrassed. It's just stupid," Marcia said.

"Bullshit," Sara said, raising her eyebrows.

"Marcia's right," Andrew said, throwing the paper aside. "Fuck 'em. And the movie starts in twenty minutes, so let's get going."

"What are we seeing again?" Sara asked with dread in her voice.

"*Un Chien Andalou,*" Marcia and Andrew said together.

Sara threw her head back and sighed.

"It's a revival. Remastered and everything," Marcia said, her eyes pleading. Driving to the little art house cinema just outside of town and watching old movies had been part of Marcia's *Let's watch real films!* initiative. It drove Sara nuts.

"I hate those depressing old European films. Why can't we just get some pot and pizza and rent an action flick?" Sara said.

"I'm game for that," Andrew said.

"Again?" Marcia said, and she looked to Andrew for support.

Andrew stood up. "*Un Chien Andalou* is short, Sara. Besides, maybe you'll pick up some French."

"I'm not even sure that I'll be in France."

"You're going to backpack around Europe and not go to France?" Marcia asked.

Andrew snorted, and both girls looked at him. Sara's year-after-high-school backpacking plans grated on him for reasons he was unable to define. It just all seemed so stereotypical. "Marcia's right. Go to France, see the Louvre, stay in hostels, write in a journal, get a tan, and contract herpes," he said.

"Jealous?" Sara shot back.

"Please stop arguing," Marcia said.

"And for your information," Sara continued, "I always use condoms. Not that either of you would know anything about that."

He scowled and crossed his arms over his chest, wounded at this reminder of his virginity.

Marcia cleared her throat and said, "Actually, condoms don't really protect against herpes, because herpes—"

"Oh, shut up, Marcia!" Sara and Andrew shouted together.

Lately they'd been bickering. It didn't help that Marcia had become infatuated with yet another medical book, this one about infectious diseases, and could not seem to stop herself from announcing these transmissible illness tidbits at the most awkward moments. *Sprinkles of anxiety to flavor your day*, Andrew called them.

"Well, if we're not going to the real movie theater," Sara said as she went behind her closet again, "I'm going to slip into something more comfortable."

"Whose car are we taking?" Andrew asked.

"Can we take both? That way you can give Marcia a ride home, and I can pick up my mom when her shift is done," Sara said.

"Or drive off alone with that sleazy projectionist," Marcia muttered.

"What was that?" Sara shouted from the closet.

"I thought Janet wasn't working nights," Andrew said, less

out of curiosity and more to prevent a spat from developing between the two girls. Andrew was more or less indifferent to Sara's occasional promiscuity with older guys, but he knew it annoyed Marcia.

"Not regularly, but she took a night shift for a friend. They're the worst. She can't get the smell of rancid milk out of her hair for days."

Sara's mother, Janet, worked at a cheese factory, and the stories she told of the place were enough to turn Marcia's vegetarianism into tentative stabs at veganism.

"You want to hang out after the movie? What time do you have to pick your mom up?" Andrew said.

"It's just easier with two cars," Sara said. Andrew and Marcia exchanged looks. She had not quite answered the question.

"I'll leave now and get tickets," he said.

"There's some cash on my dresser," Sara said.

Marcia dug around her pockets and produced a pile of lint. She looked up at Andrew, embarrassed.

"Pay me back later," he said, waving away her explanation. "You coming with me or you want to ride with Sara?"

"I think I'll go with Sara," she said.

Andrew stepped outside. It was six o'clock. The sun was just settling back into the green mountains and leaving a soft pink blush in the sky. He thought of Laura, of the color of her skin, how it was like the light of the setting sun reflected in the sky and bouncing off the clouds of a perfect spring day. Pale yet golden, cool yet warm. He sighed. Sometimes, often in fact, he wished he could stop thinking about her. He felt cursed with obsession. He considered confessing his crush to Marcia and Sara; perhaps this would ease the sting and make him feel less like an actor in his own life, pretending everything was cool when really he was half out of his mind.

He was about to drive away when Marcia came running down the steps. He smiled as she hopped into his car and buckled up.

"Sara's still messing with her clothes," she said.

Andrew shifted gears and pulled out of the driveway. He wondered if, on the way to the movies, he could get a glimpse of Laura. She would be heading to some sort of church event, even on a Friday night. Andrew thought it must be miserable to be at church all the time, but Laura and her friends always seemed happy.

The movie theater wasn't in the direction of the church, but he could take Maple Lane to Autumn Road, then loop around Hunger Street . . . yes, that would work. The circuitous route would eventually bring them to the theater. He turned the car sharply.

"Where are you going?" Marcia asked.

"Shortcut," Andrew said. He was glad that Sara hadn't come with them. Unlike Marcia, Sara would have known that he wasn't taking a shortcut and would have teased him about it. Thoughts of confession were now far away.

They drove in comfortable silence for a few minutes, the

special trick of their old friendship. Despite Sara's beauty and flirty charm, Andrew actually preferred being alone with Marcia. He often felt calm and strong when he was with her. Marcia was a small person, five feet tall and thin; she almost looked like a child. Something about Marcia's size, her fatherlessness, and even her precocious intelligence made Andrew feel like an older brother to her. He tried to treat her like the loving and protective brother that Brian had never been to him, and her own brothers had never been to her. Other times he idly fantasized about her, or Sara for that matter, and it satisfied him more than porn.

Andrew and Marcia had become friends when they were in the sixth grade. He had seen Marcia around at school. She was new to town. She had been born in Korea but was white, a paradox that intrigued and repelled some of his classmates. "That's just weird!" had been the common refrain.

When she was young, Marcia had had a subtle but strange global accent, having attended an English language school for the children of diplomats, politicians, and other international types. Her accent was gone, but her speech, especially at times of great emotion, was still peppered with the occasional "Bollocks!" or "Shiza!" or "When I go to University—I mean *college*."

Marcia's father had been a military doctor stationed in Korea. While volunteering at a free clinic, he was brutally murdered by an insane patient. Marcia's family moved back to the States shortly after the tragedy.

People were kind to them but left them alone. Marcia's

brothers were older than she was and very close in age to each other, sixteen and seventeen when they moved to town. The brothers had passed imperceptibly through high school, quietly scoring the highest marks in everything and then vanishing into college. They had attended the same state university on modest academic scholarships. Neither studied medicine.

He slowed down as they drove past Laura's church. A large placard on the lawn read ALL ANSWERS HERE! About a dozen cars were parked in the lot. He thought he saw a flicker of long amber hair out of the corner of his eye, but when he turned his head, it was gone. He silently cursed.

"Sometimes I wish I were religious," Marcia said.

"Oh?"

"I kind of envy people who have that."

"All the answers?" Andrew said.

Marcia laughed. "Yes, that. But also . . . peace, calm, certainty in the face of a storm."

"But religion has caused a lot of conflict and oppression, even warfare. Maybe religion *is* the storm."

"That's true."

"I don't know. I'd never really thought about it," Andrew said.

"No?"

"I mean, I figure we're all going to die someday, and it'll be just like before we were born."

"Nothing?"

"Nothing."

"And while we're here?"

"If you need God or Buddha or whatever to help you through life, that's . . . fine, I guess."

"As long as you're not causing wars."

"Yeah, exactly."

"It sounds so simple, talking about it in your car," Marcia said with a nervous laugh. "You know, it's weird that they're even here."

"What do you mean?"

"The 'All Answers' church. I think they're pretty conservative. *Here*, in liberal Vermont?"

"Please. That kind of stuff is all over the place. Vermont's not special. There's poverty and drugs and all kinds of shit. We're just like every place else."

"Maybe," she said.

"Need plus fear plus ignorance equals religion."

"That's pretty harsh, Drew," she said as she looked out the window.

Drew. She had invoked the childhood nickname she'd given him years ago. She rarely used it now, and when she did it usually meant, as when she swore in German, that her emotions were running high. He mentally noted all this and bit back a sarcastic retort. Besides, he wasn't even sure he felt that way about religion; it just sounded cool. Every once in a while he was meaner than he'd intended to be, like an instinct he couldn't control. It happened with his mom sometimes, and now it had happened with Marcia, who was probably talking about religion in the first place because of her father, the eminent surgeon who loomed large in her imagination but dim in her memory. He tried to think of something comforting to say, but Marcia was prickly about her family's past. He glanced at the clock and pressed the gas pedal harder. The movie started in five minutes. Sara was a fast driver and would not have taken his ridiculous "shortcut." She could be there already.

But she wasn't. They left Sara's ticket at the window and entered the already darkened theater. It smelled like nutritional yeast and hot oil. They sat down just as the movie began.

As the images flickered before him, Andrew realized that there was no dialogue at all. Maybe Sara had found this out and decided not to come. He leaned back. She'd probably be outside when the film ended. He put his arm around the back of Marcia's chair and glanced at her. She looked anxious.

"You okay?" he whispered.

She nodded, not taking her eyes away from the screen. She flinched at what she saw.

5

"I WONDER WHERE SHE IS?"

"What do you mean?"

"I mean—I—I don't want to be here," Marcia said. Her voice cracked and gave way to sobs.

Not for the first time that night, he pressed his fingertips to the corners of his eyes and tried to push the tears back.

They had sunk to the floor with their backs against the wall of room seven in the intensive care unit. They had not stopped holding hands for two hours. Now their fingers lay loosely intertwined, their palms sweaty with fear and with the constant hopeless pressing of skin on skin. Across from them lay Sara. Motionless, supine, comatose, beautiful Sara.

"There are so many tubes," said Andrew, who was now gasping with the effort not to cry.

"I know."

"So many things coming out of her."

"I know, I *know*."

They'd had this conversation many times that night. A kind nurse had explained to them what all the tubes were for. *This one helps her breathe, this one sucks out the secretions that congeal in her throat, this one drains her urine, this one reads the blood pressure in her heart, this one feeds her, these ones deliver medication to her bloodstream.*

"Oh. Oh. Oh," they'd said in response.

They were permitted to stay in the room as long as they promised to be quiet and not touch *anything*. Sara's mother was heavily sedated and half-conscious in the waiting room. A few of her friends from work had come to sit with her and help fill out paperwork. Sara had no siblings, no father to speak of, no cousins or aunts or uncles. There was a grandmother, somewhere, but Janet and her mother had not spoken in years.

Sara only has us, Andrew thought, and it made him feel protective and scared all at once. He heard Janet moaning from the waiting area. He glanced at Marcia, who was frowning and crying and picking at a bleeding hangnail on her thumb.

"Stop that," Andrew said. He pried her fingers off her thumb and found himself clutching her wrists as she tried to pull away.

"Maybe you two should get something to eat."

Andrew looked up as one of the nurses entered the room. He noticed that she was carrying a diaper. Didn't Sara have a tube for that? Then it hit him, and he felt stupid and disgusted and mad at himself. He also didn't want Marcia, who'd been to hysterics and back again three times that night, to see the diaper. Through some empathetic telepathy the nurse hid the diaper behind her back while Marcia wiped the dribbling tears from her cheeks.

"You're right," Andrew said to the nurse. He stood up. Marcia stayed on the floor, staring at Sara. He gave the nurse an embarrassed shrug and hoisted Marcia to her feet.

With his arm around her shoulders, Andrew carefully guided Marcia through the ICU. The ICU was a large, white, U-shaped hallway with four rooms on each side and a nurse's station in the center. There were no doors in the ICU. There was just an open frame through which a person could hurriedly pass in an emergency. There were curtains in the rooms, but the walls facing the nurse's station consisted of large clear windows so the patients could be continuously observed. Television screens displayed the brainwaves and heart rhythms of those being monitored.

The first thing Andrew had noticed about the ICU was that it wasn't as bustling as he imagined it would be. It wasn't like the TV shows he'd seen where people in hospitals were in constant motion and yelling orders at one another. In fact, many of the nurses and doctors seemed to speak in a deliberately quiet way. The machines that beeped and whirred had an almost muffled quality. Or was that just him? Andrew had a curious sense of drifting, as if the ICU were a spaceship and he were a humble passenger. He was on the wrong deck and belonged somewhere else and was being told to go to his assigned area.

When they walked past the waiting room, Andrew gently moved Marcia to the other side of his body so that he, not Marcia, was facing Janet and her friends. Before Janet had been sedated, she'd kept grabbing Marcia by the shoulders and saying "Marcia! Marcia!" in an insensible, questioning tone of voice. He looked in on the women, who were crying and holding hands. Janet was lying on her back on the couch. Her face looked sluggish, and her mouth curved down into a sickly and unnatural-looking frown.

Janet was usually such a fun person. "You look like I need a drink," she'd say to Andrew when she came home from a late shift and found him writing hopeless Laura poems in her living room, Sara and Marcia fast asleep on the couch and curled around each other like puppies. She'd make him a Pop-Tart and pour herself a glass of wine. They'd talk about her job and his college prospects. Janet was interested, unlike his own parents.

When Andrew and Marcia reached the hallway, he released her and they walked toward the elevator. He pushed the button for the first floor and crossed his arms over his chest. The doors closed. They looked at each other.

"I could kill that guy," he said.

"He's already dead," Marcia said.

"I know that. I'm just saying."

They didn't know much. Sara had been speeding, but the guy who'd hit her had been drunk. He crashed through his windshield and split his head open on the street. Sara's car tumbled and tumbled. It tumbled down into a granite ravine. Sara was, in the muttered words of one of the doctors who'd been swarming around, "a vegetable."

"That's not certain," another doctor in a long white coat had said quickly to Janet. But Janet was already screaming.

The elevator stopped, and the doors slid open with a jarring chunky sound, as if the mechanics of the thing weren't lined up properly. Andrew followed Marcia out into the hallway. A directory in front of them indicated that they should take a left for the cafeteria. They walked a few steps and were met by the congested and comforting smell of hot grease. They bought doughnuts and coffee.

The lights were low in the seating area. The only other occupant was a sleeping doctor in green scrubs and a wrinkled white jacket. He looked young. He was slumped over a table, his breathing heavy and uneven. *That'll be Marcia in a few years,* Andrew thought. He looked at her serious little face and wondered if she were thinking the same thing. They sat down and picked at their doughnuts. Andrew cleared his throat.

"Why did one doctor say she'd be a vegetable and the other said that maybe she'd recover?" he asked.

"Because they disagree?"

Andrew looked out the window, but it was so dark, inside and out, that he couldn't see anything, not even his own reflection. He turned back to Marcia. She was a certified Mensa brain; she generally knew a little something about everything. She leaned back in her chair. She had chocolate on her face, and for some reason this irritated the hell out of him.

"You've got food on your face," he said.

She turned to inspect herself in the window.

"You can't see yourself. I tried," he said.

"What do you want from me?" she snapped.

A high-pitched beeping sound made them both jump. The doctor awoke with a start. He grabbed his pager from his waist and leaped up from the table, running off in the direction of the elevators. They stared after him.

"Listen, after the swelling in her brain goes down, they'll need to assess how much damage has been done. See how much she's retained. That's why no one knows for sure," she said.

"How do you know that?"

"I heard one of the doctors saying it to another doctor," she said.

"They all seemed to say something different. How do you know who to believe?"

"The guy with the longest coat said the thing about the swelling."

"So length of coat indicates degree of knowledge?"

"Interns, residents, attendings—the higher up the food chain, the longer the white coat."

"Really?"

"Really." She took another bite of her doughnut.

"So, what's next? More surgery or something?"

She swallowed. "Andrew, I really don't know."

6

ANDREW NEEDED TO CHECK ON BECKY. It was still dark when he entered through the back door. She met him at once, sniffing his hands and looking into his face. He let her out so she could relieve herself, but instead of leaping around and straining for a longer walk, she sat down at his feet. He sat down as well, and saw a faint reflection of himself in her eyes. On the wet grass in the gray light he wrapped his arms around her and cried.

He lay on his back. Becky flopped beside him and rested her head on his stomach. The sky began to reflect an in-between hour, where a few stars still glimmered beyond the orange yellow light. It was a special time of day, the moments before dawn. Everything looked more intense, like the vivid colors of the atmosphere that proceed a storm. He'd spent many mornings enjoying this time of day with Sara and Marcia.

The summer they'd been thirteen, they'd snuck out of their

homes at night to meet one another on the playground of their old middle school. Marcia had been especially excited by these clandestine gatherings. It had been fun to watch her as she ran around the jungle gym and recited Allen Ginsberg poems. They'd been studying sixties literature in school, and Marcia had taken to saying "I dig it!" in response to everything that excited or pleased her. It had been as if the night air had given her a sense of freedom. Andrew had known that sneaking out was the most rebellious thing Marcia had ever done. Part of him had felt that her excitement was pedestrian and typical. Childish. He had resisted the urge to feel giddy with her.

Marcia would be expecting him back at the hospital pretty soon, but Andrew felt so tired that he didn't think it was safe to drive. *Just a ten-minute nap,* he thought as he crept up the stairs and into his room. He swaddled himself in the mess of sheets and blankets and clothes on his bed. Becky leaped up beside him, and he embraced her as he fell into a thick and dreamless sleep.

"Andrew, wake up."

He opened his eyes and stared around.

"Phone's for you." It was his mother's voice calling from the other side of his bedroom door.

"Okay, hold on." Andrew glanced at the clock and saw that it was twelve thirty. "Shit! Where's Becky?" he asked as he got up and opened the door.

His mother held the phone against her chest. "It's okay. I let the dog out," she said.

"You did?" he asked, rubbing his eyes with one hand and reaching for the phone with the other.

She handed him the phone. "I'm sorry about your friend," she said. She lightly touched his arm. He stared at her wildly for a moment. His heart flipped and plummeted at the same time. Was Sara dead? Was that why she was sorry?

"Marcia?" Andrew shouted into the phone. His mom walked away.

"I'm at the hospital. Nothing's changed. I mean, it's still kind of touch-and-go. Why are you yelling?"

"I thought . . . never mind. I closed my eyes for one minute and passed out."

"Don't worry about it. We're just sitting around. But whatever they gave Janet is wearing off, so she's a little more with it."

"I'll be there soon." He started to hang up, then stopped. "Marcia?"

"Yeah?"

"What did you say to my mom?"

"That Sara got into an accident and is a vegetable. You know, maybe."

He was shocked at the flatness of her voice.

"Oh," he said.

Andrew brushed his teeth and splashed water onto his face. He inspected himself, something he generally avoided. His light gray eyes looked back at him, heavily bagged and red-rimmed and bleary. Growing up, Andrew had hated their strange color, which he thought made him look girlish, but Sara had told him they were wonderful. Sexy. *Sara.*

He blinked back tears as he ran down the stairs. Andrew stopped when he saw the broad back of his father at the kitchen counter. Like Brian, his father was a big man—a very big man. His massive shoulders tapered down to an impressive torso and stocky strong legs. Andrew was tall, but he had his mother's lean and lanky frame. His father half turned when he heard Andrew.

"Hey," Andrew said as he grabbed a granola bar. He scanned the kitchen counter. There were several empty beer cans, crushed, lying about.

"Where you going?" his father said.

"Hospital. Mom tell you?"

"Something about one of your friends?"

"Yeah."

"The smart one or the pretty one?"

"Jesus, Dad."

"Excuse me?"

"The pretty one."

"Too bad."

Andrew glared at a spot just beyond his father's coffee.

"That didn't sound right. It's too bad either way. Your brother's home in a week or so, maybe sooner."

Andrew threw the granola bar wrapper in the trash.

"I said your brother's home—"

"I heard you."

Slowly, his father stood up. Andrew braced himself. His dad hadn't hit him in a while, but his moods were unpredictable. And the Return of Brian usually corresponded with an uptake in his dad's drinking, which was weird, because he adored Brian.

"Doug! I need your help with this window," Andrew's mother called from upstairs.

"What?" his father said. Andrew took the opportunity to slip out the kitchen door as his parents continued to yell up and down the stairs to each other.

When he got to the hospital, he decided to skip the elevator. As he dashed up the stairs, it occurred to him that he didn't have to rush. Why was he rushing as if Sara's life depended on him being present? There were doctors, nurses, medicines, tubes, pumps, vents—all sorts of things were keeping her alive. None of these things had anything to do with him. And if she was dead, there was nothing he could do anyway. Nothing except comfort Marcia and Janet.

He stopped running and then stopped moving altogether. He closed his eyes and saw white stars of light against the black of his lids. An image of Sara floated before him. Her eyes were open, their expression soft but faraway. Then the image changed, and it was Sara rolling around on her back and laughing at something he had said, some small sarcastic quip that was maybe not that funny at all but that Sara had found hysterical, or at least pretended to. The image changed again and it was Laura, only it was Sara, too. A Sara-fied Laura, a Laura-fied Sara. Beautiful and horrifying.

When he got to the ICU, he saw Marcia right away. She was listening to one of the doctors as he spoke to Janet. Janet looked stupefied and pale. She swayed from foot to foot as the doctor spoke. Janet was in perfect contrast to Marcia, who stood like a statue with her arms crossed and her gaze fixed. Andrew hung back, unsure what to do. He shuffled around and ran one of his hands over the back of his neck.

In response to one of Marcia's questions, the doctor tipped his head from side to side as if considering something not worth considering. He wore a long white coat and had white hair. His face was small and intent, not unlike Marcia's, and on his wrist a bright gold watch flashed occasionally from beneath his coat sleeve. He reached out and squeezed Janet's shoulder, then turned and smiled at Marcia in a manner that seemed to say, *Okay, then, take care.*

Janet went into Sara's room. Andrew walked toward Marcia, who looked at him dispassionately as he approached. If it were possible, he felt even more uncomfortable.

"Any news?" he asked.

"Not really."

"How is she?"

"The same, I think. I haven't been in there too much. I wanted to give Janet her space," Marcia said.

"Are Janet's friends still here?" he asked.

"Most of them are gone. I think they're staying here in shifts."

Marcia smiled at something behind him. Andrew turned and saw one of the nurses bustling toward them.

"Hi, Meg," Marcia said.

"Hello, Marcia. Is this your friend?"

"This is Andrew."

Meg was an older woman, pretty in a faded, farm-girl kind of way. She looked smart and efficient. As she spoke, she flicked her eyes back and forth between him and Marcia.

"Marcia said she wanted to help with Sara's care. I think it's best if you two just sit and talk quietly to Sara and her mother for now. I'll let you know if I need your help."

"Thank you, Meg," Marcia said.

"Yes, th-thank you," Andrew stammered. Meg nodded and walked away.

"I like her. Susan, too," Marcia said.

"The nurse from last night?"

"The nurse's aide today."

"Oh," Andrew said. He jingled his keys in his coat pocket. In a few short hours, while he had slept, Marcia had taken steps to master the situation, or at least play an active part.

"Shall we?" Marcia asked as she gestured toward room seven. Andrew followed her.

Everything looked the same as before, only now the room was brightly lit and Andrew could see things more clearly. The pumps turned and beeped and blinked. Janet sat on Sara's right side and held one of her hands. She did not look up when Andrew and Marcia entered. Janet looked like she'd aged ten years overnight. Her skin was somehow heavy and thick. Unlike her daughter, Janet had never been a beauty. Her features were plain, her body slender but shapeless. The only thing mother and daughter had in common was their hair. Janet's hair was blonde and messy and, Andrew thought for the first time, kind of sexy. He had a wild urge to push the tendrils out of her eyes. He shook his head. What was wrong with him? He reached out to her, hesitated a moment, then patted her back. She gave him a closed-lipped, dead-eyed smile.

"We were going to sit with you for a while, unless you'd like us to get you something to eat. Or bugger off," Marcia said. Janet turned her wary smile to Marcia.

"No, sweetheart. Don't bugger off." She looked back at her comatose daughter. Marcia plopped into a chair on Sara's left and proceeded to stare at Sara. Marcia's expression was strange, unreadable, not unlike the expression she'd had as she gazed at Sara's closet door, so long ago, it seemed. Marcia looked like she, too, had aged rapidly overnight. Was that how he looked?

He glanced around for another chair, but there was none. Feeling annoyed, and then annoyed at himself for being annoyed, he leaned up against the wall and forced himself to look at Sara. Still beautiful, still Sara, only sleeping. One of the nurses, or aides, or perhaps even Marcia, had arranged Sara's blankets and hospital gown so that the places where the tubes entered her body were more or less covered. For what felt like the millionth time in the last twenty-four hours, Andrew blinked back tears. And it was through this slightly watery vision that he perceived there was something off about Sara's expression. It was not just the tube that was helping her breathe. It was not just the blank inward gaze of sleep. It was something else, something lacking. Her lips were dry and pale. Her skin seemed to hang down, as if clinging to her bones. Her eyes were not closed in sleep as he'd first thought, but rather cast downward in despair. Sara never cast her eyes downward. There was no gaze on earth that she didn't meet with equanimity, or at least with confidence.

He wondered what Sara was thinking and feeling. Was she scared? Was she in pain? Was being in a coma like sleep, or was it deeper than sleep?

I wonder where she is? Marcia had said last night. Andrew shivered. He wondered the same thing.

7

PEOPLE AT SCHOOL WERE VORACIOUS.

How's Sara?

How is she?

Are you okay?

Where's Marcia?

How's her mom?

What happened, exactly?

I heard she was with a guy.

I heard you were all in the same car.

I heard at the last minute you switched cars or something.

Is she okay?

Are you okay?

Is Marcia okay?

Are you okay, okay, okay?

Andrew slunk around the building like an alley cat. He avoided gazes, tried to avoid conversations, shrunk from outstretched hands. Some students, maybe even most, seemed truly concerned about Sara, but even their sincerity stank of intrusion. That jock she was sort of dating, Kyle, followed him around the school, clearly dying to talk, but Andrew felt ungenerous and angry. *Leave her alone,* he thought.

Finals were at the end of the week, and even at the best of times, classes at this point in the year bordered on anarchy. Even Marcia knew she wasn't missing anything. He didn't know why he came, but he didn't want to be at the hospital, either. He felt utterly useless—was, in fact, utterly useless to Sara.

Marcia was distant and uncommunicative. She'd been "participating in Sara's care" by helping with her bed bath. Andrew had made some meek noises of protest, saying that Sara might not have wanted Marcia to do that, but Marcia insisted that they might never know what Sara had wanted, and it was her responsibility to keep her comfortable. This was true to a certain extent, Andrew had to admit. The nurses and aides seemed so overburdened that Sara's morning bath was merely perfunctory, whereas Marcia washed and braided Sara's hair and cleansed her face with special products. Sara truly did seem more comfortable after Marcia settled her in bed, but the shivers of disapproval that coursed up and down his spine told him otherwise. But what did he know? Andrew was constantly being reminded of how little he knew. Smart, capable Marcia with her tireless thirst to improve Sara's condition frightened and overwhelmed him. And poor Janet seemed to want and even need Marcia's take-charge handling of the situation.

Andrew hung back, confused, upset, in the way. Marcia had poor eyesight but could no longer be bothered with contacts, so she wore an enormous old pair of glasses. Her owlish brown eyes, huge and intense behind the thick frames, red-rimmed from lack of sleep, sometimes focused on Andrew with an expression of vague confusion at his presence. It was a relief to get out of there, even if it meant just going back to school.

He lowered his head onto his desk and pressed his cheek against the cool surface. He closed his eyes.

"Andrew?"

He looked up. His AP English teacher, Mr. Gonzalez, was looking at him with concern. His classmates averted their eyes.

"Yeah?" he said. "I mean, sorry. Do you want me to talk . . . or something?"

Mr. Gonzalez could usually rely on him to join in if the class discussion was flagging or not getting off the ground at all. Andrew was a good sport in his English classes. But now he didn't even know what was going on, hadn't even read the assignment.

"No, that's all right. Why don't you take the rest of the day off?" Mr. Gonzalez said.

"It's almost the end of the day anyway," Andrew said.

"I know. You can stay if you want. Your choice."

"Okay," Andrew said. He stood up and gathered his books

into his backpack. Everyone seemed to be watching. He quickly walked out of the room.

He was almost disappointed. English was his favorite class, and Mr. Gonzalez his favorite teacher. It had, in fact, been the last class of his high school career. What a way to end it all. Sara would have laughed. He made fists with his hands and banged them into the lockers.

Far down the hallway, a door swung open. It was Laura.

It was *Laura.*

She was wearing a silky beige dress that almost matched the color of her skin. Her golden amber hair was flowing around her face. She walked toward him and took his shoulders in both her hands. Her grip was firm, confident.

"Laura," he said.

Her dark blue eyes seemed to take up the entirety of his vision. He was stunned.

"I'm so sorry about Sara," she said. She was steadfast and calm.

"I—" he said. He dropped his gaze to the floor. To his horror, he started to cry.

"Let's talk," she said. The bell rang, a cacophony of doors slammed open, and students began surging around them. Laura's hands slid from his shoulders, and she placed something in his palm. Then she was gone. He opened his hand. It was a piece of paper with her phone number and, next to it, a penciled drawing of a cross.

8

WHEN HE GOT HOME, he placed the piece of paper on the kitchen counter and stared at it for a few minutes. He smoothed it out with his fingertips, crumpled it up, and smoothed it out again. Becky trotted into the kitchen and gently nudged him. Becky no longer charged at the door and threw herself at him when he got home. She was getting old, he thought. He took her out for a walk, and for the first time in a long time he carefully avoided Laura's house.

The piece of paper was now in his pocket, burning the proverbial hole. He kept worrying it between his fingers, but then it occurred to him that he might smear the number off or accidentally tear it to shreds. He took it out and made sure it was still legible and whole.

He and Becky had been ambling around for a while when he realized that he was running late for work.

Andrew guessed that Avella Pharmaceuticals employed about a quarter of the town. There were white-collar executives, secretaries, janitors, security, and grounds crew. Then there were consulting doctors and nurses. Local artists had been hired to beautify the interior with paintings and sculptures. There was even an on-site yoga instructor. The Maple Momma catering company hauled lunch up the mountain every day.

Avella was also magnificent to look at. It was a series of large white buildings that were built into the valley of a mountain range. The drive up was steep, hence the moniker "up the mountain" when anyone referred to it, but Andrew knew the phrase meant something about money and class too. It was always kind of fun to downshift his hatchback and crawl up to the gates of Avella. The grounds were kept beautiful by the maintenance department, which quadrupled in size during the warmer months by hiring temporary workers like him. The temps were usually high school or college students.

Andrew arrived just in time. The crew assembled outside the main shed and waited for Neal, the manager, before starting their shift.

"Workin' today?" Cory asked, and spit liberally on the ground. He narrowly avoided his own shoe. Cory was a philosophy major at Cornell. He wore circular wire-rimmed glasses and shaved his goatee for the summers he worked at Avella. It made Andrew laugh, the way these educated college kids affected the speech and style of working-class men.

"That's why I'm here," Andrew said.

"How's Brian?" Cory asked. Cory was two years older than Andrew and always acted as though he and Brian were old friends. Andrew knew very well that Cory was the kind of guy who Brian had probably shoved into lockers for fun.

Andrew shrugged. Cory grunted. The rest of the crew assembled. There were a few new guys who Andrew didn't recognize, and some old-timers, actual working-class men, who said hello to him.

"Andrew, Cheeve, and Ben: pond duty. Get in," Neal said. "The rest of you"—Neal glanced at his watch—"start on the bushes on West End. We'll meet up at seventeen hundred hours."

Andrew was glad to be picked to go into Neal's cart. That usually meant harder work, special projects, but it also meant hanging out with Neal. The men grumbled in unison and went on to their various tasks. Andrew got into the back of the cart. Ben, Neal's son, sat next to his father, and Cheever, an old-timer, sat next to Andrew. Andrew nodded to Cheeve, who nodded back and then spit on the road. Cheeve was extremely intelligent, but unlike the college boys he didn't show it off *or* try to hide it. Cheeve in the cart meant that something sophisticated and mathematical was going on. Andrew was worried; he was good at carrying stuff and digging stuff up, not planning things.

"Okay back there, son?" Neal asked.

"Me? Fine, thank you," Andrew said.

"Cheeve?"

"Ayup," Cheeve said.

Neal was a small, compact man. Strong, graceful. He seemed to expend the precise amount of energy required for the task at hand. He inspired respect because he moved with enormous physical confidence despite his lack of size. He was also compassionate and intelligent, gruff but loyal. Neal's son, Ben, was mentally disabled in some subtle, barely discernible way. Ben's age was impossible to determine. His face and its expressions were childlike, but his hands were a little wrinkled, and his hair had a few gray strands. Like his father, Ben was strong and small. He did exactly what was asked of him without an ounce of servility or obsequiousness, but he couldn't do anything too complicated. Andrew admired the father and son—was, in fact, rather jealous of their bond.

"Heard about that accident?" Neal said.

"Damn shame," said Cheeve.

"Did you know that girl, Andrew?" Neal asked.

"No," Andrew said quickly. He did not want to cry in front of these guys. Then he felt ashamed and said, "I mean, yes, I know her."

"Okay," Neal said. The subject was promptly dropped as Neal and Cheeve started talking about the pond.

When they reached the site, they got out of the cart and reviewed the specs, which Andrew pretended to understand but did not. Neal pointed out various areas that needed to be built up with cement. There was a lot of talk involving equations and chemicals. Cheeve took a sharp pencil from behind his ear and chewed on the eraser while he studied the plans.

"Andrew, you go with Ben," Neal said.

Andrew nervously followed Ben down a path toward a large pile of bagged unmixed cement.

"Uh, what are we doing exactly?" Andrew asked Ben.

"Haulin' bags of dirt," Ben said.

"Oh, okay."

"Over there," Ben said as he pointed to a distance some ten yards off where a cement mixer sat next to other large pieces of machinery.

"Okay," Andrew said. He wondered why the cement hadn't simply been dropped off by the mixer, but he decided not to ask. Andrew occasionally got the impression that Neal created work for his son—not all the time, but every once in a while—when there was nothing else to do. Neal liked to keep Ben close.

"How's about I carry the first bag over, and then when I get there, you start in with the next bag?" Ben said.

"Sounds good."

Ben lugged the first bag over his shoulder and started walking. When he had almost reached the mixer, he turned slightly and nodded. Andrew nodded back, picked up a bag, and followed him. In this way the two of them would constantly cross paths and be able to smile or nod or speak briefly to one another during the work, but not be under the pressure of having to make constant small talk.

Ben liked to make little subtle games out of his workday. When he mowed lawns, Neal always assigned him a partner. Ben made it so that you would start at opposite ends of the field and then mow toward one another to meet in the middle. The organization of it was soothing to him, but he also derived a companionable pleasure from it, a pleasure to which Andrew was compassionate. Andrew knew he wasn't the best temp worker on the Avella grounds crew, but he almost always got picked to go in Neal's cart simply because he was nice to Ben.

The bags were heavy, and Andrew felt himself tiring after the first hour. He was hungry and thirsty. Every few minutes he checked his pocket and felt the note from Laura. Half of him was saying, *Yes, this is it!* The other half was disgusted with the whole situation. He should be thinking about Sara, not Laura. Laura wanted to counsel and comfort him because of the accident, not because she wanted to hang out with him. And even if she did, how could he possibly be excited and happy about that when Sara was in a goddamn coma? He felt like an asshole. He dropped one of the bags and gave it a hearty kick.

"What did you do that for?" Ben said. He came up behind Andrew and added his bag to the pile.

"I don't know, man."

"Okay," Ben said. He turned around and walked away. "Little break then?" he said over his shoulder.

"Yeah."

They sat under the shade of a weeping willow and drank water mixed with orange Tang. Andrew reached into his pocket and pulled out the piece of paper. He stared at the tiny cross next to Laura's phone number. It occurred to him that a cross was a very strange symbol. After all, it was an instrument of torture.

Jesus, man or God or whatever he was, had died in agony. If Jesus had died on the rack, would pretty girls wear gold-dipped racks around their delicate necks? Would sugared racks decorate bakery buns at Easter? He imagined Laura sketching him love notes peppered with racks. *I can't call her,* he thought. Maybe she felt sorry for him, maybe she even felt really bad about Sara, but she was just doing this because of her religion. It was an obligation, nothing more. He would destroy the note. That was the right thing to do. Or was it? He tried to conjure up Sara in his mind. Sara was their unofficial leader. She called the shots, doled out the advice, led by example. Now she was beyond him, beyond helpless. *Where was she?* He lowered his head in his hands.

"Are you all right?" Ben looked at him uncertainly.

Andrew realized he was agitating Ben. "I'm okay. Let's get going." Andrew stood and clapped him on the back. Ben smiled shyly.

Andrew hoisted a bag over his shoulder and groaned. He watched Ben as he walked toward the mixer with his own easily lifted bag of cement. The sun was in front of him, and Andrew squinted to see Ben turn and wave. He started after him, half dragging his bag. Andrew didn't play sports during the school year and always began the summer feeling a little weak. The bag pressed down on his back, the sun beat down on his head, and in his heart he thought, *I can't call her, I can't call her, I can't call her . . . can I?*

9

HE DREADED GOING BACK TO the hospital. It had only been four days since the accident, but it felt more like four months. Marcia spent her days and nights there, curled up in a ball on one of the chairs in the lounge. She had learned how to suction secretions from Sara's throat, something she was so good at that the nurses let her do it with minimal supervision. The suctioning made Andrew feel nauseated, and he had to leave the room whenever it had to be done. While Janet recovered her senses and Andrew shuffled around the hallways, Marcia had become the captain, the steward, the commanding officer. It was both like and unlike her. It mystified Andrew.

He wondered who was looking after Marcia's mom, and if he ought to check in on her himself. He could swing by before he went to see Sara. Anything, he thought guiltily, to postpone his visit to the hospital.

Marcia's mom was like that old lady in *Great Expectations* whose fiancé jilted her at the altar. The one who forever wore her wedding dress, forever stopped her clocks, and ceased to move forward in life. After her husband had been murdered, Marcia's mom froze herself in a sustained posture of pure grief. There were times, Marcia had confessed to Andrew, that her mom would not speak for weeks. She loved her daughter, but she drifted about her life, and Marcia's life, as if she were a cool, inconsequential breeze on a summer's day. Those were the good days. Other days she would lie in bed, unable to get up, refusing both food and water from her frightened daughter.

Over the years Marcia's mom had gotten a little better. When Marcia was fourteen, she had suggested, and then insisted, that her mother seek help. Mrs. Stryker was now taking medications, but refused to see a therapist. The all-day-in-bed jags had ceased, but the great gulfs of self-imposed silences had not.

Andrew got out of the car and knocked on the door. There was no answer. He looked up at the second-floor window and thought he saw a pair of eyes watching him. A lacy curtain dropped, and the eyes were gone. The door opened suddenly and Andrew stepped back.

"Marcia!" he said.

"Hey," she said, "what are you doing here?"

"I thought I'd check on your mom. Nice to see you out of the hospital."

"I'm going back in a minute. We need to talk."

"What's up?" Andrew said as he slipped through the door.

"Come upstairs," Marcia said.

Andrew had long legs, and he usually took stairs two at time. But at Marcia's house he moved as quietly and unobtrusively as possible. This seemed to be a kind of unwritten rule. Andrew always felt a little nervous in Marcia's house. Marcia and her mother were small people, but their house felt too small, almost shrunken. The furniture was stiff, old-fashioned, and uncomfortably tiny. There was some kind of bizarre Victorian-meets-Asian theme to the décor: bronze statues and red kimonos hung next to prissy lace curtains, a painting of the Buddha in a minuscule, claustrophobic, carpeted bathroom. Empty golden birdcages hung about the ceilings.

When they reached Marcia's bedroom, she closed the door behind her and gestured for him to sit. He sat at her desk and said, "So what's happening?"

"Sara's been transferred."

"To another floor?"

"No. Out of state. To New Hampshire."

"What? When?" *Why didn't you call me?* Andrew thought, but squelched the question in his head.

"Hours ago," she said. "It's a huge teaching hospital. There's a special floor for patients like her. More resources, rehab for when she wakes up. They couldn't really keep her at St. Peter's anyway."

"But she's okay?"

"Out of the ICU. Stable enough to transfer, anyhow."

"That's great," Andrew said.

"She could wake up, you know."

"Like that guy. The 'moving through darkness' guy."

Marcia didn't respond. A man two doors down from Sara had awoken from a brief coma and kept saying that he'd been "moving through darkness." He'd said it to the doctors, nurses, his wife, and Andrew and Marcia as he was wheeled through the hallways. He didn't seem scared, exactly, but he wasn't happy either. It was more like he was flabbergasted and desperate to communicate what he'd been through. *I was moving through darkness, moving through darkness! Do you know what I mean? Do you understand?*

Andrew noticed that Marcia's suitcases were out. "Wait, you're going too?" he said.

"Yes."

"Marcia—"

"Janet can't take that much time off of work. If she takes a leave of absence, she won't get paid, and more important, she won't get insurance." Marcia paused, then said, "She's going to make me the proxy."

"Whoa. Really?"

"I'm eighteen," Marcia said, her chin set in a stubborn line. "Besides, I won't make actual decisions. It's just so someone is there to talk to the doctors when Janet is working."

"That sounds like a lot to take on."

"Yeah," Marcia said vaguely. She turned from him and opened her top dresser drawer.

"Marcia," he said.

She didn't respond.

"Marcia, talk to me." Andrew stood up and grabbed her arm. Marcia was tossing her clothes haphazardly into a suitcase. She dropped a shirt onto the carpet. They both stared at it. It was Sara's shirt; Marcia must have borrowed it. They were always borrowing each other's clothes. Andrew picked it up. It was light green with little painted pink flowers in a circle at the center. A favorite with both of the girls, it was cute without being cloying. The shirt hung off of Marcia's small frame in a way that looked ragged and elegant. On Sara it looked kind of hippie and sweet.

"Sara's shirt?" he said.

"It was mine originally. Not that it matters."

Andrew handed the shirt to her. "This is kind of nuts. You know that, right?"

"Drew, you realize that Janet has no one else. *Sara* has no one else."

He looked around her room. It was so neat and clean: books and notebooks all lined up, the bed carefully made, and through a crack in her closet, her graduation gown pressed and hung. "What about graduation?" he asked.

"Give me a break. I'll pick up my diploma later. Jason can make the damn speech."

"Sara wanted you to do that speech!"

"I'm not going to break down and cry in front of a bunch of people I don't care about!"

Andrew opened his mouth to protest, thought about it, then

closed his mouth. "Okay," he said. "I get that. What about finals?"

"Done and done."

"No shit?" Andrew said, almost smiling. "When?"

"About an hour ago. I only had two anyway because with my grades, I got opted out of the rest. Mr. Thibault let me take the physics and English back to back."

"Awesome."

"I know. They were actually"—and here Marcia smiled too—"the most stress-free exams I've ever taken. I didn't think about it, didn't even study."

"More important things to worry about?"

"You can say that again."

"So, where are you going to stay?"

"The hospital has a place for families of long-term patients. It's like a motel. Janet will come up on her days off."

"I don't know about this, Mar," Andrew said. He wanted to say more, but Marcia had a point. And who better than Marcia to deal with all this medical shit? Who better than Marcia, who was used to taking care of her mother, who was going to be a doctor in a few years?

"Your mom's cool with this?" he asked.

"More or less. I'm leaving for college in a couple of months anyway. Now it's just like I'm leaving a little earlier."

"Hmm," Andrew said.

"Why is this so weird for you? Actually, I wanted to know if you'd come too."

"What?" He had not for a moment considered this option.

He felt ashamed. Then he thought of the hospital, of Marcia's eager role in all the proceedings, of his own helplessness. He sat down at Marcia's desk and ran his hands through his hair. He felt the note in his pocket.

"What are you doing?" Marcia asked.

"Nothing," he said. He pulled his hand out of his pocket and stood.

"Look, I understand if you can't go. I mean, you have your job and your dog and stuff. . . ."

And Laura's phone number, Andrew thought with a vertiginous lurch of guilt. He struggled to push Laura out of his mind.

"Your parents probably wouldn't want you to come," she said.

"Brian is home this summer."

"Oh, shit," Marcia said. She placed her hand on his arm.

"It's fine. It's whatever."

"That sucks."

"Seriously, it's fine."

"Well, then . . . come with me," Marcia said. "Come with us," she urged.

Andrew turned away. He didn't want to go. And there *was* his dog and his job. Those were real things for which he was responsible. He couldn't just bail. But the truth was, he couldn't stand the thought of watching Marcia fuss over Sara's body. He couldn't do those things for Sara, and he wasn't sure that Marcia should be doing them either. And *fuck fuck fuck* . . . he wanted to call Laura, connect with Laura, be with Laura.

"Listen," he said, "I really do want to help."

"It's a nice hospital," she said.

Hospitals. The toneless hallways that seemed to never end, to rise up at you as in a nightmare. The smells, the noise, the worried or anguished expressions of the patients and their families, the calm, thoughtful blankness of the doctors and nurses. And Sara, half dead, lying in a puddle of tubes and diapers and despair.

"That's great," he said.

She must have heard the hesitation and dread in his voice because she turned away and said, "It's okay, Andrew. You don't have to go. There won't even be enough room for the three of us when Janet comes."

"I could sleep on the floor," he said, but already he felt a rush of relief followed by more guilt.

"Don't be silly. And I get it about your dog and stuff." Her voice was cool. "You can visit."

Marcia handed him a piece of paper on which she'd written different phone numbers. "That's where I'll be," she said. "I'll call you with updates."

He put the numbers in the same pocket as Laura's note and closed his hand tightly around both. He squeezed until it hurt.

10

"HEY, FAGGOT, YOU HOME?"

Andrew was sitting up in bed and doodling in his journal when he heard this pronouncement. Becky, who had been peacefully dozing, awoke with a start. She barked softly. Andrew tucked his notebook under his mattress. The page he'd been drawing on was filled with sketches of Laura surrounded by question marks and crosses.

He stood up and looked at Becky. "Let's get this over with," he said. Was it his imagination, or did she grimly nod?

When they got downstairs, the television was blaring, the sink was running, the back door was open, and Brian was shouting into the phone.

"Yeah, yeah. I'm back. I don't know. A few weeks? Coach's got something going on in Tampa in August. So, whatever, maybe I'm down there and . . . hey, don't touch that! Let it get cold," Brian said to Andrew as Andrew reached to turn off the sink.

"There's ice," Andrew said.

"Then get me some," Brian said.

"Go fuck yourself," Andrew said, but Brian had already resumed his conversation on the phone. A curious feature of Brian's massive physicality was that he was always hot. He wore shorts in the winter, cranked down thermostats, complained bitterly about the lack of central air in the house. He was like a gigantic engine for an industrial complex—vibrating, sweating, making infernal noises, producing vast amounts of pollutant energy and expending it into the atmosphere.

And the beast needed to be fed and watered, Andrew thought bitterly. Brian liked hot food and cold drinks. Their mom usually had a few bottles of sports drinks in the freezer. Andrew grabbed a red one and threw it at Brian's head. Brian caught it, of course. He caught it without looking, without thinking. He caught it with an easy absentmindedness, a powerful, effortless grace. Andrew had thrown the bottle awkwardly and hard, but somehow, as it neared Brian, it seemed to slow down, to arc in the air with beauty, as if merely being in Brian's presence altered its flight trajectory. Brian was, if nothing else, a superb athlete.

"What's going on with your friend? The hot one," Brian asked over his shoulder, the phone pressed to his chest.

Andrew was about to answer, or perhaps just curse at him again, but before he could get a word out, Brian was once again yelling into the phone.

"I'm here, I'm here. Got to do dinner or something with the folks. Then I'll come out. Pick me up. No, dude, you drive. I want to get fucked-up."

Andrew emptied a can of dog food into a clean bowl and placed it in the microwave. Becky waited at his feet while her food heated up.

"Oh, hell yeah, it's on!" Brian said, and slammed the phone down. He opened the bottle of sports drink and squeezed some of it into his mouth. It had already gone partly slushy from the warmth of his hands. He brushed past Andrew and knelt down to Becky. "You're getting old, girl," he said. Becky sniffed Brian's hand and turned her head away. Andrew took her food out of the microwave and tested it with his fingers to make sure it wasn't too hot. It was, so he mixed in some cold water with a fork. He felt Brian's eyes on his back. Andrew braced himself as Brian cuffed his neck.

"God, you're such a fag," he said softly.

He bound up the stairs. After a few moments Andrew heard the shower running.

Fucking Brian. The prodigal douche-bag returns.

What's going on with your friend? The hot one. Andrew closed his eyes and leaned against the fridge. Again he wondered where Sara was. In a kind of otherworld? Asleep and yet not asleep? Moving through darkness? Maybe it was like a nightmare from which she could not awake, no matter how hard she tried, no matter how loud her subconscious screamed—she was trapped. It was horrible to think about.

"Why is the door open?" his mother said. She had just come

home from work, and her arms were full of groceries. Andrew took the bags from her.

"Why do you think?" he said.

"Brian?" she said. Her voice was tentative, anxious.

"In the shower," he said.

"Your father and I thought we'd go to the steakhouse." She looked at Andrew out of the corners of her eyes. This was their routine, and he knew his part perfectly.

"I've got plans later. Sorry," he said.

"Okay," she said, relieved.

He was about to say something mean but stopped himself. Of course she didn't want to referee him and Brian. That was pretty understandable. He started to put the groceries away.

"How's your friend?" she said.

"The same, I guess," he said.

He heard the bathroom door slam open and Brian whistling as he walked to his bedroom. His mom was arranging a snack of pretzels and fruit on a platter. She'd always babied Brian; perhaps he demanded that kind of treatment. A few moments later Brian came down the stairs, and she squealed with delight. He briefly embraced her.

"Hey, Mommers," Brian said. He went right for the platter and grabbed a handful of pretzels. "This homo here can eat the fruit."

"Brian," their mom said.

"It's okay, Mom," Andrew said. He picked up Becky's empty bowl and washed it. He couldn't care less what Brian said or did. He had made a decision. He was going to call Laura.

11

SHE WAS WAITING ON HER porch and staring off into the distance. As he drew closer to her, his heart beat faster and his palms started to sweat. *Calm the fuck down,* he told himself. He was a few yards from her now. She turned toward him and smiled. Her dark blue irises looked even larger than usual, like when a child widens her eyes before crying or telling a lie. Or both. She raised her hand in a half wave, blushed a little, then brushed a loose strand of hair behind her ear.

Calm down.

She wore jeans and sneakers and a pink T-shirt. A sweatshirt was wrapped around her waist. She stood and came down the stairs when he reached the porch.

He was with Laura, and this wasn't a dream. They were side by side. It was so windy that the pink ribbon holding her hair had been blown out and tossed down the street. Andrew was going to chase after it, when she touched his forearm and said, "Leave it." Now the long amber strands whipped around her face and occasionally grazed his left shoulder. The little brief bites of contact between her hair and his body made Andrew feel crazy.

He was glad for the cold wind. Sultry weather would have killed him. A hot still day and the nearness of Laura might have driven him to commit some rash act of foolishness, like a confession of love, or do something lustful and insane like . . . He looked up at the sky. A gray sky, a slight drizzle, and the sun hanging behind the clouds like a hazy pearl. He looked at Laura, who was grabbing handfuls of her hair and twirling it around her fingers. A nervous gesture?

"I'm so glad you finally called," she said.

"Me too," he said. He had restrained himself from contacting Laura until after graduation.

"I just wanted to express my condolences about Sara," she said.

"She's not dead," Andrew said, then regretted his abrupt tone.

"I know that," Laura said while looking at him carefully. "But I'm sorry all the same."

Andrew nodded.

"So, Sara is . . ." Laura let the question hang in the air.

"She's in a coma. She's on a ventilator, too. They don't know how much brain damage there is. They were able to get her off the vent for a little bit, but then she got worse and they had to put her back on it. She keeps getting pneumonia."

"That must be really hard to watch."

"I wouldn't know. She got transferred to a big hospital in New Hampshire. Marcia is with her. She calls with updates and stuff." Andrew felt the color rise in his cheeks, partly because Laura had put her hand on his back, and partly because he felt like he might cry. He thought of the brief and sometimes terse phone conversations that had been occurring between him and Marcia every few days.

How is she?

The same.

And you?

Fine.

Andrew and Laura walked in silence for a few minutes. He felt like he had betrayed Sara by talking about her condition so openly. He felt confused and overwhelmed by Laura. His happiness to be with her was also excruciating. *Just calm down and be cool,* he thought, but he couldn't think of anything cool to say.

"We missed you at graduation," she said.

"How was it?"

"It was really great. And Jason said a lot of nice things about Sara."

"He must have been thrilled," Andrew said.

"What do you mean?"

"Getting to make the speech. Because Marcia wasn't there."

"Oh, Marcia was the real valedictorian?"

"Yes, of course." Andrew felt annoyed. Didn't everyone know how smart Marcia was?

"Oh. Well, I feel sad for her. I mean, it would have been her big moment."

"To tell you the truth, she was dreading it. She's very . . . shy."

"Oh?"

Andrew fell silent. He did not want to talk about Marcia. Graduation had occurred so close to the accident that Andrew had decided to skip it. The protestations of his parents were mild. Like Marcia, he took his exams, picked up his diploma, and called it a day.

"How are you feeling about everything?" Laura asked.

"Fine. Thanks for asking," he said.

"People care," she said.

"That's really nice," he said.

"I think of Sara sometimes—you know, in my prayers," she said.

"That's cool," he said.

"Sometimes . . ." Laura paused and looked at him. "Sometimes I think it helps to focus on someone you care about with . . . with, like, greater intensity than normal. I mean, more intense than usual. Um, does that make sense?" she asked, and gave a nervous little laugh. Her fingers shook, and she clasped her hands behind her back.

"Sure, yeah, that makes sense," he said.

"Like, you know, focused intensity," she said.

A fog began to clear for Andrew. "You mean prayer? So, prayer is just intense focus?" he said.

"Well, not just—" she said.

"No, of course not," he said.

Andrew thought of one of Janet's friends—Helen, who wasn't really a friend but someone from the cheese factory who had showed up at the hospital one day to offer her *support*. Helen was pushy and unpleasant. She kept crowing about the power of prayer and gripping a Bible in her hands as though it were an oxygen tank and she couldn't breathe without it. Eventually, in a rare show of her pre-accident self, Janet told Helen that she smelled like rancid whey, and the stench was making her ill.

It was different with Laura. They were just talking, right? And the idea that she was trying to lure him into her faith was paranoid and mean. Or maybe not. He needed to make things clear.

"I don't believe in that stuff, Laura."

"That's okay," she said quickly. Her hands fluttered out from behind her back, and she crossed her arms in front of her chest. She looked at the ground and rose up and down on her toes; she was either nervous or impatient or both. It was strange, because she'd been so calm and confident when she'd first given him the note. Andrew wondered if maybe she'd been compelled by someone, somehow, to have this conversation with him. Maybe it had something to do with her church. He had a feeling that these religious types went after people when they were grieving and vulnerable. But Laura wasn't like that, was she? Or maybe she didn't want to be like that. He felt sorry for her, but then he thought, *Screw it. I've got to keep this going.*

"Religion is really interesting, though. In literature and films and paintings and stuff. It's always a big deal. A big th-theme, I mean," he stuttered, then continued in a hurry. "It's interesting, you know, in a conceptual way . . ." His voice trailed off. *Stop babbling.*

"Never mind," Laura said. "I mean, it's okay." She cleared her throat. "Would you like me to go to the hospital with you or something? Is it very far?"

"No," Andrew said. "I mean, yes, it's a few hours. But I don't think you should come." A protective feeling for Sara reared up inside him as he raised his eyes to Laura. He didn't want the hottest girl in their class staring down at the second-hottest girl in their class. It would somehow diminish Sara even further and complete Laura's absolute and incontestable triumph. But he knew such thoughts were ridiculous, petty, and strange. He knew that Laura and Sara were both incapable of thinking about the situation as he did. "I think I'm going crazy," he said.

He started to walk away, but she followed him.

"I want to show you something," she said. She lightly tugged him in the direction of the park on the outskirts of their neighborhood. He followed her.

Halgin Park was twenty square miles of protected state forest. The first few miles were outfitted with fitness paths, community shelters, and picnicking sites. Farther in it became wilder, acres and acres of woods with occasional man-made or animal-made trails. They crossed paths with a few joggers who said hello or smiled at them. A very thin woman wearing weights strapped to her ankles and wrists seemed to frown at Andrew. Or perhaps she was just concentrating on her own misery, he thought. Brian used to wear a kind of weighted vest while he was training for football season. He came home sweating rivers, smelling terrible, and idly basking in the adoring gazes of their parents.

"This is a deer path," Laura said, interrupting Andrew's thoughts.

"How can you tell?"

"Because it's so thin. They have small feet and they walk single file. They're very graceful."

"Yeah. Beautiful. Sometimes my dad and Brian make noises about hunting them, but it never happens."

"Because they don't want to kill them?"

"Inertia. They'd rather sit on the couch and watch the game. Or at least my dad would. But I don't think anything would stop Brian if you gave him a gun and a license to shoot it."

Laura turned around and looked at him, her eyes searching his face. He held his breath. Laura said she was taking him to a special place where she liked to pray. Andrew assumed they were going to Shaman's Point, a sun-drenched valley that appeared like a miracle in the deepest part of the woods. Andrew didn't know if Laura knew the unofficial name of the clearing, and he wasn't sure that she'd like it, given its witchcrafty tang.

He was realizing that Laura was curiously, beautifully ignorant of the local customs and culture of other people her age. Even though they'd attended the same schools and grown up in the same neighborhood, she and her religious kinsmen were somehow isolated from the larger world to which Andrew belonged. Laura didn't know that half the kids in their high school went to Shaman's Point to make out or have sex. She didn't know that this wasn't a deer path they were walking on, but cleverly made to look like one.

"Brian's your brother?" she asked.

And she didn't know who Brian was. Andrew felt a warmth in his body that spread up through his heart and reached into his throat.

"Yeah. He's three years older than me. He was a big star on the football team. Plays college, too," he said.

"Oh," she said, and continued to walk.

The canopy of green above them grew thicker and thicker. The sun-dappled light faded, and soon they were enclosed in the daytime semidarkness of a mature forest. He heard the soft rustle of leaves as small animals scurried past. He blinked as his eyes adjusted. The scent of pine became almost sticky in its sweetness. He could feel the wet of the air on his lips and cheeks.

Laura.

Andrew shoved his hands into his pockets, where he fingered pieces of lint that gathered in the corners.

"Careful," Laura said. She stepped gingerly around tree roots and fallen branches. The valley was just up ahead. A ray of sunlight hit the path in front of them and cast a glow over Laura. Her hair was parted, and the nape of her neck was just visible. Andrew gazed hungrily at that patch of bare skin. It wasn't so much that he wanted to kiss her as that he wanted to pull her to him and press his face into her neck. He was right behind her, inches from her.

Then they were in the valley. Sunlight was everywhere at once. Laura took off in a sprint. Andrew jumped. *Shit,* he thought. What was she doing? Was she running from him? He must have scared her. Breathing down her neck like some hulking monster. Fuck! Then Laura, mid-sprint, leaped up into the air like a ballet dancer and twirled around. She shouted to him, but he couldn't understand her.

"What?" he yelled back.

She ran closer until she was about five yards from him. She was laughing and smiling. Andrew had never seen her so happy, so unreserved.

"Come on," she said, and took off in another direction.

Andrew was not about to start running around.

"I like watching you," he said to her retreating form, knowing she couldn't hear him. He was baffled and charmed by this childlike side of her. She continued to dash around the field. He was almost embarrassed by the whole scene. Laura was so terribly pretty, and the field so picturesque, that it seemed like she was filming a commercial for panty liners.

He caught up to her at the rocks, the most appealing part of Shaman's Point. The six huge concave formations were smooth enough to sit on comfortably for hours. They looked as if they'd been hollowed out by the ocean, which they probably had been. He knew one of the rocks had a fish fossil on its side, but you had to hunt around to find it. Andrew smiled to himself. Another thing not to mention to Laura. Her parents, or perhaps her church, had arranged for her to leave class whenever the science teacher discussed evolution. Andrew felt bad for her when this happened. "Laura," Ms. Devaux would say. "We're going to talk about Darwin now." With a small, frightened, apologetic nod, Laura would get up and leave class with her eyes on the ground. A few people would usually chuckle, and girls who were jealous of Laura's beauty would make catty comments. But never Marcia or Sara. They just weren't like that.

Laura sat on the largest rock and waved him over. He sat next to her and waited as she caught her breath. His first kiss had been on this very rock. He and his one and only girlfriend, Rachel, had made out and fumbled around with each other's bodies on an almost daily basis for three months when they were fourteen. She dumped him right before sophomore year, after a mutually unsatisfying and almost entirely physical relationship.

"Want to pray?" Laura asked. She was catching her breath and grinning at him.

"Seriously?" Andrew said.

"Why not? I like praying when I'm happy like this."

"So you jog around before you pray? What if you're at home? Do you bust out some push-ups and sit-ups and then start?"

Laura looked baffled before she realized that Andrew was teasing. She burst out laughing. When her giggles subsided, she took on a serious expression. Her shift in mood, from hilarity to grimness, came too quickly, too suddenly. It puzzled Andrew. Before Laura could open her mouth, Andrew spoke.

"Thanks for showing me this place. It's really pretty."

"You're welcome," she said. "Let's pray."

Andrew was about to object when Laura picked up one of his hands. He wanted to entwine his fingers with hers, but she held his hand in her palms as if it were an injured bird. He felt his body go almost limp, and lowered his head.

Laura began, "Heavenly Father, we ask that you grace Sara—"

"No," Andrew said, "not Sara."

Laura dropped his hand. "What?"

"Not Sara, okay? I'm—" He groped for words, hot with shame. "I'm not ready for that."

Laura tapped her fingertips on her thigh and leaned back. Her honey-colored hair fell all around her shoulders and framed her face. One day in English class Mr. Gonzalez had given them an article about words in other languages for which there were no direct English translations. *Cafuné* had been Andrew's favorite. It was Brazilian Portuguese for "to tenderly run one's fingers through someone's hair." Andrew wondered what Laura would do if he tried to *cafuné* her.

"Okay," she said. "Let's just try something more general."

"Fine," Andrew said.

Laura lowered her head, and Andrew followed suit, but this time she did not take his hand. She murmured something, and Andrew leaned closer to her on the pretense of trying to hear her. Or *was* he trying to hear her? He wasn't even sure anymore. He was lost in all the sunlight. What was she saying? The Lord's Prayer? No, it didn't sound like that. He tried to follow along with her, hoping she'd touch him again. He felt like he could relate to bits and snatches of what she was saying. "Our savior . . . sin . . . save us . . . Jesus . . ." He'd heard something like these words before, in movies and books, or from some small corner of his childhood when his mom took them to church on Christmas Eve.

He closed his eyes. Laura's voice faded in and out like a radio station playing his favorite song, only he couldn't quite get the reception because he was in the car and driving away. Driving away with Sara. Going for some ice cream or just driving around for fun and for the meditative calm of the rhythmic wheels on the road. A gently rocking car. Sara in the backseat. Not just in the backseat but strapped in like a baby. Then he realized he was sitting right next to her. Who was driving? He was too scared to look. His heartbeat was fast, too fast, and he could hear it pounding in his ears. No, not pounding, *fluttering.* The sunlight came in through his lids and settled behind his eyes in spots and waves and jagged flashes. Now his heart seemed to hover in his chest like a hummingbird. He couldn't keep up. He couldn't stay here. He gasped and rose to his feet. Laura opened her eyes and looked at him, her expression both elated and curious.

"I think I'm having a panic attack or something," he said.

"Andrew?"

He walked away and tried to steady his breathing. It was so bright. He felt like he might faint. He heard Laura's footsteps behind, running to catch up.

"Andrew! Did you . . . ?" She put a hand on Andrew's shoulder. He whirled around and grabbed her. He buried his face in her hair. Her body was stiff, her arms at her sides. Andrew was gripping her so hard that she couldn't have hugged him back if she'd wanted to. They stayed this way for some moments. Slowly, he released her.

They walked back to their neighborhood in near silence. Every once in a while Laura asked Andrew if he was okay.

"It can be frightening the first time," she said. *Yes, it certainly can,* he thought. Laura asked him if he would come to her house that night. He nodded. *Of course I will.*

Andrew lay on his bed with one hand under his head, the other draped on his stomach. He stared at the ceiling. Becky was asleep on the floor, snoring. That snoring was getting louder, Andrew thought. He should call the vet. Loud snoring in big dogs was bad, wasn't it? He tried to get up but could not. He scratched at his belly button, a nervous gesture that he'd developed when he was little and that his mother detested. Once he'd picked at his belly button until it bled and he'd gotten an infection. He glanced down. *I'm literally navel gazing,* he thought.

He had a strong desire to talk to Sara and Marcia. The two of them would be able to break this down and give him some perspective. They wouldn't mind that Andrew had never told them about his Laura obsession. Besides, who was he kidding? They'd probably guessed by now anyway. Marcia would gently suggest that it might not be altogether ethically sound to pretend to have a religious experience to get into the pants of a naive girl. *Not above board,* Marcia would say, whereas Sara would uncompromisingly be in favor of Andrew doing what it took to get some action. *Whatever, Marcia,* Sara would say. *It would be good for Laura, too. Those superreligious kids get all freaked out about sex. It's not healthy. Next time, Andrew, start twitching like you're having a seizure, then tell Laura that God spoke to you and told you that she should—* And then Marcia would interrupt, her cool brown eyes on his face, her hands covering Sara's mouth, her voice saying, *Unless you actually had a religious experience. Did you, Andrew?*

He wasn't sure what had happened to him. He'd never had a religious experience before, or a panic attack, for that matter, unless you counted his shitty nightmares. He felt like whatever had happened to him at Shaman's Point had more to do with his desire for Laura and his grief for Sara. It was all mixed up. It had nothing to do with God. And besides, maybe he'd just been dehydrated or something.

Andrew sat up. Becky stretched and walked over to him. She put her great big head on his leg. There had been some stiffness in her walk lately. The vet's number was programmed into the phone downstairs. *Get up,* he told himself. Becky stood.

"Not you," he said out loud, rubbing her cheekbones. Andrew had ceased to be surprised by his telepathy with Becky. He got up and walked downstairs. He picked up the phone and thought about calling the hospital. He wasn't allowed to ask about Sara, but he could ask for Marcia, and she would give him an update. An update. *Nothing's changed. Sara's in a coma. If she wakes up at all, she might never walk again, talk again, eat real food again, have sex, fall in love.*

Fuck God, he thought, and slammed the phone down.

12

THE LIGHTS WERE DIM in the windows of Laura's house. She'd told him to come over at eight. He wondered if her parents had gone out and if they were going to be alone. Then he remembered that Laura had lots of little brothers and sisters. She had older siblings too, who were at college or out of the country. Andrew couldn't keep track of her family—in fact, he'd never really tried. All he knew was that none of them were attractive. Laura was a genetic miracle among them.

As he drew closer to the house he saw that several cars were parked outside on the street. He could hear voices and the sound of laughter. Someone was strumming a guitar. Andrew stopped, rolled his eyes, and gazed heavenward.

"Really?" he said to the sky. There was nothing Andrew hated so much as an acoustic guitar-led sing-along, a rather inconvenient dislike if you grew up in Vermont. He realized even before he rang the doorbell that this was some of kind of Friday-night youth prayer group jamboree. He had not been prepared for this.

A guy about his age or older answered the door. He was taller than Andrew, who at six two was fairly tall himself. The guy had a friendly smile and a crushing handshake. His fingers seemed to wrap around Andrew's wrist like snakes.

"You must be Andy," he said.

"Andrew."

"Nice to meet you. We're so glad you came. I'm John."

"What's up?" Andrew said.

"Come on in, my brother." John opened the door wider and gestured for Andrew to enter. John had a large tattoo of a blue cross running down one of his arms. He was muscular, Andrew noted, and his longish blond hair reached just above his shoulders. A born-again surfer dude.

He was led through a small kitchen. The countertops were worn and wooden. There was no food out, but it smelled like tomato sauce and garlic bread. A pile of clean dishes was neatly stacked in the drying rack. Pots, pans, and woven baskets hung from hooks in the ceiling. A cool breeze gently rustled the warm air. As Andrew looked around, he felt a kind of sick longing that made his hands tremble. Not longing for Laura, exactly, but for something else—her kitchen, her dishes.

"You hungry? There's plenty of food left," John said.

"I ate. Thanks." Andrew was intrigued. Did that mean that John had been invited to dinner sometime earlier and Andrew had not? Something about John's manner suggested he was overly familiar with the house: guiding Andrew around, showing him where to put his shoes, offering him food. Andrew looked sideways at John and again noted how strong he looked and the easy, athletic grace with which he moved. John reminded him of Brian. Andrew felt himself hardening his heart against this surfer dude Jesus freak with the freakishly large hands.

He followed John into the den, where eight or nine kids about Andrew's age lay draped over the couches and one another. Laura was on the floor. Another girl who Andrew recognized from school was seated above Laura on one of the couches. Laura's head was in this girl's lap. The girl stroked Laura's hair as she chatted with a goateed guy on the couch.

Andrew felt John's hand lightly graze the small of his back, and it made him jump. John smiled at him and then brought his hand up Andrew's back and clapped him on the shoulder.

"Everyone, this is Andrew," John said.

Andrew was greeted with a chorus of *Hey!* and *What's up?* Laura smiled at him but said nothing. John sat beside her and took up the guitar. The room was dimly lit by a few candles. Beanbags and pillows were scattered about.

"Come sit here, Andrew," said a guy's voice from a corner of the room. Andrew felt uncomfortable as he walked over. Laura had not yet said anything to him, and he didn't want to go bounding up to her like an overeager puppy.

"I'm Matt," the guy said as he stood up to shake Andrew's hand. Matt looked vaguely familiar. He had an androgynous haircut and bright blue eyes. A pretty boy, he might be called, if Andrew thought in such terms, which he generally did not. Matt looked like the kind of pop star who would appeal to shrieking preadolescent girls and their bored suburban mothers. He wore a wooden cross on a leather string around his neck. When Andrew shook hands with him, he felt something sharp in his palm and noticed that Matt wore a large thumb ring with some words inscribed on the metal.

"We're so glad you're here," Matt said. As he spoke he seemed to give Andrew a sympathetic, meaningful look.

"Oh. Thanks," Andrew said.

Matt smiled and sat down. Andrew glanced around. He wasn't sure where to sit.

A pretty girl was sitting next to Matt. She inched over, creating a small space between them. As Andrew began to sit down, Matt and the girl each took one of his arms in their hands and pulled, guiding him to the floor. He was more or less squished in between them. The girl shifted around until her leg was draped over his thigh. Matt turned his head toward John and discussed which song to sing next.

"Is that better?" she asked.

"What? Yes, this is fine," Andrew said. She had a thin body and soft brown eyes, light brown hair, and a very slight overbite.

She rubbed her thumb inside her upper lip as she spoke; perhaps she was self-conscious about her teeth. She wore a blue T-shirt—thin, like her, and the material looked worn. He could see the little threads hanging off her sleeves; he could see the outline of her small breasts.

"I'm Carrie," she said.

"Andrew." He extended his hand. She shook it lightly, but her touch lingered a moment.

"You just graduated with Laura?" she asked.

"Yup. Where do you go to school?" She looked too young to have graduated.

"Windham. I'll be a junior, like Matt," she said.

"Cool. Thinking about college?"

"Not yet."

"Plenty of time."

"I'll be going on my mission first. Some kids do it after college, but I'd like to go before." Now her thumb was back at her mouth. She bit the tip of it and shifted her gaze toward one of the candles on the floor.

"Ah," Andrew said. He looked toward Laura, who was leafing through some sheet music.

The guitar started strumming with greater purpose, and John hummed a few notes. Matt joined in, trying to get in tune with him. Andrew bristled. *Here it comes,* he thought. Then he felt Carrie's hand and her wet little thumb on his arm.

"I heard you had quite an experience the other day," she said.

Andrew nodded but didn't speak. He wondered what Laura had told these people. Carrie smiled. She seemed like a good sport. He leaned forward and whispered conspiratorially, "Do I have to sing?"

"No," she whispered back.

Laura's prayer group started to sing.

> In the darkness of the early morn,
> You stood against the light.
> Behind you, beside me,
> It grew bright, it grew bright.

They were all good singers. Laura, whose voice was the most beautiful, was singing quietly, as though not to overwhelm the others. John sang the loudest, tossing his hair and weaving back and forth in time with the music. *What a tool*, Andrew thought. He tried to concentrate on the pleasure of Carrie's thigh on top of his own. He imagined it was Laura sitting next to him.

> I close my eyes,
> But you're still there
> Inside me, beside me.
> It's all right, it's all right.

Now Carrie was rocking side to side, her shoulder brushing up against him as she closed her eyes and sang.

Grace me with your love,
Oh, the mercy of your touch.

With her eyes still closed, Carrie took his hand and gripped it tightly. *Well then, this is kind of awesome,* Andrew thought, but it was not Carrie whom he wanted. He was smart enough to realize she didn't want him, either. One thing Andrew prided himself on was his ability to keep his cool around pretty girls and their meaningless flirting. He knew that he'd learned this trick from Sara, who, throughout their friendship, had always flirted with him, touched him, put her head on his shoulder when they studied from the same book, and settled herself into his chest when they watched movies. He knew that the physical intimacy between him and Sara had made him seem pretty cool, thereby easing his passage through high school. She had emboldened his sense of self with her friendship, her affection, her love. Because of Sara, his identity had been transformed from Brian Genter's geeky little brother to that of a quiet, smart guy who was somehow on touchy-feely terms with one of the hottest girls in school.

Beside me, inside me,
An angel in my life, in my life.

What was *up* with these lyrics? But now he was trembling and thinking about Sara. Sara in the cafeteria, flopping down in between him and Marcia and instantly making them cool. Sara in his car, turning up the music and howling out the window. Sara in her bathroom, half naked, flirtatious, and making him feel attractive and . . . confident. His eyes welled up. The singing grew louder. He covered his face with his hands and tried to control himself. Matt put his arm around Andrew's shoulders, and at first Andrew felt a violent urge to shrug him off. But then Carrie released his hand and encircled his waist with her tiny arm. He leaned back into them both and quietly cried.

They spent the rest of the evening eating potato chips and singing. Andrew found the songs to be a strange mixture of moving and laughable, but he didn't laugh. The truth was, Andrew felt better than he had in weeks. The candlelight was soft, everyone was nice and much more down-to-earth than he had expected. The only drawback was Laura, who was absorbed with one person or another, never him. Whenever he managed to catch her eye from across the room, she smiled at him, but her smile was a dazzling brightness that lacked any true connection.

The group seemed to be taking a break. They were milling about the house now, getting more soda and breaking off into smaller groups. He stood up to stretch his legs and thought about going outside to get some fresh air. Maybe Laura would like to join him? He looked over at her. She smiled again, but this time she gave him a slight wink. His heart leaped as he started to walk toward her.

"Do you have a headache?" It was John, who towered above Andrew. "It helps to rub here," John said. He made small circular movements with his fingers on Andrew's temples. John's hands blocked Andrew's peripheral vision so that Andrew was forced to lock eyes with him.

"I don't have a headache," Andrew said.

"That's cool, man," John said as he dropped his hands. "I'm really into alternative therapies. And, you know, sometimes I get a headache after I cry."

I will hit this guy, Andrew thought. Instead he glanced away, toward Laura, who was hugging the guy with the goatee.

John followed Andrew's gaze. "That's Seth. He's going to Ghana at the end of the summer."

"No shit?" Andrew said, raising his eyebrows.

"Yeah, no shit," John said flatly.

For a moment Andrew felt that the brotherly love pretense was off. Was John a rival for Laura's affections? Was pretty boy Matt? Seth? Were they all bullshitting about Jesus? Or was it real? Or both? It was just too much.

"I have to go," Andrew said. He made for the door, not stopping to say good-bye to Carrie or even Laura, who had pretty much ignored him all evening anyway and was probably still hugging Goatee Seth.

"Wait, man. Wait. Andy!" John came after him. "Take this," he said. It was a Bible. "Just take it, no big deal," John said.

Andrew was about to refuse but stopped at the look in John's eyes. There was something painful in his expression, even tragic. Andrew blinked, and the pained expression was gone. Perhaps he had imagined it. He reached out and took the Bible.

"Thanks," he said.

"You're welcome," John said as Andrew slipped out the door.

He walked briskly down the street and tried not to look back. He felt the hairs stand up on the back of his neck. Maybe Laura was peeking at him through the windows.

13

HIS FATHER WAS UP. He saw the eerie blue light of the television flickering out the living room windows. He went in through the kitchen door and quietly greeted Becky. He heard his father laugh. How drunk was that laugh? Andrew was skilled at gauging the sobriety of his father based on his laughter, his snorting, his incoherent mumblings—even the way he moved around the house. Slightly drunk and he might verbally lay into Andrew about some minor infraction like leaving Becky's dirty bowls in the sink. Very drunk meant that he would totally ignore Andrew but might suddenly, and without warning, grab him or throw a punch—although this hadn't happened in a while. Rip-roaring past-the-point-of-no-return drunk meant that Andrew did not exist.

Andrew decided that his father wasn't quite drunk enough.

His mother was probably asleep, and Brian was out doing whatever Brian did on a Friday night. For a second he felt a stab of pity for his father. He had so looked forward to Brian coming home, and Brian probably didn't spend any real time with him. Andrew motioned for Becky to follow him out the door. They walked down the street together, free from the house, inhaling the starlight.

His father's drinking had gotten worse after Brian left for college. Brian's stunning success on the football field, his golden boy status in their town (Brian "the Great" Genter), had been a source of continual happiness and pride for their father. Brian had enjoyed being petted and worshipped by everyone around him—their dad played a major role in this behavior. But all the dick sucking had made Brian an asshole. He seldom called. He spent most of the summer away or with his friends. He was home for two days during Christmas break and spent the rest of the time somewhere else.

Until now it had not occurred to Andrew that Brian might be purposely staying away. That Brian's relationship with their father, which appeared to be close, might in reality be strained. It must have been weird for Brian to realize, if he did realize, that their father lived through his athletic successes.

As with their father when he was extremely drunk or completely sober, Andrew more or less did not exist to Brian. Brian would occasionally punch him in the arm, cuff his neck, and call him a fag, or something similar. This was the only way he had of communicating whatever affection or disdain he felt for his younger brother. A few times a year they mumbled hello and good-bye to each other, but that was it in terms of neutral interactions.

Andrew walked Becky to Halgin Park. They stood under the last streetlamp at the edge of the woods as Andrew contemplated whether he should go in at this time of night. He heard the river gurgling in the darkness beyond. Salamander River skirted the perimeter of the park and flowed into the lake. On warm days Andrew would take Becky for a swim either at the lake or just to splash around in the river.

It was a relatively warm night, and Becky started panting and galloping around the riverbank.

"It's kind of dark out, Becks," Andrew said.

Becky whined and touched his feet with her paws.

"I don't have a flashlight."

Becky started to dance around in circles, lifting her limbs up and down very quickly. When Becky had been a puppy, Andrew had enjoyed her I-want-something dance so much that he encouraged it by giving in to whatever it was she was demanding.

Becky had actually been a gift to Brian. For several months Brian had been begging his parents to give him a puppy for his twelfth birthday. All his friends had dogs, he argued, and he promised to take care of it. At Brian's party his wish was granted. There were many pictures taken that day of Brian and his friends running around the yard, playing games, and eating cake. Two rolls of film were allotted to the opening of his many presents, puppy included.

Andrew kept one particular picture from that day. In the picture, Brian is holding the puppy and smiling for the camera. Their mother is looking at Brian with an expression of delight. All Brian's friends are looking at Brian and the puppy with jealousy and rapture. Andrew lies underneath a chair that had been dragged in from the kitchen. He is squeezed between the legs of the chair, on which sits his father, who is also grinning at Brian. His uncle (now dead) took the picture. The only living things in the room who are not looking at Brian are Andrew and the puppy, who are staring intensely at each other.

Brian grew tired of Becky within a matter of weeks. He didn't really have time to take proper care of a dog because of all his practices and games and general lack of awareness of anything but himself. It took a while for their parents to realize that Andrew, not Brian, was Becky's caretaker. Andrew fed and walked her. He prompted his parents to take her to the vet when she was sick or due for a physical. He kept her vaccination record in a worn manila envelope in the top drawer of his desk.

Becky continued with her tap dance. "Fine. But I'm leashing you," Andrew said. He reached into his pocket and put her leash on, which she generally didn't need because she followed all Andrew's commands.

They walked to the river. Andrew stumbled a bit in the darkness, but Becky was surefooted. He sat on the edge of the river in the wet grass while Becky splashed around. He heard rather than watched her. He lay back on the grass and examined the sky.

Marcia had once taught him and Sara how to identify all the major constellations. All he could recognize now was the Big Dipper. With his hand he traced the outline of it and thought about that wacky prayer group. The winks, the smiles, the caressing hands, the overly long hugs—what exactly was being communicated? Maybe they were all just sexually frustrated. He could relate. Andrew wondered where Laura's parents had been. Probably they had their own prayer group somewhere else.

The dew from the grass tickled the hair on his arms. He sat up. It occurred to him that he couldn't hear Becky. He groped around and realized he was no longer holding the handle of her leash. It must have slipped out of his hand.

"Becky!" he shouted, and stood up.

Silence answered him.

"Becky, come here. Come here *now.*" Andrew strained to hear a pant or a bark, but all he heard was the gurgling of the river.

"Becky, come!"

Andrew approached the river and squinted up and down its length. He couldn't see anything. He walked a few feet upstream and shouted some more. Then a few feet downstream. His foot slipped, and he cursed as his knee smashed into a rock. As he hoisted himself up he fell again, and half his body went sliding into the water. He was alarmed at how cold the water was, and how strong the current. He pulled himself to the bank and tried to catch his breath. A sliver of light beamed down on him. He gazed up at the full moon, briefly revealed between the clouds. The light illuminated his surroundings. He looked around and said, "Becky?" in a tone so soft that it was almost a whisper. Then he said her name again, louder this time. There was no answer. There was nothing.

He lunged toward the river, shouting and tripping on slippery rocks. Upstream or down? *Up,* he decided. He fell several times before he realized that he could make more progress running on the side of the river instead of in it.

But along the bank there were thorny branches and pricker bushes. He fought a rising hysteria as he crashed through the woods. The river grew thinner here. He had made the wrong choice. Becky would have traveled downstream, where the water grew deep and still before it entered the lake.

He turned and ran. He breathed hard, gasping almost, as panic overtook him. He blundered forward, fell again, felt something wet trickle into his eyes, rubbed at it, and kept going. He shouted Becky's name until his voice was hoarse. He tasted something metallic in his mouth and spit. *Becky's a good swimmer,* he chanted to himself like a prayer. *Becky's a good swimmer.*

He was worried that she might be drowning somewhere and unable to bark, so he leaped back into the water and pushed along. He stretched his arms out to his sides as he moved, hoping that he might catch her if he couldn't see her in the darkness. The river was now chest deep, and its movement toward the lake was deceptively slow. Some tenacious power kept pulling his feet out from under him.

"Becky!" he yelled, but his voice was weak. He swam and ran and thrashed along, wildly waving his arms at his sides. Then a mess of weeds wrapped around his ankles and gently tugged him down. When his head went under the water, he panicked and swallowed. He opened his eyes, but all he could see was watery blackness. *Moving through darkness.* He wanted to scream.

Andrew kicked at the weeds that gripped his feet. He came back up, sputtering and dragging his body over the bank. Muddy water came out of his mouth when he coughed. His eyes stung terribly. In the distance, behind him, he heard a bark.

"Becky," he said, attempting to stand. She thundered toward him. When they were close enough to touch, Andrew wrapped his arms around her and Becky embraced him back, sitting upright with her paws around his shoulders. She whined and licked at his various wounds. He felt dizzy. Then he heard himself muttering a small prayer of thanks, repeating some of the words and phrases that he'd heard at Laura's house.

He lay on his back and caught his breath. The moonlight broke through the clouds again, and Andrew saw that he had traveled pretty far; the lake was just up ahead. He stood up, using Becky for support. They picked their way through the brush until they were walking back along the bank of the river.

Andrew coughed again and spit out the metallic-tasting liquid in his mouth. He touched his hand to his lips and then examined his fingertips—blood. He wiped his hand on the side of his pants. Everything hurt all at once. His head, legs, arms, back, and even his kneecaps ached. Becky trotted beside him with her head down. Either she was tired out or she had reflected and was ashamed of her part in the evening's drama. Andrew patted her head and said, "It's okay. It was my fault."

The house was silent when Andrew returned. He carried Becky through the kitchen and up the stairs so that she wouldn't get her muddy paws all over the place. Then he dried her off with some towels in his room and told her he'd give her a hot bath the next day. She inhaled some jerky treats, settled in next to his bed, and fell asleep. Andrew went to the bathroom to assess the damage. He had some scrapes on his legs and a gash on his left arm that was long but not too deep. He assumed he had bit the inside of his mouth one of the times he'd fallen. He raised his hands to his scalp and felt a sticky mess of hair and blood.

He took a hot shower and dressed his various scrapes with Band-Aids, gauze, and antibiotic ointment. The gash on his arm had stopped bleeding, as had the cut on his head, but the pain from the wounds diffused throughout his body into a single dull ache.

The moment before he closed his eyes, he had a fleeting fantasy of telling Laura that he had gotten beat up. Who knows? She might be into that.

14

ANDREW STUMBLED DOWN TO THE KITCHEN and made a pot of coffee. He had the worst headache of his life. The scratches and cuts on his face seemed to itch and ripple in rhythm with the pulse in his temples. Images from the night before came back to him in weird flashes: John's hand on his back, Laura's brilliant smile, the moonlight on the water.

God, my head hurts, he thought.

He tried to distract himself from the pain by glancing through his college paperwork. He had qualified for a work-study program where he'd be shelving books part-time at the library. He could either make his paycheck apply toward his tuition, or it could be extra money in his pocket.

Since he was twelve years old, Andrew had almost always had some type of part-time work: delivering newspapers, washing dishes, making photocopies at his father's real estate office, or tending to the palatial grounds at Avella. Andrew was good at work, especially if it was monotonous and lonesome. He could disappear into a task, committing his whole self to its completion. Shelving books at the library answered all his needs for employment.

He wondered if Marcia had qualified for work-study. Probably she had. He assumed that her father's life insurance policy had dwindled away by now. Marcia's mother was not capable of working, given her depression. Andrew thought that Marcia's successful brothers supplemented their income, but he wasn't sure, and Marcia never talked about it. Jack was a lawyer in New York City, and Walter was a banker of some sort. Walter lived in New Jersey and rarely visited.

"What happened to you?"

Andrew was startled out of his thoughts by his mother's voice. He looked at her in a daze. She seemed upset.

"Becky and I were in the woods last night. I tripped and fell."

"That's it?" she said.

"I didn't get beat up," he said.

"You're sure?"

"Yes, I'm sure."

They looked away from each other. When she reached for the coffeepot, Andrew got her a mug from the cupboard and held it steady as she poured herself a cup.

"Is the paper here?" she asked.

"Not here yet. Or maybe it is. I don't know," Andrew said. He put her coffee cup on the counter and walked down the hallway to the front door. He saw the Bible that John had given him on the floor and quickly picked it up and stashed it under a pile of his old schoolbooks. He doubted that either of his parents would care, but he wanted his bizarre foray into Christianity to be a secret from them. He grabbed the newspaper from the front steps and was ambling down the hallway when he heard the back door open and his brother come in. Andrew put the paper on the kitchen counter and grabbed the cordless phone.

"Hi, baby," their mother said.

"Hey," Brian said.

Andrew was about to go upstairs when Brian stopped him.

"What happened to you?" he asked.

"Tripped in the woods."

"That's weird."

"Why would that be weird?"

"I don't know." Brian shrugged and dropped onto a stool. He groaned and clutched his head. He looked like shit.

"Rough night?" their mother said to Brian.

"Nah," he said. "Are you sure you're okay?" he asked Andrew. Andrew was taken aback. He could not recall a time that Brian had ever been concerned about him.

"Why do you care?" he said, retreating up the stairs.

"Hey," he said when he got Marcia on the phone. "How is she?"

"The same," Marcia said.

"And you?"

"Fine. Kind of tired."

"So, what's the plan?"

"Watch and wait."

"And the pneumonia?"

"A little better," Marcia said.

"Oh, good. That's good." Andrew cleared his throat.

"So, what have you been up to?" she asked.

He decided to be honest. "Hanging out with a bunch of born-again Christians."

"So, you're finally making a play for Laura Lettel?"

Of course she knew. Andrew sighed.

"You know, I don't think she's actually born-again," Marcia said.

"They're extreme Christian something."

"What are they like?"

"They're really, like, I don't know. Kinda nice. Very touchy-feely. There's this big guy, John. He seems kind of older, kind of in charge. He was a little too eager."

"Too eager for what?"

"Shit, I don't know. To convert me, I guess." Marcia listened while Andrew went on to describe the people he'd met at the prayer group. She laughed slightly when he told her about how affectionate they'd all been.

"Most of them weren't from our school. Except for Laura and this one other guy. I think he's a junior. Matt something. He was okay."

"Matt Denver?"

"I guess. You know him?"

"Not really. I think he and Laura used to go out."

Andrew's stomach backflipped to the floor. "Oh," he said. *Not possible,* he thought immediately. He'd been following Laura around for three years. How could he have missed a boyfriend? On the other hand, Laura was often inaccessible. He only really saw her in the hallways and the occasional shared class. Maybe she and Matt were still going out?

"Brian home yet?" Marcia asked, interrupting his thoughts.

"Yes. Christ, he's such an ass."

"Just let it go. Or try to. You're almost out of there."

"I know. It was weird. This morning he was all worried about me or something."

"Why?"

"I tripped in the woods and got a little bruised up," he said. "Actually, it was more than that." Andrew took a deep breath before he continued. It was a relief to be telling the truth about the other night. He hadn't yet grappled with how awful it had all been. "Becky jumped in the river, and I almost lost her. Then I jumped in after her and almost drowned."

"Are you kidding me?"

"Maybe I'm exaggerating. But I did go under for a few

moments. I felt like I couldn't get air. The water was so cold and—and, Marcia, remember what that guy said about moving through darkness?"

"What? Um, no," she said. She sounded distracted.

"You know, the guy in the mini-coma. When he woke up, he kept telling everybody about how it was like 'moving through darkness.' I think I felt that way for a second. Do you think that Sara—"

"I have to go."

"Oh, okay, well—"

"Bye."

The line clicked off. Andrew listened to the dial tone for a few seconds before hanging up. Marcia had sounded kind of angry. Had something happened to Sara? He was further from them both than he'd ever felt in his life, and just when he needed them the most.

15

HE TOOK BECKY OUT for a long walk, avoiding the woods. She stuck close to his side. The more he thought about it, the more he felt that Marcia had ended their phone call because she'd been pissed at him, not because something new had happened to Sara. Perhaps she didn't want to hear about him trying to pursue some girl while she, Marcia, tended to their sick friend. But maybe it wasn't all about Laura. He didn't like to admit it, even to himself, but last night, and in the woods with Laura, he'd felt *something*. It had been cathartic to cry about Sara with all those people around, offering him their support, looking at him with affection and sympathy in their eyes. No one had talked to him about Jesus or pushed anything like that. It had been weird, for sure, but not *that* weird. They were nice.

The house was empty when he got back. The three of them

had gone out somewhere, probably to buy Brian a big greasy breakfast to work off his hangover. There was a note on the kitchen counter that read *Someone named Matt called. He said to meet them at the church if you can. He's there already.* The note was in his mother's handwriting.

Andrew felt funny about going to their church. It was a Saturday, however, so he didn't think he'd have to endure a service and a bunch of prying adults. He called Laura's house, but no one answered. Not even a machine picked up. He wondered why Matt, not Laura, was calling him. Was Laura trying to maneuver away from him? He grabbed his car keys and left.

Laura's church wasn't a white-steepled New England beauty like on all the picture postcards of Vermont. It looked like a small office building. It was plain, square, and beige, with ample parking. You wouldn't even know it was a church if it weren't for the small cross and the ALL ANSWERS HERE! placard. There were a few men doing lawn work. As soon as Andrew got out of his car, one of them waved to him and said, "They're out back."

"Oh. Thanks," Andrew said. Apparently he was expected. As he walked around the building, he heard singing. Choir practice? Andrew thought he had made it pretty clear the night before that he wasn't going to sing. When he got to the back of the building, he saw John carrying boxes of produce.

"Hey," Andrew said.

"Hey, man!" John said. "I'm glad you came."

"Me too."

John peered at him. "Are you okay?"

"Tripped in the woods. I'm fine," Andrew said. "Can I help you with those?"

"I've got it. Come on down." John gestured with his head toward a door that was propped open. Andrew followed him inside. Now he could hear the music more clearly. It was reggae. He and John were in a small dark hallway. Off to one side was a set of stairs from which the reggae, and the smell of food, was emerging.

Andrew looked at John questioningly.

"Soup kitchen," John said.

"Cool," Andrew said.

At the bottom of the stairs was a brightly lit industrial-looking kitchen. There were two stoves, two refrigerators, and one enormous sink. The walls were lined with hanging pots and pans, some of which were huge and battered with age. Large metal prep tables were everywhere. A paint-spattered boom box blasted Bob Marley. The kitchen was filled with teenagers, some of whom he recognized from the night before. It was a little chaotic, but everyone seemed to move with purpose and intent. It was like a colony of worker ants, Andrew thought. And where was their queen? He looked around for Laura. A quick scan confirmed that she wasn't there.

"Got the veggies," John said, heaving the boxes onto a prep

table. The table shuddered under the sudden weight.

"You need a reimburse?" asked Carrie.

"Nope. Just bad enough to be free," John said.

This was followed by a few cheers and a chorus of groans.

"Free is free," Matt said. He noticed Andrew and motioned him over.

"Can someone say fruit flies?" said another girl. Andrew chuckled.

"I'll get the vinegar," John said.

Matt was chopping onions at one of the tables. Andrew saw that he had a wide berth. The pile of onions was pretty impressive. So was the gigantic knife that Matt wielded.

"Please tell me you can stand onions," Matt said.

"I can," Andrew said. For whatever mysterious reason, Andrew's eyes did not tear up around onions.

"Yes!" Matt said. He pumped his knife in the air. "I'm not alone anymore."

"Take it easy there," Andrew said.

Andrew washed his hands and selected a knife, much more reasonably sized than the one Matt had. People smiled and said hello to him, danced around to the reggae, threw flour at one another. It was dorky, but the overall vibe was nice.

"What happened to your face?" Matt asked quietly once Andrew joined him at the table.

"Just some bullshit. Nothing. I mean, I tripped in the woods," he said.

"Okay. If you ever want to talk . . ."

"About tripping?" Andrew said, but he was touched by the sympathy in Matt's voice. He also noticed that Matt was chopping his onions very haphazardly.

"Here, let me show you something," Andrew said. "Chop the onion in half first. Now hold it like this. Put your knife right up against your fingers, almost against your nails. As you slice, just keep sliding your fingers back. Let the knife do the work. Make sense?"

"I won't cut myself?"

"You won't cut yourself. Slice with the knife, slide your fingers back, slice with the knife, slide your fingers back. It's all one motion."

Matt did as he was instructed. "Seems slower," he said.

"At first," Andrew said. "Once you get it, you'll go really fast. See? Watch." Andrew demonstrated his onion-cutting technique. Perfect half-moons shredded out beneath his hands.

"Damn," Matt said. "Check this out."

Andrew suppressed a pleased grin when a group of people gathered around to watch him.

"How professional," someone whispered in his ear. It was Carrie. He turned to say something to her. But just then John asked for her help on the other side of the room.

"You want *me* to help you carry that stuff?" she said as she walked away. Andrew privately agreed with her. Carrie was tiny—why would John want her to help haul heavy boxes? But maybe John had a thing for her. Andrew wanted to figure out the social dynamics of the group. He continued cutting the onions as the rest of the crowd dispersed, intent on completing their own tasks.

"Where did you learn that?" Matt asked.

"I worked as a dishwasher at the co-op. The chef there was amazing. Like, this French-trained dude. His assistant was this local kid who was always high. He was nice enough, just stoned out of his gourd. One day Chef was really behind, so he taught me how to cut onions."

"Did the stoner do the dishes?"

"Please."

"Did you turn him in?"

"What? To my boss or something?"

"Or the police," Matt said solemnly.

"No, man, no," Andrew said with a chuckle.

"You're at Avella now, right?" Matt said.

"How did you know?"

"Someone must have told me," Matt said vaguely.

Someone, Andrew thought. Had they been talking about him? Discussing him during secret meetings? He heard raucous laughter, and when he looked up, he saw John carrying a sack of potatoes in one arm and Carrie in the other.

"Cute," Andrew said, motioning his knife toward Carrie. Matt seemed perturbed.

"Yeah," Matt said. "John's always messing around."

"I mean Carrie. She's cute."

"Oh, I know what you meant, sorry. You're right."

Matt seemed uncomfortable. Maybe talking about cute girls in the basement of his church was against their doctrine, or Matt's personal code of ethics. But Andrew didn't want to drop it. He wanted to steer the conversation toward Laura.

"Speaking of which, where's Laura?"

Matt dropped his knife and instinctively reached to catch it. Andrew grabbed his wrist just in time. The knife clattered to the floor. A few people looked up.

"You guys all right?" John asked, appearing suddenly beside Andrew.

"I'm fine," said Andrew.

"Me too," Matt said. He walked away. "I just need to get some air. Back in a sec."

Andrew watched Matt as he slipped between the prep tables and headed up the stairs. So Matt was touchy about Laura. There must be something there.

"I can help you finish," John said. He picked up Matt's knife and brought it to the sink. He came back a few moments later, and the two of them put their heads down and chopped, no small talk. Like Andrew, John knew how to work, and Andrew respected that. When they had finished chopping the onions, they piled them into a huge bowl and brought them over to the stove.

"Are we making soup?" Andrew asked.

"Some kind of stew. I never know. I just carry stuff and chop stuff," John said.

Andrew noticed that John's eyes were watery and red. Even his face looked a bit puffy. "Shit, John, you should've let me finish the onions."

"I'm okay," John said.

Two youngish-looking girls and a guy came to take the onions over to the stove. They thanked Andrew, and one of the girls, who couldn't have been more than thirteen, said, "God bless you," to Andrew.

"Thanks," Andrew said.

"You want a tour?" John asked.

"I can keep chopping stuff," Andrew said.

"That part's over. We're not much use here now. I can show you the chapel," he said.

"I think I'd rather not. Or maybe later." The God Bless You Girl had freaked Andrew out. She was so young, so very sure of herself, so content. It was eerie. "Where's Laura?"

"Hmm, let's see. She wasn't here? Probably with Chip," John said.

"Who?" Andrew said, but someone asked John for help and he was already walking away. John, Matt, Seth, now Chip . . . who were all these guys in Laura's life? Andrew wiped down the table and threw away the onion skins. After that, he wasn't sure what to do with himself. Matt still hadn't surfaced, and the only people left were the pious-looking tweens at the stove.

Everyone else had cleaned up and gone off on some other duties.

"Now where did all those little ants go?" he muttered to himself.

"Little what?" said a voice behind him.

Andrew turned, embarrassed. The speaker was a girl about his age or older. She was very thin, rather pointy-looking, and she had short brown hair and small dark eyes. She was frowning at Andrew. She was dressed in jean shorts and a tank top.

"Sorry, just talking to myself," Andrew said.

The girl stepped forward. Her face was very close to his, and the somewhat accusing expression in her eyes did not change. "So, you're the new guy," she said.

"Um . . ." Andrew began.

"Nice shorts," Matt said. He walked toward them. Andrew was glad to see him again.

"Shut up," said the girl, but she grinned.

"This is Karen," Matt said.

Andrew extended his hand. Karen looked at it for a moment before taking it. She very faintly snorted as she shook his hand. Her grip was firm.

"I'm Andrew," he said.

"I know," she said.

"Be nice," said Matt.

"Whatever. I'll be downstairs," she said.

"Karen's moody," Matt said, once Karen had walked away.

"Did I do something to offend her?" Andrew asked.

"I'm sure you didn't. Let's get the banquet hall ready."

Andrew followed Matt toward the stairs. He wondered where Karen was going, as there was apparently a level even farther down than this one. Was Laura down there too?

16

MATT BROUGHT ANDREW TO a bright room that had been made up as a kind of makeshift cafeteria. A few kids were setting up tables and chairs. Andrew didn't recognize anyone. It was as though the church had an inexhaustible army of teenagers to do their bidding. These kids seemed more serious, more subdued than the reggae-dancing bunch downstairs. The mood of solemnity affected him, too. He and Matt grabbed some collapsible tables that were stacked against the wall and set them up around the room. The tables were heavy. Andrew was in better shape now that he'd been working at Avella, but Matt struggled. They worked hard.

"When do people come for the food?" Andrew asked.

"Five o'clock," Matt said, out of breath.

"It's really nice that you guys do this."

"Thanks. It's cool that you're here," Matt said.

"Will we serve the food?"

"If you want," Matt said.

When they were finished, they carried dishes up from the kitchen. Andrew felt good. He'd never done any volunteer work before. He crouched underneath one of the tables so he could plug in a hot plate for the soup. When he crawled back out, someone had extended their hand to help him up. He took the hand and came face-to-face with one of the solemn teenagers. He was pale with very dark slicked-down hair and light blue eyes. "Have you accepted Jesus?" the guy asked.

"Not yet," Andrew said. He'd planned an answer to this question in advance.

"He's waiting for you."

"All right," Andrew said. He tried to pull his hand away, but the guy clasped it tightly. A girl came over and put her arm around Andrew's shoulders. Her hair was pulled into a fierce ponytail, and her expression was comically grumpy. The two of them closed their eyes and murmured. Andrew was spooked, but he didn't want to shake them off, either.

"Come on, you two, back to work," Matt said.

"We're almost finished," said the guy.

"Finished what?" Andrew said, and this time he did pull his hand away.

The guy didn't answer. The girl kept murmuring, her arm firmly around Andrew's shoulders.

"Kylie, Jeb, I'm serious," Matt said. He walked over to them and pried the girl's hand off Andrew's shoulders. The two of them dispersed, the guy mumbling something about Matt being "too cool."

"Well, that was weird," Andrew said.

"Sorry about that."

"Maybe I should go. I seem to be causing a stir."

"What are you talking about?" Matt said.

Andrew thought about Karen's catty attitude and comment about him being "the new guy." He was beginning to like Matt, and John, too, for that matter, but this was going further than he'd intended. He took his keys out his pocket and glanced at his watch. "I really need to get going anyway," he said.

"Want to see Laura?" Matt said.

"What?"

"She's picking flowers for the tables. She's out back."

Andrew *did* want to see Laura. His pleasant feelings about helping out were mitigated by the suspicion that he was being manipulated, but damn it, he wanted to see Laura.

"I'll bring you over there," Matt said.

This is getting weirder and weirder, Andrew thought. He felt like Laura was being dangled in front of him like a carrot or a longed-for present. *For Christ's sake,* he thought, *she's not a prize heifer; she's a person.* And this final thought at least brought some resolve.

"Yes, I'd like to see her," he said. "Just tell me where she is and I'll go myself."

"Go out the door you came in, and walk straight. It goes

right into a field." Matt spoke with casual nonchalance, as if it were all no big deal. Andrew thanked him and left the banquet hall. When he walked out the door, again he saw John, who was loading boxes into the back of a pickup truck. John waved, but Andrew regarded him warily.

He walked into the field, feeling as though he were being watched. He shrugged off the feeling. Probably just paranoia. Now he thought perhaps he had overreacted. They weren't the Children of the Corn; they were just really religious, right? The grass in the field grew thicker and longer. He stumbled, and something clattered and cracked under his feet.

"Shit," he said. He leaned down to examine what he'd broken. It was a Mason jar.

"Hi there," Laura said.

Andrew looked up. Her hair was down, her dress was white, and her arms were full of flowers.

"Hi," he croaked.

"What are you doing?"

He stood up and noticed that her feet were bare. "Don't move," he said.

Laura, who had been advancing toward him, now froze. "A snake? Don't tell me it's a snake. I'll totally scream."

"It's not a snake—"

"Ohmygod, it's a snake." She dropped the flowers. "And I just took the Lord's name in vain." She pressed her hands to her mouth. She seemed on the verge of screaming. "And what happened to you?"

"Laura, chill out. First of all, there is no snake. Second, I tripped in the woods last night. And thirdly, I just stepped on a jar. In fact"—he looked around—"why are there Mason jars everywhere?"

"I put the flowers in them."

"Where are your shoes?"

"Over there, I think." Laura pointed.

"Okay. Just stay there. I'll go get them."

"Thanks," Laura said. She bent down to pick up the flowers.

Andrew waded out into the field, searching for her shoes. He realized after a few minutes that he wasn't going to find them. "Did you leave them by a rock or a tree or anything?"

"Um, no, I just kicked them off."

He poked around some more, scanning the ground. He was reminded of when he'd first fallen in love with Laura. It had been their sophomore year. He'd been studying geometry in the library. He had finally worked out a difficult problem and had been taking a break by leaning back in his chair and stretching. He'd glanced around and seen her. She'd been leaning up against the stacks in the classics section. Like a lot of guys, he'd thought Laura was very pretty. But he had never been obsessed with her or anything.

He wasn't able to tell what she'd been reading, but she'd been absorbed. She'd worn sandals and shorts. Then it had happened. Without looking up from her book she'd slipped the sandal off her right foot and used her toes to scratch her left ankle. She'd put her sandal back on, turned the page, and sighed. It'd been as if a thousand stars had burst in his brain and descended into his body. He'd suddenly felt hyperalert and hyperaware. All his senses had sharpened, and the room and Laura had come into startling focus. The smell of pencil eraser and lead, the glare of the fluorescent lights, and *Laura, Laura, Laura.* Just standing there, just reading with a little smile on her face, just breathing and being alive.

He had never been the same. It had been as though he'd dove into a dream, or awoke from one, and the new reality, the Laura reality, was the only life he'd ever known. And it didn't matter if he was eating or playing with Becky or fighting with his parents or horsing around with Sara and Marcia—another part of him was constantly preoccupied with Laura. Now he was always half present; he couldn't stop thinking about her if he tried. And he had tried—he had. It was impossible, it was depressing, it was all-consuming misery. It was that kind of love.

"I can't find them," he said.

"Shoot," Laura said. "We'd better get back."

"Why did you take your shoes off?"

"Oh, I don't know. I like the feel of the grass between my toes. I like—" She giggled. "I like picking flowers in my bare feet." She had gathered all her flowers into a single bouquet. The sun shone brightly behind her, creating a hazy halo around her amber hair.

"And exercising before you pray," said Andrew as he reached her.

"That too," she said. "Can you help me over the glass?" She placed one arm around his neck, and he picked her up easily. His heart felt like a caged animal in his chest.

"Can we make it back?" she asked.

"No problem," Andrew said. He walked slowly back to the church parking lot.

"Did you have fun in the kitchen?"

"Sure, yeah."

"Don't try to convince me or anything," she said with a laugh.

"Sorry," he said. He wondered if he should put her down, as they were way past the broken glass. But she didn't seem to mind being carried, and he certainly didn't mind carrying her.

"Do you need convincing?" she asked.

"About what?" he said.

She wrapped her other arm around his neck and balanced the bouquet on her stomach and chest. To his mortification, Andrew sneezed. He sneezed and sneezed again.

"Oh no—allergies?" she asked, trying to angle the flowers away from his face.

"I'm fine," Andrew said, who was commanding superhuman strength to prevent himself from sneezing again. "Why Mason jars?" he asked.

"You can only preserve food in them once, just to be safe. Then after you eat the food, you have all these jars," she said.

"Ah," Andrew said. "Ah, ah, ah, *choo*!" He turned his head away at the last moment. He felt two thin streams of mucus running out his nose and down his face. *Unfuckingbelievable,* he thought. Laura lowered her face, either from disgust or compassion or both. They'd reached the edge of the parking lot. John ran up to them.

"What's going on?" he said, his voice sounding the least friendly that Andrew had ever heard. With a quick motion Laura twisted her body and leaped out of his arms. Andrew gave way to a fit of sneezing. Through a haze of snot, breathlessness, and bone-chilling embarrassment, Andrew heard Laura explaining to John about her shoes.

"Here, here," John said. He took off his shirt and handed it to him.

"Dude, I'm not going to take—" And he sneezed again, twice, then three times.

John shoved his shirt in Andrew's face. It was rank with man sweat. Andrew wiped his nose and face. A few people in the parking lot, including Karen and Carrie, were watching. He heard someone laughing.

"Listen," John said, standing close to him and almost whispering. "I know today was weird. And now this. Just go home and take some allergy medicine. It's all good, okay? I really think you should go home right now."

John rubbed his neck briefly and hard before he and his impossibly chiseled torso and his stupid long hair and his arm around Laura's waist disappeared into the church.

17

He threw John's shirt into the backseat of his car and slammed the door. He'd had Laura *in his arms,* and all he could do was talk about Mason jars and have a sneezing fit. He banged on the steering wheel and shouted. All he wanted was to crawl into a hole. He needed to reflect on the utter weirdness of the entire afternoon. He also wanted desperately to talk to Marcia and Sara. Thoughts of Sara, of his need of her, brought him back to a depressing shame spiral.

The house looked different when he pulled into his driveway. He couldn't put his finger on it, but when he got out of his car, he felt an inkling of dread. As he neared the back door, he heard his parents fighting.

"Shut the fuck up. I mean it, Sharon." Andrew rushed through the door. His father rarely used his mother's name, and if he did, it meant things were seriously bad between them.

"I'm home!" he shouted. For a few seconds he was met with dead silence. His father walked slowly into the kitchen. He looked terrible and terrifying. His mouth was set in a deep frown, his face ruddy.

"Dad," he said.

"I presume you've heard the news?" From the other room, his mother let out a strangled sob. Andrew tried to maneuver around his father. "Mom, are you okay?"

"She's fine," his father said. "Brian's been arrested."

Andrew froze. "For what?" he asked. His mother cried louder, harder.

"I said shut up!" his father barked. This time Andrew did push around him, narrowly avoiding his massive outstretched arm. His mom was on the couch, crying. He sat next to her. She was upset but seemed otherwise unharmed. He put his hand tentatively on her knee.

"Mom?" he said.

"It'll be on the news!" she wailed. His father stomped up the stairs, cursing. Andrew didn't press her. After a few moments her tears subsided and she stood up. She took a deep breath and turned toward him.

"Brian's been arrested for assault. It was him and some other guys. But it's all lies. All of it. Brian wouldn't hurt . . . Brian wouldn't hurt someone like that!"

"Hurt someone like what?"

"You know, it was a girl."

"What? Rape?" Andrew gripped the edge of the couch. He felt like he was going to be sick.

"Andrew, I said it's all lies! Brian said so."

"Who is she? Is she okay?"

"What? I—I don't know!" his mother said. She turned and left the room. His father was yelling into the phone and walking down the hallway and turning on the radio. All these sounds were muffled and strange and seemed to be coming from deep within Andrew's head.

"Andrew, come here!" his father said.

As Andrew walked up the stairs he saw Becky poke her head outside of his room. With a slight gesture Andrew indicated that she should stay. Her great black body disappeared behind the door like a seal slipping back into the ocean.

"Fill up the car," his father said as he handed Andrew twenty dollars.

"Where are you going?" Andrew said.

"Dexter," his father said. Dexter was a small town up north. Why had Brian been all the way up there? He looked at his father, who now looked purposeful, energetic, and angry in an excited way. Andrew turned away in disgust. *Fucking Brian,* he thought. *Motherfucking Brian.* He shook his head to clear the images that came to him. He did not want to think about it.

Andrew rarely drove his parents' car. His own car was a beat-up '85 Corolla hatchback with a standard shift. He had paid for it after two summers at Avella. His parents' car was an automatic, and Andrew awkwardly adjusted to driving it, his left foot constantly looking for a clutch that wasn't there.

A morbid satisfaction crept into his heart. Driving this car was a grand but stupid metaphor for himself and his relationship with his family. An ill fit. A pointless groping for something that did not exist.

It cost thirty dollars to fill the tank. His parents must be going to bail Brian out or visit him. He got them a couple of coffees and placed them in the cup holders. He took pleasure in the fact that his thoughtfulness toward them would be unappreciated and unnoticed. He was the sniveling resentful good son. Perhaps they sensed this and disliked him the more for it. His dad did, anyway. He could never quite tell with his mom.

He stopped at a red light and stared at the dashboard. It was clean in here. His mother got carsick easily so she had the car washed, inside and out, almost every month. The car was a year old, but it still smelled like a new car. It was a strangely intoxicating scent. Why was that? Then he remembered: Sara had once said that the smell turned her on, that one day she wanted to have sex in a new car. They had been driving around in Jack's new car. He was home for Christmas and had let Marcia borrow it, a brave as well as generous gesture because Marcia was a terrible driver. Overly cautious, afraid of hurting herself or others, she crept around the streets like an old lady. She gripped the wheel, staring straight in front of her, refusing both Sara's and Andrew's offers to drive. "One day I'd really like to have sex in a new car," Sara said. There was an awkward silence. Then Marcia said stiffly, "Today will not be that day, Sara." They had all burst out laughing.

When Andrew got back home, his parents were dressed, packed, and ready to go. His father was still talking on the phone, and his mother was bustling around the kitchen and running her hands along countertops in a frantic and pointless manner.

"This could ruin him." Her voice cracked. Like a child, she covered her face with her hands. Andrew was touched.

"It's okay, Mom," he said.

"It's not okay!"

"Fine. Whatever," Andrew said. He tossed the keys on the counter and went upstairs.

"Whatever. That's your answer for everything!" his mother shouted to his back.

"It's as good an answer as any," he said.

He was about to go to his room to get Becky when his father hung up the phone and said, "Hey."

"Yes?" Andrew said.

"What happened to your face?" His father looked at him and then at the ground. He jiggled his leg restlessly and cleared his throat a few times.

He thinks he might've done this to me, Andrew realized. The thought made him feel annoyed and vaguely satisfied and even a little sorry for his father.

"I tripped in the woods. I'm fine," Andrew said. He tried to sound reassuring, then wondered why. *Oh, fuck him,* he thought.

"The charges might not stick, in which case we'll raise hell for an early bail," his father said.

"Okay."

"Or we might be back Monday if it takes that long."

"Okay."

"When are you leaving for college?"

"Month and a half."

"You're almost eighteen, right?"

"That's right."

His father reached into his back pocket and took out his wallet. "There's not much in the house. Do you need money for groceries?"

"No. I'll increase my hours at Avella. I was planning to anyway."

"Oh." His father turned to go and said as he was leaving, "We're going to beat this thing."

"Okay," Andrew said.

Andrew didn't watch as his parents pulled out of the driveway and drove down the street. He wondered if his mother shed tears into her coffee, thick with cream and sticky with sugar, just how she liked it.

18

BECKY CAME OUT OF ANDREW'S room and dropped her leash at his feet. He took her for a long walk, his mind blank. When he got home, he watched television and paced the house. He kept an ear out for news about his brother. His mother was right, of course; whatever Brian and his friends had done would make some sort of headline. Andrew shuddered. What had Brian done? Andrew knew that his older brother had the capacity for violence. It was his trademark on the field.

Andrew had never felt more separate from his family. For a long time he'd felt and been treated like a bizarre sort of visitor. A quiet houseguest with a dog. He sometimes wondered if he even loved his family. His mom tugged at his heartstrings occasionally, but his father? Brian? Andrew thought Brian probably deserved whatever was coming to him. But even this

Andrew did not feel strongly about. He wanted nothing to do with *them* or *their* problems.

He flipped around the different news stations and satisfied himself that there was nothing about Brian. Emotionally, he didn't think he felt terribly invested in whatever was going on with his brother. But in terms of his own self-interest, Andrew was keenly aware that word would get around, and it would eventually affect him and everything he was up to.

And what was he up to, exactly? He wasn't even sure. *Making a play for Laura Lettel.* That was what Marcia had said. But was he making a play or planning an invasion? Sometimes he felt less like he was in love and more like he was a hunter. A predator. Camouflaging himself, blending in with her habitat, negotiating with her guardians. He'd had a setback today, for sure, but now he was determined. Holding Laura in the field had felt so natural, so right. He could have put her down after they'd gotten away from the broken glass, but she had wound her other arm around his neck almost to avoid being put down, to sustain the embrace . . . and maybe even something more?

He remembered those moments at Shaman's Point. When he'd either had a panic attack or . . . Or what? Felt the grace of God? Been touched by Jesus? That weird kid in the church had said that Jesus was waiting for him. *Just like I'm waiting for Laura,* he thought. *Only now I'm not waiting anymore, now I'm trying to get her.* Was Jesus trying to get him? Sending out messengers, signs, temptations? It couldn't possibly work like that. Maybe he was just losing his mind.

He wanted to talk to Marcia, but at this hour she would be at the hospital. Sara did not have a phone in her room, something to do with her lousy insurance, so he could only reach Marcia at the nurses' station. It made their conversations short and probably accounted for some of the awkwardness as well. He weighed the options and decided to call her anyway.

"I'm sorry about the other day," she said after he got her on the phone.

"It's okay. I know you're under a lot of stress."

"Sara's doing fine. Stable."

"Breathing tube out?"

"They don't want to chance it again."

"Bummer."

"Maybe in a few weeks. They're not sure."

"Good, that's good."

"I can't talk for too long," Marcia said. She sounded apologetic, and Andrew could hear the nurses and doctors murmuring in the background.

"Shit, I'm sorry. I had to talk to you."

"Are you all right?"

"I'm fine. Will you call me from your motel?"

"Sure thing," she said. "But I might stay here tonight. Grand rounds are tomorrow morning, and if I'm not here at the ass crack of dawn, I'll miss the pulmonologist."

"Okay."

"Seriously, it's like Where's Waldo? with that guy."

Andrew heard one of the nurses giggle. "No problem," he said. "Whenever you get a chance."

They said good-bye and hung up. Marcia had more important things to do. It was understandable. He stared at the phone in his hands.

When he had left the church, he'd needed to be alone, to get away from his humiliation and his new weirdo religious friends. Now he found himself very much missing their company.

19

"DO YOU THINK HE DID IT?" Matt asked.

"I do," Andrew said. They were walking through the woods of Halgin Park. *These Jesus kids sure love their nature walks,* Andrew thought.

"How can you be sure? I mean, you don't know anything yet."

"I know enough."

"What do you mean?"

"I know Brian. It hasn't always been easy at home."

"I sensed that."

"Did you?"

"Sort of," Matt said. "Is your dad like that too?"

"He is," Andrew said, surprised. "What are you, clairvoyant or something?"

"Nah, nothing like that."

Andrew wondered if he seemed like the kind of person who had been bullied. Did he come off as downtrodden or wimpy? The thought embarrassed him. Matt seemed to sense this as well.

"You were a big help at the soup kitchen yesterday. Did you enjoy it?" Matt asked.

"I did. How did it go?"

"It was fine. The usual crowd."

"You have regulars?"

"Oh yeah. The numbers swell when it gets cold, when the economy is bad, and sometimes for no reason at all. Or no reason that I can tell, anyway," Matt said.

"Is there—and I don't mean to offend you or anything—"

"You can ask me anything," Matt said.

"Is there, like, a religious component to the food you serve people?"

Matt laughed. "You mean, do we lure people into the church in order to save them?"

"I don't mean it like that," Andrew said. He brushed a spider off his arm.

"It's okay. Because that's exactly what we do. Wait, turn around." Andrew complied and felt Matt hitting more bugs off his back. "You must have walked through some webs or something."

"Gross."

"Check me?"

Andrew inspected his back and shoulders for spiders.

"You're clean," he said.

"Anyway, I know what you're thinking: like, that's bad or something. But when I talk to someone about Jesus, I'm speaking from my heart. I *want* them to feel better. I *want* to help them. The best thing in my life is my faith. Maybe it can be for them, too. And sometimes it's just more subtle than that. My love for them, my desire to help—they're in the food I prepare, the respect that I try and show them, that kind of thing, you know?"

"So you don't just talk about Jesus."

"Not at all."

"You don't talk to me about Jesus."

"Everyone needs to go at their own pace."

"And mine is glacial, right? Is that what you're saying?"

"Come on, Andrew. You really want to talk about this?"

"No, I guess I don't," Andrew said, but it wasn't exactly true. He did kind of want to talk about it. Whatever *it* was. The details of Matt and Laura's religion didn't really interest him; rather, it was their faith that he found fascinating—especially Laura's. To Andrew, Laura's faith meant she was capable of an unwavering devotion to an idea, or a set of ideas, whereas he felt devotion only to physical things, real things, things you could touch, like Laura.

"This place reminds me of someone," Matt said suddenly. He glanced around.

"Oh yeah?" Andrew said. He was barely listening, lost in another Laura fantasy.

"Someone who was really important to me once. Who still is."

Laura, he thought. They were circling the topic of Laura, talking and not talking about Laura. He brought his attention fully on Matt.

"I come here a lot," Matt said.

"To remind yourself of that person?"

"Sort of. Or to remind me of what that person meant to me, of their struggle," he said. "I've never told anyone about this before."

Andrew thought for a moment. *Was* Matt talking about Laura? Or maybe he was talking about John. Now Andrew felt nervous too. He almost didn't want to know. But he also sensed that Matt wanted to unburden himself and perhaps needed some encouragement. Andrew was still an outsider, and Matt clearly needed to talk to someone besides his friends in the youth group. He recalled Matt's compassion toward him, toward everyone, and his subtle and not-so-subtle ways of defending Andrew against the more aggressive members at the church. And it was very kind of Matt to hear him out about Brian. Andrew had never had a close male friend. It had always been just him and Marcia, then him and Marcia and Sara.

"It's okay, man," Andrew said. "Tell me about it."

"You can't— It's a secret," Matt said, running his hand through his hair.

"Don't worry about it," Andrew said.

"Seriously, there would be repercussions for this person if it got out."

"You can trust me."

Matt nodded. "Okay. Until we're sixteen, we do this summer camp thing."

"Vacation Bible School?" Andrew said, suppressing a laugh.

"Yeah, yeah, I know. Totally corny. But it's actually a lot of fun. During the day it's almost like regular camp. Hiking, swimming, archery, all that stuff. But every night we light a bonfire, get into a big circle, and we sing and pray. It's really intense. I can't even describe it. It's amazing."

"Wow," Andrew said, thinking it sounded kind of cheesy.

"It's like an out-of-body experience."

Andrew stopped short. "Really?" He thought of that day at Shaman's Point with Laura. He hadn't felt out of his body exactly, but he hadn't felt *in* it either. "Go on."

"Yeah. But it's not quite out-of-body, either, because it's so physical. Does that make sense?"

Andrew thought it did kind of make sense. But he asked, "What do you mean?"

"Don't laugh, okay?"

"I won't."

Matt stopped and looked around again. All Andrew could hear was the babble of the brook, a sound that was no longer pleasant to him after the incident with Becky. The wind picked up and made a whistling sound through the trees. It was eerie, but they were definitely alone.

"Some nights we'd do a hug spiral," Matt said.

Andrew wasn't sure what he had expected, but this wasn't it. "A what now?"

"You get in a straight line and hold hands. Then the first person starts the spiral by hugging the person next to them. You spiral into each other until you're this huge hugging circle."

"Okay . . ." Andrew said, raising his eyebrows.

"I said don't laugh."

"Am I laughing?"

"No. Sorry."

Matt turned and resumed walking. Andrew followed him. They were silent for a few minutes. Andrew cleared his throat.

"So, the hugging spiral."

"We're all spiraled in, hugging and praying and singing. And it's, like, really intense. I usually keep my eyes closed—I mean, I always keep my eyes closed when I'm praying. My eyes are closed and I'm praying and really feeling God's love for us all and our love for one another. And then, suddenly, and I don't even know why, I open my eyes. And my counselor, Chip, his eyes are open too. And we're right across from each other, spiraled in, and our faces are like almost pressed together. We're, like, eyeball to eyeball, you know?"

"Um, you do this spiral shit with the counselors?" Andrew said.

"Yes. Dude, that's not the point at all," Matt said.

"Sorry, go on."

"Chip's eyes were so sad. I mean, painfully, horribly sad. I thought he was dying or something."

"Shit."

"Afterward, when everyone was getting ready for bed, Chip asked me to go for a walk. That part is kind of weird, because we're all supposed to just turn in, you know?"

That part is weird? Andrew thought. But he said, "What happened on the walk?"

"Nothing happened," Matt said quickly. "I mean, we walked a long way. And we didn't say much to each other. But every once in a while, he'd stop and point back to the fires and lights of the campsite and say, 'See that, Matt? That's my faith.' We got farther and farther away, and it got darker and darker. The campsite was fading behind us until we could just barely see it. And he said again, 'That's my faith.' Then we were completely in the dark and I couldn't see anything at all. Not even my hand in front of my face. And then Chip said, 'This is my faith.' We just stood there in the dark."

"Huh," Andrew said.

"He's the youth pastor now."

"Well, maybe he had a change of heart. Or found his faith or whatever."

"Found his faith or whatever," Matt repeated softly. He appeared lost in his own thoughts. They walked in silence for quite some time. Andrew wasn't sure what to say.

Matt cleared his throat. "Sorry if it was weird for you to hear about that."

"Not at all," Andrew said.

"I mean, if you didn't grow up in this . . ." His voice trailed off. He was a few feet ahead of Andrew on the trail, and Andrew could barely hear him.

"Grow up with what?" Andrew asked.

"With Jesus," Matt said. He turned around and reached out his hand. Andrew was embarrassed, but Matt seemed so earnest. They shook hands. The mood lightened.

"Hey, we're back," Andrew said, looking up and seeing his car.

"I took us in a circle," Matt said.

"How old is this youth pastor guy?" Andrew asked. Matt seemed to consider the question unimportant.

"Oh, I don't know. In his thirties, maybe? Ask Laura. They're really tight."

20

HIS PARENTS HAD CALLED the night before and said that Brian's bail hearing had been set for Monday morning. In all likelihood the three of them would be back that afternoon. Andrew had not slept well. He was plagued by more nightmares and had also become obsessed with this Chip character, who was apparently so close to Laura.

He tried calling Laura, but the phone just rang and rang. He had, in fact, tried calling Laura a few times since their walk, but no one would answer, or at best a little brother or sister would pick up and supposedly take a message. Laura never called back. She had a huge family, he reasoned. It was probably chaos most of the time. Marcia hadn't called him back either, and he didn't want to bother her. He decided to focus his energies back on his job, at least for the time being.

Avella had always been a part-time job for Andrew, but he needed more money for college. He also wanted to spend the least amount of time possible at home. By six a.m. Monday morning Andrew was standing outside Neal's office. He knew the morning crew started at six thirty. The office was in a shed where they stored all the equipment. The shed was partially in the woods surrounding Avella, and also in the shadow of one of the taller buildings. It was dark and quiet most of the time.

Neal and Ben pulled up in a sporty pink convertible. Andrew had expected them to be in a pickup truck. His thoughts must have been reflected in his face because when Neal got out he said, "My wife's car. She wants me to fix the air conditioner."

"Mom's got the rig!" said Ben, who seemed to find this greatly amusing. He got out of the car and came right up to Andrew.

"Hey, Ben," Andrew said.

"You're on early today?" Ben said.

"Maybe," Andrew said.

"Hey, what happened?" Ben said. He touched the still large but fading bruise on Andrew's forehead.

"Why don't you get the office opened?" Neal said to Ben. Ben took the keys from his father and disappeared inside.

"Have a seat," Neal said, indicating one of the picnic tables where the crew usually broke for lunch.

They sat down. Neal leaned forward, a pleasant and noncommittal expression on his face.

"Are you all right?" Neal said.

"I need more work," Andrew said. "Do you have anything?"

"Hmmm," Neal said. He leaned back and considered the request. "Thing is, I just hired this other kid."

His heart sank. "Not a problem," he said.

"I could give you some hours here and there," Neal said.

"That would be great," Andrew said.

"But I'm fully staffed this morning."

"How about this afternoon?"

"Sure, come by this afternoon. And if you need to hang around here for the day, that's okay by me. Just pretend you're doing office work. Although really, there's nothing to be done. There's a couch in there too, if you need it."

Andrew hung his head. Neal was probably being so nice because he thought he'd gotten beat up. "Listen, I tripped in the woods," he said.

"Okay."

"No, really. Tell Ben. I don't want him to get upset."

"I will."

"There's some stuff happening with my brother."

"Ayup."

"It might get pretty ugly."

"For you?"

"Maybe."

"You remember what I told you last year," Neal said.

"Eighteen and out," Andrew said.

"Ayup," Neal said.

Last summer Andrew had gotten into a fight with his father about Becky barking at him when he'd gotten home from work. His father had grabbed his arm and left a nasty purple mark. It wasn't a big deal, but Neal had noticed. Andrew had confessed his unhappiness at home, his father's occasional drunken aggression. *Eighteen and out,* Neal had said. He'd also told Andrew about his own, and by comparison, horrifying, childhood. Neal's father had been a farmer and worked his two sons half to death. Farmers work hard, and the children of farmers work hard, but Neal's father had been perverse. He'd told his children that they were his property until they'd turned eighteen. Neal had turned eighteen and never looked back.

He must have been remembering it all, because when Andrew looked at him, he was lost in thought. He met Andrew's gaze and frowned slightly. "Let me push some numbers around," he said abruptly. "You can come on full-time."

"That's not necessary," Andrew said.

"Oh hell, Andrew, you're the only summer hire who shows up stone sober. Might as well reward good behavior."

"Thank you," he said.

Ben popped his head out the door. "Want to mow the lawns with me?"

Nine hours later he was home, dirty and exhausted. He smelled of the fuel from the lawn mowers and the grass they'd cut. No allergy attacks today; it must be only pretty flowers that set him off. His parents and brother still weren't home. Becky kept trying to lick him clean. He took her out for a quick walk, then came home and took a long shower. By the time he got out, his family was home. He could hear the three of them talking downstairs. He crept to his room and shut the door. He was very hungry but knew if he left his room, he would get pulled into their drama. An hour passed. He read, drew a picture of Laura holding a bouquet of onions, and tried to take a nap. When he couldn't stand it anymore, he got up and left his room. They were still talking in low serious murmurs. If he had his wallet and keys, he might've been able to slip out the front door unnoticed, but he'd left them on the kitchen counter.

Andrew's mom was leaning against the refrigerator, her face puffy and purple with distress. His father and Brian were seated at the kitchen stools. No one looked up when he walked in. He could just grab his stuff and bolt, but he was pissed that his father and brother sat on their asses while his mother stood.

"Why don't you sit down, Mom?" he said.

"I'm fine," she said.

"Let me get you a chair from the dining room."

"I'm—yes, thanks."

Andrew left to get a chair, but when he got back, his mother was now seated at the stool that Brian had vacated.

"Well, aren't you nice?" Brian said to him. "Are you going to ask me if I'm okay?"

"I'm going out," Andrew said. He placed the chair on the floor and reached for his keys and wallet, but Brian grabbed both.

"Don't start," their mother said.

"Start what? We never start," Andrew said.

"Where you going?" Brian said.

"Out," Andrew said.

"To church? You praying for me?"

Andrew digested this. His mom might've mentioned the phone call from Matt, or Brian could have seen the note that she'd left on the counter the day before.

"I've been working all day. I'm going to get something to eat. Please give me my stuff so I can get out of here and you three can get on with whatever it is that you're doing."

"Watch it," his dad said.

"Yeah," Brian said, getting in Andrew's face. "Watch it." Then he dropped Andrew's keys and wallet onto the floor.

Andrew knew he should just pick up his stuff and leave. That was his style, anyway, his modus operandi. He might be passive-aggressive now and then, but on principle he almost never took the bait, and rarely threw down during a confrontation. Even without Neal's advice, eighteen and out was what he'd been planning all along.

Brian stepped even closer to him, his face a mere inch or so from his own. His breath smelled like hell, and the heat that vapored from his enormous body was unreal. It was like being pressed against black pavement on a scorching summer day. It was like being smothered, trapped, pinned down.

Andrew raised his eyes to his brother. He brought his finger into Brian's chest, punctuating each word with a point. "You. Are. Horrible."

Boom!

The last thing he heard was Becky's frantic bark.

21

WHEN ANDREW WOKE UP, he was lying on the couch in the living room. Becky immediately began licking his face. She must have kept vigil by his side. A plastic bag full of melting ice was on the floor. He sat up slowly and groaned. His head hurt even worse than the morning after he'd fallen in the woods. The right side of his face was swollen and tender.

Brian had never really hit him before. Punching him in the arm and cuffing his neck were about as bad as it got. *Well,* Andrew thought, *he's upping the ante all over the place.* Then he felt terrible for thinking such a thing.

A few moments later his mother came in. "Are you okay?" she asked.

"I feel terrible," he said.

"I'm sorry," she said.

"Yeah, I know."

Becky growled and barked.

"Stop, Becky," he said.

"She's been doing that every time I try and come in."

"Sorry."

"Here's some aspirin," she said. She handed him the pills and a glass of water.

"Guess I should get out of here for a little while," Andrew said.

His mother did not dispute this. "Where can you go?" she asked.

He used to crash at Sara's when things would heat up at home, but it seemed inappropriate to try to stay with Janet now. Besides, she was probably with Sara every spare moment she had. He remembered Neal's offer of the couch in his office. And the place seemed more amenable to dogs anyway. "How long have I been out?"

"Maybe five minutes."

His mother cleared her throat and looked away.

"Can you get me the phone?" he asked.

She brought the cordless over, and he dialed Neal's number.

"There's an extra key under the mat," Neal said. "And I should tell security you're coming."

"They'll be okay with that?"

"The guy who works night shift is a buddy of mine. How long you need it for?"

Andrew held the phone to his chest. "How long will this take to blow over?" he asked his mother.

She made a helpless gesture, so familiar to him, tossing her hands in the air and letting them gently fall to her sides.

"A few days, I think," Andrew said. "And shit, I'm sorry, but I need to bring my dog."

"That's okay. The shed's huge."

"Thanks."

"You can always stay at our place," Neal said.

"No," Andrew said quickly. He did not want to pollute Neal and Ben with the mess that was his family, his life. "That won't be necessary."

Andrew hung up the phone and handed it back to his mom. His head pounded as he stood up. He took a deep breath as a wave of nausea came over him. He sat back down. "Where are they?" he asked.

"Out. I don't know," she said.

"Who brought me in here?" he said.

"Your brother," she said.

This time Andrew stood up and stayed up. "Please don't call him that," he said.

He threw some clothes and his toothbrush into his backpack. He was about to walk out the door with Becky when his mother stopped him and handed him a plastic bag. It was full of granola bars and dog food.

"Thanks," he said. He turned to go.

"Andrew?"

"Yes?" His hand was on the knob.

"This church stuff that you're doing. Is it because—" The phone rang. She dashed away to answer it. "Where are you?" he heard her ask. He left the house.

He stopped at a fast-food restaurant and got some burgers. He even gave one to Becky, a sinful treat for a good dog on a terrible night. He drove to Avella and was waved in by the security guard, who looked like Neal but wasn't.

Inside, he lay back on the office couch, which was more comfortable than he'd expected. Becky fell asleep immediately, as the innocent will do. He watched her breathe. He envied her. He closed his eyes and tried to sleep.

He heard a little tinkling noise. He sat up and looked around the office. It was small and cramped and dimly lit by the security light, always on just outside the front door. He felt the shed behind him, a vast dark space, too large for the modest amount of equipment that was needed for the grounds. He stood up, felt dizzy, and sat back down. Becky slept on, and he wished that she would wake up. He heard the tinkling noise again. *It could be anything,* he thought. An animal, water, anything. His heart beat loudly in his ears.

He'd been so cool and calm with his mother, like it was no big deal that his brother had knocked him unconscious. He wanted to cry. He actually tried to cry, thinking it would give him some relief from his feelings. He reached out to Becky but stopped. She needed her rest.

Calm down, he told himself.

He got his backpack out, thinking he'd eat more and feel better. When he opened his bag, he saw the Bible that John had given him. His mom must have stuck it in there with the granola bars. He remembered having stacked it under a pile of books in the hallway. She had found it and probably wondered about it. He half wished they could've continued their conversation before he'd left the house. *No,* he thought, *no.* He had learned to immediately squash down any desire to be closer to his mother, or to reach some sort of understanding with her. It was just too painful to think about.

He hadn't even glanced at the Bible since that night at Laura's house. He pulled it out and thumbed through it. He was shocked to discover that passages had been outlined and pages marked. He looked at the inside of the front cover, where a name was written. *John Taylor.* Andrew thought John had given him some generic Bible. He figured that the group stockpiled them and handed them out like Halloween candy, which perhaps they did, but this had been John's Bible, his personal tome. Andrew was touched, flabbergasted, annoyed. He was also comforted. It felt heavy in his hands, substantive and real. The gold trim on the pages was worn down, the cover was soft, the lettering faded. This Bible was precious, beloved. He tucked it close to his chest, lay down, and fell asleep.

22

HE WAS AWAKENED BY Ben the following morning.

"You trip in the woods again?" he asked, peering at Andrew.

"Yeah. I've got to stop doing that," Andrew said. He sat up and tucked the Bible into his backpack.

"You need a flashlight," Ben said.

"I need a coffee," Andrew said. "And some aspirin."

Ben handed him a white bag. Andrew took it and looked inside. An egg sandwich and a cup of coffee.

"Thanks, man," Andrew said.

"Dad bought it. There are some pills here somewhere." Ben started searching around the office.

"Don't worry about that. Where's your dad?" he asked between mouthfuls of food. "And where's my dog?"

"With Dad. He likes dogs."

"Cool."

"You feel okay?"

"Actually," Andrew said, "I don't feel that bad." He didn't. His head hurt, but not terribly, and he felt well rested, even unburdened.

The door swung open, and Becky and Neal walked in. Becky settled herself half on the couch and half in Andrew's lap.

"This okay?" Andrew said to Neal, indicating Becky.

"Oh yeah. Reminds me of my old pup," Neal said. "That's quite a goose egg you got there," he added, pointing to Andrew's head. Andrew felt his forehead. There was a sizeable lump. He finished his sandwich and thanked Neal again. Ben took Becky out to the back of the shed.

"She'll have to hang out there during the day," Neal said.

"That's fine. She's old. She sleeps most of the day anyway."

"You need to talk?"

"I need to work," Andrew said.

"Good boy," Neal said. "Up and at 'em."

At the end of the day Neal showed Andrew how to hook a hose up to the sink and take a shower. It was cold and required a lot of coordination, but in a way he'd never felt more refreshed. He wondered if Marcia had tried calling him. He thought about calling her—she obviously didn't know where he was—but he didn't think he should use the office phone for long-distance calls. He was used to being in almost daily contact with her for years. And he was lonely in the office, even with Becky.

His mom had thoughtfully included bowls and a can opener in the bag she'd given him. He wondered what she was doing now. Andrew and his mother met occasionally outside the battlefield, handing each other groceries and exchanging brief words, but that was it. Between them it was mostly a vast void of regret. He pitied her, he told himself. That was it. He cared more deeply about his dog than anyone else in that house.

He'd worked by himself most of the day, with Neal sending him out on various solitary missions. He did this perhaps to protect him from prying questions about Brian, whose crime must certainly now be public knowledge.

Neal and Ben invited Andrew over for dinner that night, but Andrew refused, saying he had plans with a friend. He thought about calling Matt but decided against it. Their talk in the woods had ended kind of oddly. He took Becky for a long walk, enjoying the grounds in a way that was usually inaccessible to him. It was like a golf course. For some reason the smooth beauty of manicured lawns was more appealing to him than untouched wilderness. He thought maybe this meant he wasn't a real Vermonter, but he'd never given a shit about that kind of thing anyway.

He opened a can of soup and heated it in a bowl in the office microwave. He was tired and satisfied with his day, but as the sky darkened he began to feel the ache of loneliness again.

He picked up John's Bible. Andrew was a good reader, and the Bible was, if nothing else, a great book. Even people who weren't religious liked the Bible for its literary value, its historical enormity, its parables, its poetry, its truths. Its awesome, inescapable Bible-ness. He turned it over in his hands. Again he felt the weight and substance. And somehow, it felt sacred, too. Was it the thing itself or all the cultural associations he had absorbed that made it seem this way? Last night he'd held it to his chest like a security blanket. The memory made him blush.

He opened it and read.

After ten pages, however, he closed it in frustration. It was just boring. He didn't connect with it. The opening was kind of awesome, but after that the words seemed to blur into meaningless spillage. How did people read this thing? How did they find in it truth and beauty? He thumbed the pages, letting them slide through his fingers like an animated flip-book. He decided he would read the passages that John had marked. Mostly, John had underlined words that were already written in red, the words of Jesus. He read the Sermon on the Mount, he read the Ask, Seek, Knock speech. It was all fine; it was great, even. But he was unmoved. He tried to disassociate from his natural skepticism and sarcasm, the inner reel of "whatever" that played in his head, but he couldn't. He just couldn't. He didn't understand this heavy, worn thing, these red words, this beloved object of another person. *This doesn't belong to me,* he decided.

He found a phone book in the office and called John. A few minutes later he was on his way to meet him downtown.

23

Andrew pulled up to the curb outside the city center. The city center was a kind of mini mall that housed a few restaurants and stores. It was an incongruous structure among the small shops and quaint buildings of their modest downtown. Like Laura's church, it was more a generic office space than a thing of beauty. The building was dark. John stood on the sidewalk.

"Hey," Andrew said out his window.

"It's closed," John said. They had talked about getting some pizza or coffee, but ten p.m. in a mid-size Vermont town meant everyone was already at home either asleep or drunk or stoned.

"I figured," Andrew said. "Let's just go for a drive."

"Okay," John said. He stood on the sidewalk, shifting slightly from foot to foot.

"Are you all right?" Andrew said.

"Sorry. Let's do it," John said. He got in and buckled up. He drummed his fingers on the dashboard. He seemed to be very slightly trembling. His jeans were worn, and his shirt, dark red, looked threadbare. In fact, Andrew thought, all John's clothes were a little ragged and secondhand-looking. He felt bad about the T-shirt he'd blown his nose on and neglected to wash. It was still in the backseat, in fact. He hoped John wouldn't notice.

"I think you may have given this to me by accident," Andrew said as he held up John's Bible. John looked both surprised and affronted.

"No way, man. It was a gift."

"It just seems really personal," Andrew said. John looked embarrassed.

Andrew realized that he was being kind of a jerk. "Sorry. I just wanted to make sure you didn't give it to me by mistake and wanted it back."

John looked out the window. Andrew tossed the Bible in the backseat and cleared his throat. "Where to?" he asked.

"Wherever," John said. He peered at Andrew. "Wow! You sure did swell up from the other day."

"Oh yeah. This is something new. Actually, I got hit."

"What?"

"It was over some shit with my brother."

"I'm sorry."

"I'm fine."

"I heard about that thing with your brother."

"When?"

"A few days ago. Before the soup kitchen."

"Really?" Andrew said. He was surprised. "Then you knew before I did. Who did you hear it from?"

"Just around. How are you feeling about it?"

"I don't feel anything about it. I mean, fuck, I feel bad for the girl."

"So, you think he did it? Or he participated in it?"

"Yeah."

"I heard, um, I heard that maybe she was a prostitute or something and that they just didn't pay her. Not that any part of that's okay," John added quickly.

Andrew digested this information. He gripped the steering wheel and said, "Well, that adds up to rape, doesn't it?"

The word *rape* seemed to ring out in the car like a bell. It silenced them both for several minutes.

"Want to talk about something else?" said John.

"Yeah. Let's talk about Jesus."

"Are you being sarcastic?"

"Yeah," he said. Then: "No, actually, I'm not."

"What do you want to know?" John asked.

"When were you saved?"

"We're not, like, born-again."

"So what's the proper vernacular?"

"I guess we say 'found.' Either that or 'accepted into your heart.'"

"So, when did you find or accept Jesus?"

"October 2, 1993."

"You know the exact date?"

"I know the exact moment. Two a.m. Because that's what it is: a moment in time. And nothing is ever the same. You're not the same. Everything changes. Everything suddenly makes sense. Your heart opens."

As John spoke he seemed to gain confidence, even happiness. He stopped jittering, and his voice was lighter, less tentative. "It's hard to describe. He's just there for you, and He's beautiful. He's love."

"But how do you know? What happens that makes you know you found Him, or that He's in your heart?"

"You just know."

"What leads up to it? I mean, it doesn't just suddenly happen out of the blue, right? You've got to be looking for it or studying it, right? There's a human influence. A cultural influence. Do you know what I mean?"

"Yes," John said slowly. "For some people it does just happen, like you said, out of the blue. But for others it is a search. You read the Bible, you connect with other people who are already there."

"Like what I'm doing?" Andrew said.

"Looking for it?" John said. He shifted around in the passenger seat.

"You can lower the seat back if you want," Andrew said.

"I'm fine. Anyway, sometimes a darkness, a dark event,

can lead you to search. You start asking questions."

He's talking about Sara's accident, Andrew thought. He looked over at John, who had grown quiet and thoughtful. Maybe he was talking about his own struggle. *Why do I always think it's about me?*

"Tell me more about your moment," Andrew said.

"There was a lot of stuff going on. I was living in a bad way. And then I hit rock bottom . . . and then I found Him," John said abruptly.

"Oh," Andrew said.

"What about you? Have you been searching?" John said.

Andrew wanted to blurt out that he was in love with Laura, that he would do or say anything to get closer to Laura. But he also knew it was more nuanced than that. At Shaman's Point, and in the river where he'd almost lost Becky, he'd felt—he didn't know another way to describe it—*moved*. Like when you read a great book or a poem and something inside you shifted— or opened, for that matter.

"I guess I've been searching," Andrew said.

"We have a study group tomorrow night if you want to join. You're not really supposed to come until you've accepted Jesus, but . . ."

"Nah, I don't want to make anyone uncomfortable," Andrew said, thinking of his day at the soup kitchen.

"The group is really small. Just me, Matt, Seth, Laura, some- times Chip."

"Oh?" Andrew said.

"Come to Laura's tomorrow night at six."

"I don't know," Andrew said, but he'd already made up his mind to go.

"It's up to you," John said.

Andrew's mind worked rapidly. If he went to a study group, he'd have to be prepared to say something coherent and sincere-sounding about the Bible. What could he say that would impress Laura? What could he find in its pages that would actually resonate with him? When he called John, he'd meant, in a way, to come clean. But this new opportunity confused his intentions. He'd get to be with Laura again and see her interact with what he'd come to think of as the mysterious men in her life. Were they all in love with her? Were they a bunch of pathetic fawning eunuchs? And why was she apparently the only female in their cozy little study group?

"Listen, I want to be honest with you," Andrew said.

"Yes?" John said. He started his drumming fingers on the dashboard again.

"I'm wearing a mask," he said. "I'm pretending. Sort of, anyway."

"That's okay. That's what the search is like for some people. They feel almost phony, as if they're acting out the motions."

"Isn't that a lie?"

"It's just more subtle than that, Andrew, more complicated. Have you ever heard the phrase 'fake it until you make it'?"

"Yeah. That's, like, an alcoholic thing." Andrew wondered if maybe that was what John meant when he'd said he'd hit rock bottom.

"It's like that for some people," John said.

"So you're literally saying to pretend to believe until you actually believe? That can't be right. Is that actually okay with your"—Andrew hesitated, groping for the right words—"your people?"

"My people," John said thoughtfully. "That 'fake it until you make it' phrase doesn't quite fit. It's hard to explain."

"Did you feel that you were faking it or subtly faking it before you found Him?" Andrew pressed.

John was silent for a long time. A long, long time, for miles. The atmosphere in the car was thick with sadness, although it was difficult to figure out what aspects of the situation suggested that feeling. He briefly considered bringing the conversation around to Laura, but something about John made him resist that urge, even dulled its impulse.

"John?"

"What? Where are we?" he said. He seemed startled by the sound of Andrew's voice.

Andrew had driven down Route 2. They were in Turbury, a town so tiny that the gas station, convenience store, and post office were all combined. It made him think of how he, Sara, and Marcia used to drive around when there was nothing else to do. He remembered his last drive with Marcia, the day of the accident, when they had talked about religion. Andrew had been so flippant, so brutal, so unconcerned. *It sounds so simple, talking about it in your car.* That was what Marcia had said, but it hadn't been simple or easy for her. And it wasn't simple or easy for him, either, not now anyway, and it certainly wasn't for John, whose expression was pained, whose hands and jaw were clenched.

"We're nowhere," Andrew said. "I'll take you home."

24

THE NEXT DAY ANDREW SPENT his lunch break skimming the Bible for something he could talk about at the study group. He read a little Old Testament and a little New Testament. Again he felt bored and frustrated.

He got permission from Neal to use the office for a long-distance call. Marcia wasn't at her hotel or the hospital, but one of the nurses told Andrew, even though she wasn't supposed to, that Sara was doing just fine. "Her status hasn't changed," she said. Andrew wondered where Marcia was. Hopefully doing something unrelated to Sara. He pictured Marcia alone at the cafeteria, eating a sad slice of pizza and reading a big book of Spanish poetry.

Poetry. He grabbed his Bible again. He flipped through the pages until he found where the text was broken into lines that resembled poems: the Psalms. Poetry, or at least the beauty of it, was something he could understand. He read.

Be merciful to me, LORD, for I am faint;
O LORD, heal me, for my bones are in agony.

Finally, a connection.

When he got to Laura's house that night, one of her little sisters answered the door. She looked to be about seven or eight years old. Her hair was braided and wrapped around her head like a crown. She was pudgy and rosy cheeked.

"They're at the church. They tried to call you," she said to Andrew before he'd said a word.

"Oh," he said as she closed the door.

Andrew stood for a moment on the porch. He listened to the sounds of happiness, of children and adults giggling and having a good time. Perhaps they were playing a board game or doing something similarly wholesome.

"Was that the new kid?" he heard a woman ask.

Andrew stepped off the porch and got back into his car. He didn't like this "new kid" shit. He drove to the church. It was dark. There were only two cars in the lot. He grabbed his Bible and went to the front doors, but they were chained shut. He briefly held the large padlock and peered inside. Then he remembered to go around back.

The back door was open. He stepped inside the dark hallway. Where should he go? He figured they wouldn't be in the kitchen, so he tried some of the other doors. The floorboards creaked as he fumbled around and looked for a light switch. Then he felt a heavy hand on his shoulder.

"Shit!" he said, spinning around. He came face to face with a man.

"Don't curse in this house," the man said.

"Sorry," Andrew said.

"You're Andy?"

"Andr— Yes," Andrew said. The man had not removed his hand from Andrew's shoulder. He still hadn't found the light switch, so they were blinking at each other, trying to make each other out in the dark. *This must be Chip,* Andrew thought, breathing a little easier. He moved slightly so that Chip's hand fell off his shoulder. Something about this action seemed to break the tension between them.

"Welcome!" Chip said. Then he turned on a light. The fluorescent bulb cast a yellow glow, which was perhaps why Chip didn't look so good. He had the face and body of a young person, but his skin was gray and pale, his hair prematurely balding, his eyes bloodshot. A few brown wisps were combed over his shiny forehead. "That way," he said, and pointed down the stairs.

"You're not coming?" Andrew asked.

"Not tonight," he said.

Andrew walked down the narrow staircase. When he got to the bottom, there was another door. He looked back up the stairs, intending to thank Chip, or perhaps assure himself that he wasn't an apparition.

He was still there, still pointing. "Go on, go on," he said.

Andrew slipped through the door. He found himself in a small room lined with books. In the center of the room sat Laura, John, Matt, and Goatee Seth.

"Hey, sorry, I'm late—" he started to say.

"Shhh," Seth said.

Andrew stopped. Then he realized they were praying. Their heads were bowed and their eyes were closed. There were only four chairs in the room, and they were occupied. Laura was wearing a light blue sweater over a jean skirt. Her feet were tucked up under her. Her hair was braided and coiled around her head in the same fashion as her younger sister. They must have been playing with each other's hair. He gazed at her lovely face, at her slightly parted lips. Then he felt as if he were violating her while she communicated with her God, so he looked away. He studied the books. They were all Bibles.

He sat on the floor and opened his own Bible. While the group prayed, he read the Psalm he'd chosen, lingering over his favorite parts.

Be merciful to me, LORD, for I am faint;
O LORD, heal me, for my bones are in agony.
My soul is in anguish.
How long, O LORD, how long? . . .

I am worn out from groaning;
all night long I flood my bed with weeping
and drench my couch with tears.

"Cool," he whispered. He liked the language, which struck him as overwrought, torrid, and even erotic. The "worn out from groaning" bit also meant something to him personally. It was the way he often felt about Laura. Exhausted from wanting her and not getting what he wanted. He wondered if Laura or Matt or even John would be able to discern this in his choice of Psalm.

He looked at the silent group again. They were still at it. He forced himself to shift his gaze from Laura to Matt, from Matt to John. He even studied Goatee Seth's stern serious face. He didn't have a watch, but he felt like he'd been there for at least fifteen minutes. He wondered about Chip. He remembered the strange story that Matt had told him about Chip at the Bible camp. The incident seemed to upset Matt because of Chip's apparent loss of faith, but it bothered Andrew for other reasons. Why would the youth pastor drag Matt off in the middle of the night? Why would he confess such a thing to someone so much younger than himself? And what was he doing here now, lurking around instead of joining his flock? Andrew tried to shrug off his apprehensions. It was none of his damn business. He was here for Laura. Andrew leaned back against a wall of Bibles and closed his eyes.

"Andrew?" Someone shook him lightly.

He jerked awake. "Sorry, I must have fallen asleep," he said. He looked at Matt.

"I know you've got a demanding job," Matt said.

"Have you accepted Christ into your heart?" asked Goatee Seth.

Matt was crouching down next to him. John, Laura, and Seth were still seated in their prayer circle. John was looking at the floor, his hands loosely wound in his lap. Laura was fiddling with her necklace. Seth was frowning at him. Andrew extended his hand to Matt, who took it and hoisted him to his feet.

"Not yet," Andrew said.

25

"We start with thirty minutes or so of silent prayer," Seth said. His expression was severe, made perhaps more severe by his little beard. At first Andrew didn't respond, then he realized that something was expected of him.

"Sorry I missed the prayer part," he said. "I didn't realize the location changed."

"My fault," Matt said. "I called you at the last minute."

"Who'd you talk to?" Andrew said.

"Your mother," Matt said.

"How'd she sound?" Andrew said.

Matt was about to respond when Seth said, "And *then* we discuss a chapter and verse selected by our youth pastor. Only he couldn't be here tonight."

"Actually, I think he's here somewhere. He told me to come down here," Andrew said.

"No one is here but us," Seth said.

So he was just lurking around, Andrew thought. Out loud he said, "Whatever. Someone told me to come down here. I didn't make them up."

"No one is saying that," John said, looking up for the first time.

"This is a waste of time," Seth said.

"Let's talk about doubt," Laura said suddenly. "Doubt and belief." She looked at Andrew as she spoke. Her eyes seemed to twinkle, and she smiled invitingly. She closed her Bible and placed it on a table behind her.

"Chip said we shouldn't just talk without guidance," Seth said, holding up his Bible.

"He certainly does," Matt muttered. Only Andrew heard.

There was an uncomfortable silence. Everyone seemed to be looking at John. *He's second in command,* Andrew realized. Goatee Seth was trying to take charge, but they didn't really respect him. And John was staring at the floor again. Andrew cleared his throat.

"I picked out a Psalm that I like," he said.

"Will you read it to us?" Matt said.

"Yes, I'd like that," Laura said, ignoring Seth, who was sputtering.

Andrew opened his Bible and ran his finger along the words of Psalm 6. He felt like laughing all of a sudden. The dynamics of the group amused him. He'd expected to be out of his league, to be intellectually tested in some way that would demand he rise to the occasion, sort of like arguing with Marcia. But the study group was rudderless without Chip and with John apparently checked out.

Andrew cleared his throat and was about to read when the door opened and a girl walked in. Andrew recognized her immediately. It was Karen, the bitchy girl from the soup kitchen. She was dressed in a short tight skirt and white T-shirt that was knotted at her waist. Tan lines from her bathing suit graced her collarbones and long thin neck.

"What are you doing here?" Seth said.

"*He's* invited to your study group and I'm not?" she asked, jerking her head toward Andrew.

"John invited him. It wasn't *my* idea," Seth said.

Karen flicked her eyes at John. "Oh," she said.

Andrew looked back and forth between Seth and Karen. Those pointy severe features, he realized; they were brother and sister.

Laura rose from her seat and embraced Karen. The two girls held each other tightly for several moments until Laura pulled away. "Come on, sweetie," she said. "You know you've never shown an interest."

"I *am* interested," Karen whined. "Take me seriously."

"How can we when you barely show up for anything else?" Seth said.

"Guys, not here," Laura said.

"Laura's right," Matt said.

"We'll come back and do this right next week. And, Karen, you're welcome to join us," John said.

"Really?" She smiled at John.

John clasped his hands together and bowed his head. The others followed suit. Andrew bowed his head too, but he didn't close his eyes. John recited the Lord's Prayer. His voice dropped to a deep murmur. It was very *natural*, Andrew thought, the way they prayed together, the way they carried each other's words. It was like a beautifully rehearsed play, the actors gliding around one another like a harmonious school of pretty fish.

When they were finished, Karen and Seth slipped off together. As soon as the door closed behind them, they started to argue.

"You're so immature," Seth hissed.

"You think excluding *me* will get you in with them. . . ." Karen's voice trailed off as they walked up the stairs. Laura rolled her eyes at Matt.

They're the cool kids, Andrew thought, and Seth is an interloper who wants, as Karen put it, *in.* It didn't surprise him, now that he thought about it. John, Laura, and Matt were attractive and smart and confident. The social dynamics of their youth group resembled the social dynamics of any group of teenagers, regardless of whether Jesus was involved.

"Brother and sister?" Andrew said to no one in particular.

"Twins," Laura said.

"They really shouldn't bicker like that all the time," Matt said.

"Seth seems kind of harsh," Andrew said.

"We shouldn't talk about them when they're not here," John said.

"You're so right," Laura said to John. She smiled at him, and her eyes glowed with admiration and respect. Andrew grimaced.

"This isn't how it usually goes," Matt said to Andrew.

"Oh?" Andrew said. His eyes were on John and Laura, whose heads were close together as they examined something in her Bible. John seemed to be explaining something to her.

"Last week we were discussing the power of redemption," Matt said.

"What about it?" Andrew said, not looking at Matt and trying to hear what John was saying to Laura.

"Andrew," Matt said.

"Yeah?" Andrew said.

"Your mom. She sounded kind of upset."

Shit, Andrew thought. He hadn't thought to check in with his mother while he was staying at the Avella office. She was probably upset because of the charges. Maybe there were some new developments? He would stop by later. In the meantime he would try and salvage what he could from the study group.

"You need a ride home?" he asked Laura.

"I'm all set," she said. She barely glanced at him as she spoke.

"All right. Bye," Andrew said.

"Call me later, okay?" Matt said to Andrew.

"Sure," Andrew said. John and Laura were absorbed in their discussion. As he turned to go, he thought he glimpsed John's hand on Laura's knee.

He marched up the stairs, furious with himself, with Laura, and with John. How could he possibly compete with John? He reached the back door of the church and thrust it open. He took his Bible out of his pocket and glared at it, intending to toss it into the field.

"What am I doing?" he shouted at the book.

"What indeed?" said a voice to his left.

He turned, expecting weirdo Chip, and was nearly ready to punch him, but it was Seth who emerged from the shadows. Andrew glared at him and said nothing.

He got in his car and drove to his house to check on his mom. No one was home.

26

ON THURSDAY HIS MOM CALLED him at work. It was lunchtime. They were all huddled around the picnic tables when Neal came out of the office and told him she was on the phone.

"You should come home," she said.

"It's only been three days."

"Things are fine. Everyone feels bad about what happened."

"Please. What's really going on?"

She sighed. Andrew could picture her furrowing her brow and tapping her foot. "Reporters are sniffing around. It would look better if we were together as a family."

"Whatever," Andrew said. He hung up.

When he came out of the office, he was met with some curious gazes. Most of the week Neal had him trimming bushes by himself or mowing lawns with Ben, but he'd had to fend off some questions about Brian at the lunch hour. The old-timers were polite. Andrew admired their old-school everyone-should-mind-their-own-damn-business New Englander ethos. But they were a dying breed. The younger guys all wanted to know about the case.

"You okay?" Cory said to him.

"I'm fine," Andrew said. He sat back down and started to eat.

"Was that your brother? Or a reporter?" he pressed. Cory fiddled with his water bottle. "I heard that it was these other guys and that Brian wasn't even involved," he said.

Another college kid, Ted something, Andrew didn't know him too well, sat down next to him and Cory.

"If you ask me," Ted said loudly, "it's all bullshit."

Andrew swallowed. "What's all bullshit?"

"You know, the case. You know," Ted said with affected nonchalance. It was like he wanted to bond over it or something. It infuriated Andrew.

"I don't know. Why don't you tell me?" Andrew said. He stood up.

"Simmer down," said Neal.

"I think Ted's just saying that we all support you," Cory said.

"Well, that's fucking ridiculous," Andrew said. "I have nothing to do with it." He packed up his sandwich and walked into the office. He grabbed his Bible and stared at it. Cory knocked on the door and opened it at the same time.

"What?" Andrew said.

"Sorry about that. Ted's an ass," Cory said. "Hey, what are you reading?"

"The word of God. Why do you ask?"

"Oh."

Cory stood in the doorway, looking at him with a concerned expression on his face. Cory was like an actor who couldn't figure out his role. A bros-before-hoes type, a college intellectual, a blue-collar worker, a peacemaker nice guy—nothing fit. He was just trying his best.

"Forget it," Andrew said. "Sorry, I'm being a prick."

"No, man, that's cool. I used to go to church."

"Really?"

"Yeah." Cory came into the office and sat down at Neal's desk.

"Which church?" Andrew asked.

"Saint Mary's. Catholic."

"Do you still go?"

"Noooo," Cory said. He leaned back in the chair and stared up at the ceiling. "I don't believe in God."

"I guess I'm on the fence. I don't know."

"So what gives?"

"It's complicated. There's this girl."

"*Cherchez la femme,*" Cory said.

"Huh?"

"It's French for 'look for the woman.' When the shit hits the fan, when you're trying to figure out a mystery, or explain some inexplicable behavior, *cherchez la femme.*"

Neal poked his head in the door. "Back to work. And get your ass out of my chair," he said. Cory leaped up.

"I like that *cherchez* thing," Andrew said as they went back outside.

"French is full of stuff like that," Cory said. "Perfect phrases."

"Kinda sexist," said Andrew.

"So is the Bible," Cory said.

No one was home when he arrived. Maybe they'd planned it that way; maybe nobody cared. Becky, at least, was glad to be back. She jumped around the kitchen and sat in the place where he usually put her food bowl.

The answering machine was blinking. There were two messages from reporters, one message from his mother telling him not to talk to reporters, and a message from John, simply asking him to call back.

John. Andrew was both jealous and wary of John. He also felt sorry for him, and he wasn't entirely sure what inspired that feeling. But John was an avenue to Laura. He picked up on the second ring.

"I got your number from Matt. That's cool, right?"

"Yeah. Of course. What's up?"

"I just wanted to see how you're feeling."

"I'm fine." Andrew tried to relax. Why was he being such a jerk? "I've got to wash your shirt."

"Don't worry about it. Keep it."

"Um, okay."

"Anyway, I'm planning a hike," John said.

"Who's going?" Andrew said.

"Me and Matt, a few others. I'm still trying to put it all together."

Andrew thought, if Laura was going, John would have said so. But he didn't want to ask directly about her. "I kind of have a lot going on right now. And I've got work tomorrow."

"The hike's not tomorrow. I was thinking Sunday."

"Sunday? Don't you have church?"

"God is everywhere. Besides, it's a sunrise hike."

"A what?"

"We time it so that the sun hits when we're at the top of the mountain."

Andrew thought for a moment. It actually sounded kind of nice. And Laura would probably be there, right? If she wasn't, he could at least further ingratiate himself with her friends.

"Which mountain?" he asked.

"Darren. Well-marked trail. Easy climb."

"Can I bring my dog?"

"Definitely."

"Okay," Andrew said.

"Okay?"

"Yup."

"Awesome. We'll meet at Matt's house. Three thirty a.m.," John said.

"Should I bring my car?" Andrew recalled that Darren Mountain was a couple of towns over.

"I think we have enough cars. You can ride with me," John said, then added, "I'll pick you up."

"I might need my car for an emergency." Something about John's tone was bothering him. Besides, if Laura came, he might be able to drive her and have Becky take up the backseat so they could be alone.

"That's cool," John said.

A sunrise hike on a Sunday morning with a bunch of fundamentalist Christian kids. What was he getting himself into? He double-checked the answering machine and scanned the counter for notes—Marcia had apparently not called. Andrew was determined to get in touch with her. He hadn't spoken to her in almost a week, and he wanted to, badly. Marcia was *Reason*. Marcia was *Science*. Despite the spiritual distress she suffered from her father's death, her mother's illness, even Sara's accident, Andrew had no doubt that Marcia saw the forest through the trees. She was not, inherently, on the side of faith. She might envy those who had it, but it was simply not hers to have. He needed that kind of clarity. When the phone rang, he sprang up, almost, but not quite, wanting it to be Marcia over anyone else, even Laura.

"This is Glenn from the *Journal*. Is this Andrew Genter?" The man's voice was silky and deep.

"Shit," Andrew said, and hung up.

A reporter calling and asking for him by name. What the fuck was that about? The phone rang again. He let the answering machine pick up.

"Listen, Andrew, we just wanted to get your side of the story—"

Andrew picked up the phone. "Leave me alone. It has nothing to do with me."

"What doesn't?"

Andrew hung up again. This time the reporter didn't call back. He heard a car pull into the driveway. His first thought was to go upstairs to his room, but he decided to stay. The status quo needed to be reestablished. Might as well get it over with. Andrew knew how to walk away from a fight. The other night had been an aberration on *his* part; Brian had behaved exactly as was expected. *I control this,* he said to himself.

Brian walked in the door. "Hey," he said.

"What's up?" Andrew said.

"Where have you been?" he asked.

"Seriously? Mom didn't tell you?"

"No."

"Well, then, I won't either."

"Fuck you, man."

"Whatever."

Brian went into the living room and turned on the TV. He was quiet, which was weird. Usually he yelled at the players or the sportscasters. Andrew had the uncanny feeling that Brian was listening to him, just as he was listening to Brian. He grabbed the phone to call Marcia.

"Who are you calling?" Brian said.

"I've to check on Sara," Andrew said. "You know, the hot one," he added.

"The lawyer is going to call any second. Stay the fuck off the phone."

Andrew thought for a minute. He did not want to get hit again. *I control this. Eighteen and out.* He put the phone down, leashed Becky, and left.

He and Becky walked around the neighborhood slowly. He thought about visiting Laura. One of her little siblings was bound to like dogs. But he was tired, having spent the second half of the day mixing cement with Cheeve. He also didn't feel like getting all caught up with the weight of seeing her. The agonizing crush of desire he felt when he was with her was somehow made worse, even more intolerable, now that he was closer to her. He also felt somewhat unwelcome at her house. He played the cozy little scene between her and John over and over in his head. She admired John; she respected John. And John was tall and cut and good-looking. Better-looking than Pretty Boy Matt or Goatee Seth or balding Chip. Certainly better-looking than he was. He kicked a rock into the grass.

Becky woofed softly and leaned into his legs. He stumbled and caught himself. He sat on the ground and petted her for a while. Becky occasionally leaned on his legs as if to trip him. Her veterinarian said it was either a gesture of affection or a way of showing dominance. *Which is it?* Andrew had asked. *Both,* the vet said with a shrug. *They're fundamentally different from us, Andrew. You can't always equate animal behavior with human behavior. It doesn't work like that.* But despite the advice, he tried to understand Becky through the lens of human emotion. *I love you so much that I'm going to dominate you, trip you, get the better of you.* It made perfect sense, he thought.

When Andrew got back, he saw a bunch of cars in his driveway and decided that Brian must have a crew of friends over. He could hear them in the living room as he fed Becky in the kitchen.

"Don't worry about it, man. It's going to be all right."

"You don't know that," Brian said. His voice sounded weak, hollow.

"You didn't do anything, right? It'll be okay."

Must have been bad news from the lawyer, Andrew thought.

"I heard the door. Ty coming over?"

"No. It's just my brother."

"Little Andrew? Hey, buddy, get us some chips!" the voice commanded. Andrew wasn't even sure who it was; all of Brian's friends seemed interchangeable to him.

"Leave him alone," Brian said.

"But—"

"Just leave him alone. Let's get out of here. I'll drive."

Andrew was startled by Brian's command to leave him alone. He must feel guilty as hell, Andrew thought. *He must actually be guilty.* His stomach lurched with a feeling he could not identify. He quickly crept up the stairs. His mother was sitting on her bed with the door open. They exchanged the briefest of glances before he went into his own room and closed the door. He heard her walk downstairs. He thought she might be weeping. *Should I go to her? What for?* He blinked tears out of his eyes and fished his Bible out from under a pile of clothes. He held it to his chest, trying to call up that feeling of comfort it had given him when he'd spent his first night in Neal's office. It no longer seemed sacred; it had lost something. Or he had lost something.

27

ANDREW WALKED ALONG THE BEACH with bare feet. The sand felt icy and gritty between his toes. When he stopped and tried to get the grains out, he found they were impacted and had formed a kind of webbing. Disgusted, he reached for the chisel in his pocket, the one that Neal had given him, but it was gone. A yellowish moon rose high above him, casting silver and gold light along the length of the beach. He looked back and forth and saw that the shoreline was endless and the ocean was dry. He wasn't on the beach; he was in a desert. And he was alone. Alone, alone, alone.

Andrew awoke to the painful sound of the alarm clock. It made an angry beeping noise that he was not accustomed to. He usually woke up a few minutes before it went off to avoid the sound.

It was three a.m. Becky did not stir as he left the room to shower. The swelling in his face was almost completely gone. After he'd showered, dressed, and changed his shirt at least three times, Andrew went down to the kitchen and quickly drank a cup of coffee. He glanced at the clock and saw that he had to leave in five minutes.

"Becky, get up," he called.

Becky trotted down the stairs and gave him a look of irritation that made Andrew laugh. He fed her, grabbed his jacket, and stuffed some dog treats and his Bible into his pockets. After he got in the car, he realized that he'd forgotten to look for a flashlight. *Screw it,* he thought. There were bound to be extra flashlights, and he didn't want to be late picking up Laura.

Getting to drive Laura was a major coup. He had finally gotten her on the phone yesterday afternoon and casually mentioned that he had lost the directions to Matt's house. She had come up with the idea of Andrew picking her up—that way she could simply direct him to Matt's house. John was going to drive her, she'd said, but Andrew lived closer. "Makes sense," Andrew had said.

It was dark and cool at this hour of the morning. The air felt cleaner, too, as if the sky and even the air had been washed overnight. He looked up at the pale light of the moon and thought of Laura. He had set goals for himself; he had even written them down in his journal. No matter what, by week's end, he would kiss her.

Laura was waiting on the steps when he pulled up to her house. She was dazzling, even at this hour. She gave him a bright-eyed smile as she stood. She looked very young, he thought, as he studied her face and her huge blue eyes. But at second glance he saw that her T-shirt was very tight across her breasts. *Make eye contact,* he told himself. *No glancing down. Don't be a jackass about her tits.*

"Morning," she said. She got into the car and reached into the backseat to pet Becky.

"What's up?" Andrew said. He pulled away from the curb and drove down the street. She did not have a jacket. "Aren't you cold?"

"A little. But I get hot when I hike, and I don't like carrying a jacket around," she said.

"You could've left it in my car. Should we go back?"

"No, it's all right. I don't want to be late."

Andrew stopped the car. "Just wear my jacket." He fumbled as he took it off. Laura began to protest, but Andrew insisted.

"Thanks," she said. She put the jacket on. It was way too big for her. She looked cute.

"This should be fun," Andrew said.

"You seem to know what you're doing," she said.

"What?"

"Matt's house."

Andrew realized that he was driving to Matt's house without any further instruction from her.

"Oh. I kind of remember the first part of the way."

Laura smiled. As their eyes met, Andrew knew he looked sheepish.

They reached Matt's house, Laura casually offering directions along the way. John was waiting on the steps of the porch when they arrived. The porch lights cast a slight glow on the sidewalk. John stood up and came toward them when Andrew and Laura got out of the car. She and John hugged each other while Andrew tried to look indifferent.

"Where is everyone?" Laura asked.

"David and Matt are in the house with Karen. Josh and Susie should be here any minute. This is kind of big for you," John said, fingering the collar of Andrew's jacket.

"It's Andrew's," Laura said. "I was cold."

With his torn jeans and bright orange tank top, John looked even more like a surfer dude than before, if that were possible. John reached out to shake Andrew's hand but then pulled him into a backslapping man hug. It was awkward, and Andrew's face was briefly pressed against the gigantic blue cross tattoo on John's arm. Laura disappeared into the house, leaving John and Andrew to their own devices.

"About the other night . . ." John began.

"Which one?" Andrew said.

"Um, in your car," John said.

"I'm glad we got to talk," Andrew said.

"Yeah," John said. He looked as if he wanted to say more, but he didn't.

"Carrie coming?" Andrew asked.

"Nah. She's helping prepare the service today," John said.

"Bummer."

"Yeah. Carrie's a doll," John said.

Andrew crossed his arms over his chest and rocked back and forth.

"You cold?"

"I'm fine."

Embarrassed, Andrew stopped moving and shoved his hands into his pockets while John fiddled with the buttons on his own jacket.

"Look, man—" John said.

"Want to meet my dog?" Andrew turned abruptly and went to his car.

"Uh, sure," John said. He followed Andrew closely and said, "Actually, I love dogs. Always wanted one."

John and Becky greeted each other with unbridled enthusiasm; John embraced her and talked in a baby voice as Becky alternately licked his face and spun around in circles to express her joy. As the displays of mutual affection continued, Andrew began to feel jealous. He told himself to chill out. After all, it was nice for Becky to have a new friend. Marcia was a little frightened of big dogs, Becky included, but Sara used to talk to Becky in the same baby voice as John.

"Why don't you get a dog?" Andrew asked.

John was rubbing Becky's belly. He looked up and said, "My apartment building doesn't allow them. And before that, my parents . . ." John's voice trailed off as he looked away.

How old is John anyway? Andrew mused. He was solidly built, like Brian, only not so gargantuan. His features were young, he acted young, but the corners of his eyes were creased. And he had that air of tragedy about him, that quality of hurt and pain. He thought of Marcia.

"You remind me of my friend," Andrew said.

"The one in the coma?" John said softly.

What a weird thing to say, Andrew thought. In the darkness of the morning, at the distance they were standing from each other, Andrew could not see the expression on John's face. But the tenor of John's voice had changed. John's manner toward him had subtly shifted.

At that moment Laura and the rest of the group came out of the house and began to discuss driving arrangements. Karen and Goatee Seth were among them. His eyes locked with Seth for a moment. They both looked quickly away.

"Well, I rode here with Andrew . . ." Laura began.

"But his car is small, and I want to sit with you," Karen said.

"I know, I know. I want to sit with you, too," Laura said.

"I can fit two people. Someone will just have to sit in the back with my dog," Andrew said. He looked at Karen as he spoke. She narrowed her eyes at him. He studied her for a moment. Despite the pointy chin, she was pretty and had very long legs, emphasized by a pair of tiny cut-off shorts. Her top was a bit too small for her, and Andrew could see a flash of her bare midriff.

She must be cold, he thought. He shifted his gaze and noticed that Laura was watching him watch Karen.

Much to Andrew's irritation, Laura ended up riding with Seth and Karen in Matt's car (they all had something doctrinal to discuss) while John drove a couple of other kids whom Andrew had met briefly at the church. Andrew was assigned to drive David, who was Seth and Karen's twelve-year-old brother. David, like John, was a dog lover without a dog and so occupied himself with Becky in the backseat during the fifteen-minute drive to Darren Mountain.

"Having fun back there?" Andrew asked.

"Yes!" David said. "Becky is my new best friend."

Andrew thought that David was a little old to be talking like that, but he just smiled and said, "Good." Then added, "Keep that seat belt on."

It was pitch dark at the base of the mountain. Andrew blinked as he exited the car and then recalled that he didn't have a flashlight. Andrew instructed David to stay in the backseat with Becky while he went to get her leash, which was still in the pocket of his jacket.

"Can I open the windows?" David asked.

"Sure. I know it's kind of stuffy," Andrew said. His car was so old that the windows rolled down manually.

Andrew followed the sound of Laura's voice and felt along the side of Matt's car until he reached her. She and Karen were giggling about something.

"Laura?" He lightly touched her shoulder as he spoke.

Laura jumped. "Whoa! You scared me."

"Sorry. I need Becky's leash. It's in the right pocket."

Laura pulled the leash out of the pocket, and Becky's treats fell out as well. Andrew kneeled down to pick them up when a bright light suddenly enveloped them both.

"Everything okay over there?" It was John's voice. A glaring light was strapped to his forehead. Andrew and Laura held their arms up to shield their eyes.

"Yes, fine," Andrew said.

"John, turn that thing off," Laura said.

"Sorry," John said. He turned away, and for a moment Andrew and Laura were plunged into an even deeper darkness.

"I'm blinded," Andrew said, rubbing his eyes.

"I know," Laura said. She giggled, and then Andrew felt her hands on his waist. She gently turned him around. "You know where you're going?" she whispered.

"Yes," he said. He reached back in an attempt to squeeze one of her hands, but they had left his waist. Laura herself seemed to glide away behind him. *Like a wood nymph,* Andrew thought as he walked back to his car.

David had a tiny flashlight that he held under his chin to illuminate his face. As Andrew got closer, he heard David speaking to Becky.

"And the bride kept hearing that noise—*tap, tap, tap*—right on the roof of the car. But she didn't open the door because her husband told her not to, remember, Becky? So then—"

David really is a dork, Andrew thought. He smiled when he reached the car but didn't speak. He might as well let David finish his story.

"Hey!" Seth called out. "What are you doing in there?" He shone his own large flashlight into the backseat of Andrew's car, revealing a frightened-looking David, who had switched off his flashlight and was now frantically petting Becky.

"What did I tell you about those stories?" Seth said.

"I'm sorry. I was just playing around," David said. His voice quavered and his bottom lip trembled.

"Do you understand me?" Seth opened the car door.

"Take it easy," Andrew said, unsure of what was going on.

Seth ignored him. "Blasphemy. Witchcraft. If I hear that stuff one more time, I'm going to tell Mom and Dad."

David started to cry. Seth reached inside the car and took David by the wrist. David yelped and Becky growled.

Andrew moved toward them with his fists balled up. "Jesus fucking Christ, Seth—" he started.

A collective gasp erupted from the group. Andrew inwardly cursed both himself and them. *These fucking people,* he thought.

"Sorry. It's just an expression," Andrew said. He took a step back. His arms were shaking at his sides.

"Is it?" It was Karen who spoke now, stepping forward into the circle of light created by all the flashlights that shone upon Andrew.

"Okay, everybody. We're here to have a good time," John said. He appeared next to Andrew and put his arm around his shoulders. "Let's just put this behind us and start going up."

"We're going to miss the sunrise if we don't leave now," Laura said. Andrew looked in the direction of her voice but couldn't see her. A grumble rose from the group as everybody started up the trail.

"I'll go first," John said as he switched on his headlamp.

Seth still gripped the handle of Andrew's car. They exchanged a hostile glance before Seth turned and followed John. Andrew attached Becky's leash while David wiped his tears and runny nose on his shirt.

"Everyone's mad at me," he whimpered.

Andrew felt the urge to get into the car, drive to the nearest diner, and buy David some pancakes. Instead he said, "I'm not mad at you. And neither is Becky." He paused, then added, "And neither is John."

David took out his flashlight and shone it on the path in front of them. Then he slipped his free hand into Andrew's and squeezed it. David's hand was sticky and wet.

"Still," David said, "you shouldn't take the Lord's name in vain."

28

ANDREW FOCUSED ON THE LIGHT coming from John's headlamp. David had recovered from the incident with his brother and kept swinging his flashlight so that it made swirls and jags on the path. As he did this, he babbled sound effects to accompany the light show. David also tried to get Becky to play with him.

"Hey, Becky! Becky! Becky, chase after the light. Why isn't she chasing it?"

"I don't know," Andrew said.

"Oh, okay," David said with such an immediate tone of apology that Andrew felt guilty. David's gooey, damp hand still clung to him. It was gross, but also warm and oddly comforting. Andrew thought briefly of the night of Sara's accident, when he and Marcia had spent hours sitting holding hands while Marcia wept. The moist warmth of their joined palms had become oppressive to him. *For her, too, probably,* he thought now.

The voices of the people ahead of them had grown fainter, as had the light from John's headlamp.

"We'd better pick up the pace here, buddy," Andrew said.

"Okay."

They walked faster, and David tripped on something and fell down, nearly taking Andrew with him. Andrew reached under David's armpits and pulled him to his feet. The flashlight rolled away. They were in total darkness. "You all right?" he asked.

"Sorry," David said.

"Stop apologizing. Why did your flashlight go off?"

"You have to push the button constantly to make it work. There's no switch or anything."

"Shit."

"You shouldn't—"

"David, there's nothing wrong with saying *shit*." Andrew groped around in the dark, looking for the flashlight. Becky sniffed the ground and pawed at leaves.

"Hey, John!" Andrew said. No answer. Andrew shouted again.

"What's up?" John's voice seemed to come from a long way off.

"We lost our light."

"What?"

"Turn toward us!"

John obliged, and Andrew and David were immediately bathed in light. They searched until they found the absurd toy flashlight. Andrew grabbed it and shouted his thanks to John. He heard John ask the group to slow down a bit so that Andrew and David could catch up. Then he heard a girl, probably Karen, whine about not wanting to miss the sunrise.

"Everything okay back there?" It was Seth. He sounded apologetic. Andrew took hold of one of David's hands and put Becky's leash in the other.

"Don't let go," Andrew said. Then, in the direction of Seth's voice, Andrew yelled, "We're okay! I've got him."

They continued up the trail at a faster pace. Gradually, even though they couldn't see the sun, the world seemed to brighten around them. It was so subtle that at first Andrew thought it was just his eyes adjusting to the dark or his proximity to the rest of the group and all their flashlights. But then he saw that the leaves of the trees were not just green but glowing green. Soft, golden green. Somewhere, somehow, the sun was taking hold of the mountain.

He thought of Laura. Of her little hand touching his face and grazing his waist. Her skin was unbelievably soft. Like the skin of a baby or a puppy's belly. Andrew quickened his pace. He wanted to see her. He heard David panting. They were almost there. The trees got shorter and sturdier. They could see the horizon, an orange strip just barely visible beyond the mountaintop. Above the orange strip a pink glow softened the bluish blackness of the sky. The ground beneath them turned rocky and uneven. David stumbled a bit, but Andrew kept him from falling.

Andrew could now see Laura's back. Laura was very curvy. He cast his eyes up and down her. He felt a terrible urgency to be near her. An urgency that was strangely subdued by the presence of David and David's squishy hand gripping his.

She wasn't wearing his jacket anymore. Probably John was carrying it. Or Matt, who had been curiously silent during the Seth-and-David debacle. Just then David gave his hand an encouraging squeeze. *Weird,* thought Andrew. He wondered if his body was communicating his dismay. Andrew could tell that David was a hypersensitive kid who was constantly being monitored by his parents and older siblings for any infraction. He must be able to sense even the slightest glimmer of disapproval or disappointment from those around him. *Poor David,* Andrew thought. But when they got to the top of the mountain, scrambling over some rocks to reach it, Andrew automatically let go of David's hand.

He walked toward Laura. He could barely see her, and then suddenly he couldn't see her at all. Everyone had turned their flashlights off. He released the button of David's flashlight as well. Darkness. The orange strip on the horizon was just slightly bigger, the sky pinker and bluer and softer.

He stood perfectly still and silent, as did everyone else

around him, even Becky. It was as though they were compelled to be motionless. He could barely make out the faint outlines of all the still bodies around him. *Like Stonehenge,* he thought. Soft mutterings echoed in his ears. Praying? Who was praying? Then someone started to sing. He couldn't tell who was singing; he couldn't even distinguish their gender. Other voices joined the first. He tuned out the singing as he looked for Laura.

Her head was bowed and her lips moved softly. He focused on her silhouette as the world slowly brightened. Laura was like a living work of art, the best movie you'd ever seen, the prettiest painting, the perfect poem. He imagined his arms around Laura, gripping her waist and pressing his lips to hers. Burying his face in her body, running his fingers through her hair. Soft wisps of that hair were now blowing around in the wind, around her bowed head.

Cautiously, Andrew took a step forward. Brighter and brighter and brighter. And warmer, too. Then the brightness and warmth were coming from within him. The feeling of light, lush and warm, right from the center of his heart, or was it his stomach? Or was it his brain? Brighter and warmer, and he could feel himself somehow falling up.

One part of him wanted to surrender to this feeling of endless light, a feeling that came from within. Another part of him floated above and watched himself on the mountaintop. *There's Andrew,* Andrew thought. *That's me down there.*

With a gasp, Andrew sat down and clutched his heart, which

was beating so hard, it felt like a piece of machinery in his chest. He struggled to catch his breath. The inevitable hand of John was on his back, his arm.

"You okay? Are you all right?"

"I'm—" Andrew tried to say he was fine but realized he was gasping too hard and couldn't get the words out. Then Laura was at his side.

"Like in the field?" she said.

"Only worse," Andrew muttered. "Or better. I don't know."

Laura stroked the small of his back. Andrew felt her little hands and John's large ones all over his back, his neck, his head even. Laura and John's hands seemed to be overlapping each other's. As if they were petting him and each other, the three of them bound together in a strange moving embrace. And all around them the world glowed.

"It's starting," John said.

It was as though they were inside a ray of the sun. Everything was pale yellow. Everyone looked beautiful, desirable. Laura, especially. A pale golden Laura lit from within. She sat next to Andrew with her hands gently clasped around one of his wrists. Like a human handcuff, or as though she were offering his hand to the sun. John's hand slid from Andrew's back and drooped by his side, his palm open and turned upward, his eyes closed, his head bowed. The feeling of awful and absolute pity that John sometimes inspired in Andrew returned to him now with an exquisite stab.

His breath steady, his heart calm, Andrew reached out to John and touched his hand. John jumped a little, but otherwise remained perfectly still. A moment passed. Laura and John were like statues beside him. They were frozen in time.

Andrew did not want to stay inside this moment. He wanted to be an observer, an outsider looking in—not a participant. He was, he thought, the only person on the mountaintop with his eyes wide open. Everyone else's lids were closed or half closed, which he found odd, because the sunrise was so beautiful. Wasn't that why they were here? To *see* the sunrise?

Andrew glanced around and saw that David was lying on the ground with Becky flopped over his legs. They looked like they were both asleep, which perhaps they were. He smiled. That was nice. Everything was nice. He began to feel high again, floating upward inside the light. He drew his breath in sharply. He didn't want that feeling to return.

He put one hand on top of Laura's clasped hands on his arm. She immediately entwined his fingers with hers. The longed-for moment. She was inches from him, golden and praying. A gust of wind blew her hair back, revealing her face more clearly. Her ears were unpierced.

"I love having my earlobes kissed," Sara had once said to him, when they were talking about sex. "Tip for the future, Andrew," she'd said. "Really gently suck on a girl's earlobe. Bite it, even." And then she'd demonstrated what she'd meant.

So now he leaned over and gently kissed the tip of Laura's

earlobe. Startled, Laura turned her head toward him, her eyes wide and her expression enigmatic. She blinked at him, smiled, then lowered her head and began to pray once more.

He was light, floating again, but this time totally in control. He glanced at John, who still had his head bowed in prayer as well. The deep, sad, furrows around John's eyes were more pronounced in the bright light of the sun.

Andrew felt warm and sleepy. He wished he were alone with Laura. That he could take her into his arms and lean back against the rocks. Anything seemed possible in this sunlight. The sun moved across the sky, and the intensity of the brightness dimmed by slow degrees, the warm, golden light replaced by regular yellow clarity. Marcia would have liked this. Sara, too.

The group began shifting around and stretching, as if they were all waking from the same dream. John rose abruptly and walked toward the edge of the mountain. He stood with his arms crossed and his legs apart, looking down. Laura got up and drifted toward Karen. The two girls whispered to each other. Were they talking about him? But then he thought that there was no way on earth that Laura would tell Karen that he'd just kissed her ear. Andrew moved closer to the girls and strained to hear them. Karen pulled from her pocket what looked like his Bible.

"I found it on the ground. He must have dropped it," Karen said.

"So give it back to him," Laura said.

And then for some reason they both giggled.

"Hey."

Andrew looked up and saw Matt and Seth. Matt had Andrew's jacket crumpled up under one of his arms. He handed him the jacket and sat down.

"Thanks," Andrew said. "Sorry you had to carry that."

"No problem," Matt said.

Matt stretched his legs out in front of him and grabbed the toes of his sneakers, like an athlete preparing himself for a race. Seth did not sit. Andrew glanced away, looking for David and Becky. They were running around in a grassy part of the mountaintop, David's hand still gripping the handle of the leash.

"We're sorry about before," Matt said.

"It's fine," Andrew said.

"It's not fine. We've talked about this. You didn't grow up in this—" Matt said as he gestured with his arms as if to encompass all the people around them in an aerial embrace. He cleared his throat and looked at Seth, who seemed like he was pretending to read his Bible. He closed it and spoke to Andrew.

"I'm sorry too," he said.

"What's wrong with ghost stories?" Andrew asked him. Seth rolled his eyes. "I'm honestly curious," Andrew said. Seth didn't respond.

"Well, it's like—" Matt said. "Ghosts aren't real. Your soul goes to Heaven or, you know, it doesn't. The soul doesn't hang out on Earth torturing people, haunting people, possessing people. That's what we mean by blasphemy. We believe, I believe, that thinking about the soul in that way, like in a horror movie or something, is just harmful."

"Harmful to who?" Andrew asked.

"Everyone," Matt said. "The living and the dead."

"Oh," Andrew said. "What about—" He took a deep breath. He didn't want to talk about anything real in front of douche-bag Goatee Seth. But Matt seemed to read his mind.

"Your friend's soul is still here. Sara is still *here*," Matt said.

Andrew stood up and immediately felt lightheaded. He swayed slightly.

"Are you okay? Did you eat this morning? I have some crackers . . . somewhere," Matt said as he searched the pockets of his pants. Even Seth reached out as if to steady him. But Andrew regained control of himself and stepped away from them both.

"It's not a ghost story anyway," Andrew said.

"What?" Seth said.

"David's story. There's nothing supernatural about that one. It's just a stupid scary story."

"Oh," Seth said.

"We didn't know that," Matt added.

Seth looked long and hard at David, who was at that moment literally frolicking on a sunny mountaintop. "It's best not to stray into that territory," he said.

"Whatever," Andrew said. He turned toward Seth. "Where are you going, anyway?"

"What do you mean?"

"For your thing. You know, the traveling portion of your faith."

"Ghana," Seth said.

"Oh, right," Andrew said. "I knew that." Then he turned away and walked toward David and Becky. He heard Matt say his name, barely audible, but he pretended not to hear.

Off to Africa to convert the unbelieving. *Seth is pure ass hat,* he thought, but Andrew was shaken. Shaken to hear Matt refer to Sara's soul. How dare he? Laura had told all these jerks about Sara and her coma and her fucking ventilator. That was why Laura wanted to hang out with him in the first place. Because he was grieving, vulnerable, possibly convertible. Did she even really care about him? Then with a surge of shame he realized that for the past few days he hadn't really thought about Sara at all because he was so consumed with trying to connect with Laura.

With a frown on his face he reached the joyful David and Becky. "Hey," Andrew said.

"Oh, hi," David said, standing up straight and gazing at Andrew with wide eyes. Andrew noted with irritation that David had picked up on his bad mood and responded to it immediately, like a cringing dog. *We always hate the ones we hurt the most,* Andrew thought. Where had he heard that before? He felt dizzy again and sat down.

"You okay?" David asked, sitting next to him and leaning against him slightly.

"Everyone keeps asking me that," Andrew said more to himself than to David. "Maybe I'm not okay."

"Maybe," David said, shrugging. Then he looked at Andrew with an expression of such nonchalance that it made Andrew laugh. Becky flopped in between them and put her head on Andrew's knee.

"We should start heading down," John said. His voice sounded strangely harsh in the distance. John stood on the edge of a cliff with his back to the sun. His arms were crossed over his chest, and the wind blew his long hair out in front of him. He was lit from behind by golden-orange light. Andrew thought that John looked comically epic. A born-again surfer-dude warrior on the cover of a fantasy book. Andrew laughed some more. A note of hysteria tinged his voice. Becky took her head off his knee, and the ever-sensitive David squirmed around and looked confused.

"David!" Seth called.

"Better hop to," Andrew said, reeling onto his back and laughing even harder.

David ran off in the direction of his brother. Andrew stared at the sky and took some deep breaths, trying to calm down. He closed his eyes and heard footsteps. An image of Sara floated before him. She was lying in her hospital bed, back to normal, wide-awake, fully dressed, with a suggestive smile on her lips. She sat up and said, *Come on, Andrew, let's go!*

A shadow passed before his closed eyelids.

"We do a prayer circle before we go down," John said.

"You can't be too careful," Andrew said, laughing.

"What?"

"Nothing," Andrew said. He jumped up and grinned.

John was frowning and looking at Andrew with concern.

"Let's go, man," Andrew said as he swung his arm around John's shoulders in a drunken fashion. With his other hand, Andrew patted John on the chest and said, "You okay, buddy?"

"I'm fine," John said.

Together they walked toward the group of people forming a loose and uneven circle at the top of the mountain. John seemed startled by Andrew's sudden physical aggression. The intimacy that John usually initiated seemed now to have been passed on to Andrew.

"This won't do," Andrew said as his arm slid from John's shoulders and then grasped one of his hands. "C'mon, everybody, close ranks." John's hand, at first warm and dry, began to sweat profusely. The group glanced at one another and then formed a circle by holding hands.

"John?" Laura said.

John opened his mouth when Andrew said suddenly, "How about I give it a go?" He laughed by himself for a few moments. Andrew felt hysterical and almost out of control but also sort of pleased with himself and unconcerned about anyone else. An uncomfortable silence ensued while he recovered.

"I think that would be nice," John said.

"Yes, it would be," Matt said firmly.

"I think . . ." Karen began in a snotty tone of voice.

"Sweetheart, the men have spoken," Andrew said. He walked over to Karen and gently cupped her angry face in the palm of his hand. She stared back.

"How dare you . . ." she began.

"I think you have my book," Andrew said so softly that only he and Karen, and perhaps Laura who was standing next to them and looking at Andrew with her static unreadable expression, could hear.

"This is *yours*?" Karen said as she pulled the Bible from her pocket.

Andrew leaned in even closer to Karen so that he was whispering in her ear. "My boyfriend gave it to me," he said.

Karen jumped and handed him the book.

"What is wrong with you?" Seth said as he grasped Andrew's arm and yanked him away from his sister.

"The spirit's got ahold of me," Andrew said. "No hard feelings, right, Karen?"

"No," Karen said. "No hard feelings at all. We'd better get started." She glanced at her watch and Andrew noticed, without a shred of guilt, that her hands were clenched and her face was red.

"Okay, everyone, let's just chill," John said, although he spoke with less certainty in his voice than was usual for him.

Andrew opened the book and read Psalm 6 out loud, laughing

occasionally throughout, while the group lowered their heads.

"'I am worn out from groaning; all night long I flood my bed with weeping and drench my couch with tears,'" Andrew read. Then he chuckled.

John said, "Amen," and everyone else said "Amen," including Andrew, whose giddiness was stoked rather than calmed by the solemn prayer circle.

"David?" Andrew said.

"Yeah?" David said, opening his eyes and looking excited.

"Race you down the mountain?" Andrew said.

"Okay!"

Then Andrew, David, and Becky took off down the trail amid unheeded cries urging them to slow down and be careful.

They reached the bottom of the mountain well before any of the others. Becky trotted behind them, panting and wagging her tail madly. There was a craggy old water fountain at the foot of the trail from which they drank. Andrew rummaged around in his trunk for a suitable container for Becky to drink out of. He found an old Styrofoam coffee cup that he rinsed and filled with water. Becky drank while the two boys lay on the ground and panted.

"That was a pretty good Psalm that you read back there," David said.

"Oh yeah?"

"Yeah. My favorite."

"You're lying."

"Am not."

"Are too."

They heard the footsteps of the others approaching. Karen reached them first. Andrew noted that she was sweaty and breathing hard. Her cut-offs were now sitting very low on her hips and her hair was disheveled.

"Did you run after us?" Andrew asked innocently.

Karen did not respond. She drank from the fountain and handed David the keys to Matt's car.

"Get in," she said.

David leaped up, said a quick good-bye to Andrew and Becky, and then crawled into the backseat of Matt's van. Andrew thought he could hear David singing to himself.

Andrew remained stretched out on the ground with his arms under his head. He smiled at Karen, who gazed down at him, her hands on her hips like a superhero.

"You need a cape," Andrew said, and then he giggled and turned over on his side, rollicking and chuckling.

The others came out of the trail in quick succession. He could feel their eyes on him, but he didn't care. He heard them confer about driving arrangements. Bits of their whispers reached his ears.

"Someone should go with him. He's freaking out."

"He's Laura's friend."

"He's all of our friend." *Definitely Matt's voice.*

Andrew stood up and put Becky in the backseat of the car. She stretched out her body and closed her eyes. As he walked over to the group, their whispers quieted. Laura smiled at him, but he shifted his eyes away from her and grabbed Karen's wrist.

"Karen will go with me," he said.

"I don't think—" Seth began, but Karen interrupted.

"No, it's fine. We have to talk anyway," she said.

"You do?" John and Seth said together.

"Andrew—" Matt said.

"Chill out, bro," Andrew said.

Andrew led her back to his car and opened the passenger side door for her. As she got in and buckled up, he winked at her. She frowned. He walked around the front of his car and glanced casually at Laura, who looked both hurt and confused. *Now we're getting somewhere,* he thought.

29

AFTER FIVE MINUTES OF COMPLETE silence, Karen said, "That's John's book."

"Mine now."

"His name is written on the inside."

"It's not his name. It's actually a precious old collectible. It belonged to John the Baptist, not John the born-again surfer dude."

"We're not born-again. And that's a mean way to talk about someone who cares about you."

"Oh, he cares about me, all right."

Karen crossed her arms and glared at the road. "What are you saying?" she asked.

Andrew seemed to awake from a dream. Cold sweat ran down his arms. What *was* he saying? "Nothing, Karen," he said.

"Nothing what?"

"Nothing. As in, I'm not saying anything." Andrew tried to laugh, but all the mirth in his body was spent. "I'm worn out from laughing," he said.

"What?"

He glanced in the rearview mirror and didn't see any of the others behind him. He felt nervous, jittery. He decided to get off the interstate, take Route 2 back to town. Maybe the pretty drive would calm him down. He heard Karen shift around and open the window.

"Shortcut," he murmured.

"Whatever," Karen said. "Listen, Matt likes you a lot. So does Laura," she said.

"Oh yeah?"

"I think you're up to something."

"I think *you're* up to something."

"Like what?"

"You first."

"Like, messing around with what we've got. Like, not taking it seriously."

"So what? Convert me. That's your job, isn't it? Or would it help if I were half starved and from a third-world country and—"

"Fuck you."

"Tough words, Sister Karen."

"And John's struggling. Leave him alone."

"Struggling with what?" Andrew said, feeling reckless again.

Karen didn't answer him. "And speaking of struggling, tell Goatee to lay off David," Andrew said.

"David is none of your business," Karen said.

"He acts like he's seven. Does he even have any friends?" Andrew was practically yelling at this girl he barely knew.

"Do you?"

"What?"

"Oh, please! Why are you hanging out with us? Why are you messing around with John's head? Why did you pull me into this car?"

"Because you wanted to come!"

"What? What did you say?" Karen screeched.

Andrew swerved to the side of the road and stopped the car. He met her angry gaze and said, "Because this is fun."

And then Karen was unbuckling her seat belt and in his arms. She pressed her lips on his, and her tongue was like a wild animal in his mouth. She was in his lap and working her hips against him. She groaned and dug her nails into his neck. He hesitated for a fraction of a second before tearing at the buttons on her shirt. Her skin tasted like pine needles and sunshine, sap and blue sky and the flashing brilliance of a thousand stars. She reached her hand down and unzipped his pants and grabbed at him, hard, and her touch was so frenzied that it was almost painful. He seized the lever to lower the back of his seat, and together they jerked down. Then somehow her shorts were off and then her underwear was off. She was so warm, like a fever. She rocked her body on him and muttered over and over something that sounded like *help me* or *save me* or *take me*. He felt himself climaxing and dissolving and biting her in his ecstasy and her saying *ouch* and him saying *sorry* and her struggling against him and gasping and all of it happening all at once.

They lay still and panted.

Andrew ran his fingers through Karen's silky brown hair. She looked up. Their eyes met. She looked as dumbfounded as he felt. From the backseat, Becky snorted.

Karen flopped back into the passenger seat. They both fumbled with their clothes. Andrew started the car, and they drove without speaking. His heart was thumping so hard, he could feel it in his throat, his mouth, his eyes.

"Are you . . ." He groped for the right words.

"Am I what?"

"Are you okay? I mean, is everything okay?"

"I'm fine."

They said nothing more. Andrew glanced at her a few times, but she stared out the window so that he couldn't see her face.

When they reached the outskirts of town, he cleared his throat.

"Did . . . Where am I going?" he asked.

"What?" Karen seemed to come out of a trance.

"Church or home or—"

"Church," she said.

"Okay," he said.

After a few minutes he pulled up behind a long line of cars waiting to park. Karen got out of the car and walked briskly toward her church's enormous double doors and the smiling faces of the men who held them open.

30

"ANDREW? IS THAT YOU?" Marcia said.

"Who else could it be?"

"I don't know. Are you all right?"

"I just need to talk."

"I'm back at the hospital at ten—"

"Is everything okay with Sara?"

"Basically. What's up with you?" she said.

Andrew paced around his kitchen. He'd checked the whole house before he called Marcia: there was definitely no one home. Still, he was nervous. He took a deep breath.

"So I went on this sunrise hike with the Christian kids and then I outed John to this really bitchy Christian girl and then I had sex with her."

There was a long pause. Then Marcia said, "To shut her up?"

"Don't start."

"How do you know John is gay?"

"I don't even know if he's actually gay. I mean, they're all kind of affectionate, you know, touchy-feely. I didn't even know that I thought that about him until I suggested it to Karen," he said.

"Really?" Marcia said.

Andrew paused. "Yes. No. I don't know." What did he know? How long had he suspected John was gay? *Was* John gay?

Marcia cleared her throat and said, "So, you told Karen the bitch—"

"Shit."

"What is it?"

"I guess I shouldn't call her that," he said.

"She did make you a man, after all."

Andrew grunted.

"Was it her first time too?"

"I really, really, *really* doubt it."

"That's telling us something."

Andrew grabbed some crackers and stuffed them into his mouth. He was famished. Marcia continued talking. She seemed to be enjoying herself. He could tell, even over the phone.

"She's deeply religious. These kids don't believe in sex before marriage. But clearly she had it with you, and she's had it before which means . . . which means—"

"What does it mean?"

"Which means she's probably pretty conflicted herself."

"Oh," he said.

"Like John."

"Oh."

"Conflicted."

"I get it!" he said through a mouthful of cracker.

"Do you? John's kind of an alpha male, right? Handsome. One of the ringleaders?"

"Um . . ." Had he said that about John? He remembered that he'd told Marcia all about these kids a while ago. Did he say John was *handsome*? Or had he implied it somehow? But Marcia didn't wait for him to answer. She rattled on.

"Karen's in love with John. She knows that he's gay and has a thing for you. You're a surrogate John, so to speak."

Andrew sunk back on a kitchen stool. "Give me a break," he said. And then he groaned and closed his eyes. He massaged his lids. "My eyes hurt."

"Too much sun."

"What about Laura?" he asked.

"Oh my god, Andrew. You want to know if you can salvage the Laura pursuit despite the fact that you had sex with her friend this very morning?" Marcia laughed and said, "Tell me more. Tell me everything."

Andrew spent the next ten minutes piecing together his bizarre and exciting morning. He left out the part about him kissing Laura's earlobe and their having briefly held hands. He wanted to keep that private, even from Marcia.

"Poor David," Marcia said when Andrew had finished.

"Yeah."

"Poor John."

"That too," Andrew said. He rubbed a kink in his thigh and recalled how he had flung his arm around John's broad shoulders and briefly clung to the back of his neck. What had come over him? John had trembled. Andrew was ashamed at having treated him in such a cavalier way, and then disgusted at John's response, and then ashamed of feeling disgusted. But then again, maybe John wasn't gay.

"Is Karen pretty?" Marcia said.

"She's okay. She's got nice legs."

"Nice legs?"

"She has nice legs and skin."

"Lovely. But not like Laura?"

"No one is like Laura," he said.

"Sara is like Laura."

"What?"

"And Laura and Karen are close?" Marcia said.

"Yeah. Always whispering and talking."

"So Laura probably knows that Karen has sex."

"Shit!" Andrew said. "Karen wouldn't tell her though, right?"

"Karen doesn't have to. Laura may have guessed. She's probably seen her friend like this before—worked up, angry, emotional. And then some guy gets her alone."

"She came on to me. I didn't take advantage of her," Andrew said.

"Speaking of which, did you use protection?"

"I didn't even know it was happening until it was happening."

"That sounds pretty born-again."

"They're not born-again!"

"So the two girls are close, Laura's prettier than Karen, Karen probably knows you're gaga for Laura because she's used to every straight guy within a ten-mile radius being in love with Laura—"

Andrew felt uncomfortable. Like maybe Marcia was talking about herself and Sara. Marcia was cute and shy; Sara was sexy and confident. Guys were always after Sara. How had that affected their friendship? How had it affected Marcia and how she thought about herself? And why hadn't he ever considered these things before? He was about to say something stupid to Marcia about how cute she was, but she was happily occupied psychoanalyzing people she didn't know.

"So, there's this dynamic between them, this push-pull of competition. Karen never feels as if she measures up. So she compensates by sleeping with the guy who can't get Laura."

"I thought you said she slept with me because she's in love with John," Andrew said.

"That too, I think."

Andrew stood up. "David is going to catch hell for hanging out with me so much. And then I totally fucked things up for John. Those dorks are like his family, and I don't think he has family and— Fuck!" With a violent gesture he swept his arm across the counter, spilling the newspaper and box of crackers.

"Listen. You think you're this—this demonic force, excuse the pun, that's wreaking havoc on this group. But they were already screwed up to begin with, okay? Just like everybody else."

Andrew thought for a moment. It made sense. Unable to help himself, he said, "What about Laura?"

"Drew, I have to go."

"What's happening?"

"She's having a new central line put in."

"The main IV thing?"

"Yeah."

"Why?"

"I meant to call you. She's been spiking fevers. They don't know why. They figure if they replace all the lines that might help. Sometimes those can introduce infection."

"That sounds bad."

"Dr. Bavin seems confident that this will help."

"Oh. Good." He shuffled around, played with the phone cord, unsure of what to say next.

"I heard about Brian," she said.

"Fuck him," Andrew said.

"Are you okay?"

"With that? It's fucked-up, but it has nothing to do with me!"

"All right, all right, don't yell."

"Sorry."

"It's okay. I really should go."

"Talk soon?"

"Yup."

Andrew wandered into the living room and flopped onto the couch. He felt both better and worse after talking to Marcia. He had thought that losing his virginity would be pure elation, and in a way it was, but he also felt empty. There was a sort of distance between himself and his body. It had all happened so fast. And Karen had been so . . . furious. It was sexy; the memory of it was sexy, and just thinking about her angry, pointy face made him excited again. Her legs gripping him, her tongue in his mouth, the warmth of her, the smell and taste of her. Something musky and piney and dark and sweet. Did all women smell like that when they were excited? Or was it particular to Karen? He remembered her shocked perplexity when they had finished. And then that empty nauseated feeling returned, like the feeling of being excited and *not* getting satisfaction.

He groaned and put his head in his hands. Surely, he'd just exploded his relationships with his new friends. With Laura.

31

HE WOKE UP TO THE SOUND of Becky trotting around in the kitchen. He peeled himself off the couch to feed her.

It was four o'clock. What an annoying time to have woken up; now he'd be up half the night. His mom worked weekends and would probably be home soon. She worked odd hours at a big box store in Darington. She stocked shelves and kept inventory. As a result, her arms and back were often sore. Yet she rarely complained. His father, on the other hand, complained a lot about back pain. There was still no sight of Brian or his dad anywhere, for which he was grateful.

After Becky ate, he grabbed her leash and they headed out the door. As he walked along, he thought about his weird out-of-body experience on the mountaintop. The feeling of endless light. Endless sunlight and breathlessness and palpitations and general semi-hysteria. He hadn't told Marcia about that stuff either. It was like that time with Laura at Shaman's Point when he'd thought that he'd had a panic attack. *I was dehydrated and exhausted,* Andrew reasoned, *and all I'd had for breakfast was a cup of coffee.* Even Matt had said something about his needing to eat. Besides, being close to Laura always seemed to throw him for a loop. Maybe he'd had anxiety brought on by hunger or something—this thought was much less disturbing than the other possibility, the possibility that there was a God that looked down on him and . . . and did what, exactly? Make him feel crazy and be weird to John and have sex with Karen? It didn't make any sense. Laura and her friends were elated by prayer and singing and the supposed presence of their God. Maybe he'd felt that way for a moment, but mostly, he'd just felt dark and horny.

At that moment a man walked toward him. "Andy?" he asked. The man's eyes were sharp.

"Andrew."

The man just stood there, smiling. Andrew noticed a small notebook and pen in one of his hands.

"That's a great-looking dog," the man said.

"She bites."

"Bullshit."

"Fuck off."

"Well, aren't we off to a nice start," the man said as he fell into stride with Andrew. Becky dodged the man's attempts to pet her.

"I write for—" the man started.

"I don't care who you write for. I told you to fuck off," Andrew said.

"I can understand why you're upset. That shit they're saying about your brother. Him in particular. I mean, Jesus."

Andrew wondered who was saying what about Brian in particular, but he knew better than to ask. "You shouldn't take the lord's name in vain," he said.

This seemed to catch the man off guard. "Oh," he said. Then: "This could really mess things up for him."

Who cares? Andrew thought. He quickened his pace.

"You're a smart kid. Better student than your brother from what I hear." Andrew didn't respond, so the man went on, "I mean, he may have gotten the scholarships, but he was born with what he's got. Not that he didn't work hard. Because he did work hard, didn't he, Andy? Not just physically, but mentally. The way that boy plays, whew! He plays *vicious*. You got to practice that kind of mean. You got to work at it." The man had a soft voice with a low thick pitch, as though his tongue were coated in cream. Andrew felt the speed of his walk slowing to the pace of the man's soothing, creepy voice.

"Your parents must be very proud," the man said.

Andrew started to open his mouth but stopped himself. *This man is smarter than I am,* he realized, and the thought did not disturb him. *My best friend is smarter than I am. I'm used to this shit.*

"Please leave me alone," Andrew said. Becky growled softly. Startled, the man stopped as Andrew and Becky kept walking.

"I'll leave my card on the steps. Just in case you want to tell your side of the story. *Protect* your information, if you know what I mean," the man called out behind him.

Andrew didn't know and didn't care what he meant. He felt aimless and irritated. He wanted to see Laura, but he didn't know what he'd say. He vaguely wanted to get in touch with Karen somehow too. Just to make sure everything was all right. They hadn't used a condom. What if Karen got pregnant? Andrew's stomach plummeted into his shoes. That would ruin his life. Utterly ruin it. Karen probably slept around, he thought. She went nuts every so often and jumped on some hapless jerk like him. At this thought, Andrew felt terrible for Karen, and terrible, too, for thinking so harshly about her. He also wanted to have sex with her again, and this made him feel like a fiend or a hypocrite or both.

Unable to help himself, he walked to Laura's house. He loafed around for a few minutes. He heard voices inside, but he couldn't make up his mind about what to do. He had to find out if Laura knew he'd had sex with Karen.

He was just making up his mind to knock when he heard a car pull into the driveway. Laura and a little girl got out of a beat-up family van.

There were dark circles under Laura's eyes, and her skin, usually golden, was pale. Her arms were crossed in front of her chest. She seemed to slump forward. He liked the darkness under her eyes. It made her look weary in a sexy sort of way. As Andrew drew closer to her, he noticed that her lips were dry. He had a desperate urge to lick his thumb and draw it across her mouth.

Lie through your teeth, he thought. *You have nothing to lose.*

"Laura," he said.

She turned toward him, her expression calm and cool. Andrew found himself unable to speak.

"Get in the house. Help Mom with dinner," Laura instructed the girl, who was not the same girl who had answered the door for Andrew the other night, so long ago. Laura started up the steps. Andrew gently took her arm above the elbow.

"Laura," he said.

"Yes?" She did not look at him.

"I don't know . . . how I'm feeling . . . about everything. I know today was crazy." He blushed. "I just know that I want to keep spending time with the group. With you."

As usual, he had trouble reading her expression. Placid, calm, indifferent. Indifference, that was what it was. It was devastating. This morning he'd had her, hadn't he? He'd kissed her ear; she'd held his hand. And Laura was jealous when he took Karen into his car. Andrew knew enough about girls to know that he might've been able to play off that jealousy, spin it into something else. But things with Karen had gotten so out of hand.

"John was talking about a fishing trip," Laura said. "You guys should go." She started up the steps again, and his hand slid from her arm.

"Laura, don't—"

Someone shouted from inside the house. "Come and sing to us!"

"Good-bye," Laura said.

Andrew watched a sliver of her silhouette through the narrow window above the front door. Then she was a shadow disappearing up the stairs. Then a flicker of a shadow. He watched until he knew that any remnant of her shadow was just his mind playing tricks on him.

As Andrew walked away, he heard an eruption of clapping behind him, in the house, where Laura was entertaining the people she loved.

32

"THINGS ARE LOOKING UP," Brian said to him when he got home. He was tossing a tub of fake butter in the air and catching it like a baseball.

"That shit's going to splatter everywhere, and I'm going to end up cleaning it up," Andrew said. He unleashed Becky and put some treats in her bowl.

"Ass," Brian muttered.

"Mom home?"

"How should I know?" Brian put the tub on the counter and tried to pet Becky. Becky shied away. "What the fuck?" he said.

"Don't pet her while she's eating," Andrew said. "That's threatening to her."

"Fuck you," Brian said.

"Andrew!" their dad shouted from the living room.

They both froze.

"What is it?" Brian said.

"Was I talking to you?" their father said. His voice was slurred.

Brian looked at Andrew and shrugged. Andrew walked into the living room. His dad was sitting on the couch with his feet up on the coffee table, a beer in one hand and the remote control in the other.

"You talk to any reporters?" he said. He did not look at Andrew when he spoke.

"No," Andrew said. He leaned against the bookshelf, exhausted. His head and heart were consumed with Laura. The last thing he wanted was to deal with this bullshit.

"Good. Brian tell you about the girl's lawyer?"

"No," Andrew said. He was about to add *and I don't care*, but then he remembered his mantra: *eighteen and out*. He didn't say anything, but he was unable to keep himself from walking out of the living room. His dad didn't call him back. He nearly toppled over Brian in the dining room.

"Were you listening in or something?" Andrew said.

"Blow me," Brian said.

Andrew put the tub of fake butter away and walked up the stairs. He wanted to get away from his family. He wanted to get back to Laura somehow. He picked up his Bible and leafed through it. He lacked the patience and discipline to even read his favorite Psalms. He paced the room. He thought about Karen.

He thought about jerking off. He felt beyond horny, beyond restless; he felt lost. He tiptoed down the stairs. Brian and his dad were watching sports. He picked up the phone and called John, who was surprised to hear from him.

"I don't want to go on a fishing trip. Let's just hang out," Andrew spoke quickly and without thought.

"Okay, cool," John said. He sounded hesitant.

"I could get some pot or something." Andrew felt like getting fucked-up. Would John go for that? Or would he cower and faint at the suggestion?

"Um . . . sure. You could see my place. It's kind of a dump, but there's beer and stuff," John said.

"Don't call Matt."

John paused. "All right," he said.

Later that evening Andrew was walking to John's place. It wasn't too far, and Andrew knew he'd probably have a few drinks. He left Becky at home because he remembered John saying that pets weren't allowed at his apartment.

John lived on "the other side of town," a euphemism for a neighborhood with less money. Some of the asshole kids at his school used to call people from the other side of town *scumbags*. The word had lost its trendiness, but Andrew could recall his brother using it frequently and with great relish. Not that their own family was that much better off. Their dad may have worn a shirt and tie to work, but money was always tight. A local sports store had started sponsoring Brian when he wasn't even out of middle school. The store was graced with pictures of Brian smiling for the camera and holding up the equipment he got for free. *That must have been a little weird for him,* Andrew thought for the first time.

The other side of town featured several rundown apartment buildings, one of which was the one John lived in. A bunch of people sat out on their porches smoking and talking or just hanging out.

Pink chips of paint that looked like dried Pepto-Bismol were ringed around the exterior of John's apartment building like some kind of decrepit magic barrier. John lived on the second floor. The stairs creaked and groaned and smelled like piss. The hallway, however, was relatively quiet and clean. Dim flickering bulbs gave an awful, feeble light. Despite himself, Andrew felt a little uneasy. A raucous drunken laugh erupted from one of the apartments.

When he reached the door, he hesitated and glanced down the hallway. Then his body seemed to move in two directions at once; he took a step back and his fist came up and knocked on the door.

"It's open!" John shouted.

Andrew walked in. John's living room consisted of a futon couch, an old coffee table, and a television. Off to the right was a half-closed door, which must have led to John's bedroom. Down to the left was a dark, short hallway that led to a small kitchen. John had his back to Andrew and was rummaging around in the refrigerator.

"Make yourself at home. Want a beer?" John said.

"Yes," Andrew said. He took off his sweatshirt and sat on the couch, which barely rose off the ground. He stretched his long legs out in front of him and underneath the coffee table. The walls, furniture, and carpeting in John's apartment were all shades of beige. The walls had once been white but were faded and sun stained. The carpet was brown, as was the covering on the futon.

John came down the hallway carrying two beers and an unopened bag of chips in his mouth. With a deft gesture he tossed the chips on the table and handed Andrew a beer.

"It's the cheap stuff," John said.

"Whatever," Andrew said. He drank. "So you and Laura seem pretty close," he said abruptly.

"I used to live with them. With her family."

"How's that?"

"They took me in, helped me get set up with the GED program and an apartment. They even helped me get a job. That's why I feel bad sometimes. I don't know." John shook his head.

Andrew decided to drop the subject. "I meant to ask you. How did you hear about Brian? Is it on the news?"

"Just around. Not from the news. Guys at work who used to know him or went to his games and stuff," John said.

"Where do you work?"

"Giuseppe's, the granite place."

"Yeah, I know it," Andrew said.

"It's nice to be physical all day."

"I'm at Avella."

"Up the mountain?"

"Up the mountain."

John tilted his head and drank deeply from the bottle. He wiped his lips with the back of his hand. Andrew stared at his beer, thinking about his dad and Brian.

"I'm sorry," John said.

"Sorry for what?"

"For—" John made a helpless gesture with his hands, then said, "For the pain. Whatever pain he causes you."

Andrew finished his beer and belched. He didn't really like beer and had drunk his fast to keep up with John. John seemed to sense this, Andrew realized, and it made Andrew feel self-conscious and annoyed. John's empathy was like a wobbly bridge forever stretching out but never quite reaching Andrew.

"So what did you and Karen talk about?" John said. It seemed to Andrew that John was trying to sound casual.

"This and that. Nothing really."

"You guys just seemed pissed at each other," John said.

"Uh—no, it's all good. We were just talking about David."

"I mean, you just seemed kind of freaked out."

Andrew put his lips to his bottle and blew softly. It made a dull, barely audible whistling noise.

"It's nice that you've taken an interest in David," John said.

Andrew gently peeled off the label of his beer. He glanced around the room. He had been looking for the remote, but his eyes rested on John's guitar, which was leaning up against the wall.

"You play?" John asked.

"Nah."

"I can show you a few chords."

Andrew shrugged. This was more awkward than he'd anticipated. "Where are you from?"

"Colorado."

"Cool. You climb or ski?"

"Some climbing, sort of. It was a long time ago."

"My friend used to be all hot for guys with climbing gear strapped on their backs," Andrew said, then felt stupid for saying it.

"Your friend in the coma?"

"Yeah. How did you know?"

"I don't know. Something Laura said."

"What did Laura say about Sara?"

"That she was kind of boy crazy," John said.

"What?" Andrew said. Laura didn't know Sara at all. While Andrew fumed, John took another long pull from his beer. Then he looked at Andrew from the corners of his eyes.

"That's the way Laura talks. She says things like 'boy crazy' and 'jeepers,'" John said. Then they both chuckled. A shared laugh over Laura, and the ice was broken—sort of. John cleared his throat.

"Our service was amazing this morning," John said. "I wish you could have been there. It was about—"

"Do you have any pot?" Andrew asked.

John raised his eyebrows and rubbed the back of his neck with one of his large hands. Andrew merely looked at him, expressionless.

"Um, well, I could get some," John said.

"Don't bother."

"No, man, I can literally step out into the hallway and get some."

Andrew pulled out his wallet, but John waved him away. "You're my guest," he said.

Andrew took inventory of the room while he waited for John. There were no books or magazines lying about—not even the Bible. Andrew supposed that John kept that book at his bedside. He must have gotten another one after giving his to Andrew.

He peered past the partially closed door toward John's bedroom. He saw a bench press in one corner and a mattress in the other. On top of the mattress was what looked like a thin patchwork quilt. He wondered if the quilt had been handmade by Laura or her family. They seemed like quilty people. Andrew felt like getting up and running his hands across the blanket, but he thought better of it and stayed where he was.

"I'm not very good at this," John said. He toed the door closed behind him and sat next to Andrew on the futon. He pulled out a small bag of ashy-looking pot and some rolling papers. "It's been a while," he said, fumbling with the paper as he attempted to roll a joint.

"I'm not much better," Andrew said. But he gently took the misshapen joint from John's hands and packed it tighter. John lit a match, cupping it from a breeze that wasn't there, as Andrew got the joint started.

It was the harshest pot that Andrew had ever smoked. He coughed and gagged and handed it over to John just as John handed him another beer. Andrew took an enormous gulp and sat back on the couch. He looked at the ceiling and took a deep breath.

"This is rank," John said, after he'd recovered from his own fit of coughing.

"It'll do the job."

For the next hour, by some mutual unspoken agreement, they drank and smoked a lot and spoke very little. Sometimes John got up to get more beer, sometimes Andrew. John did not attempt any more God talk. At some point a bottle of whiskey appeared, and they took shots from the same dingy glass. When he was drunker and higher and gigglier than he'd been in his entire life, Andrew started to pepper John with more questions about Laura and her family.

"So, was Laura adopted or what?"

John looked at him questioningly.

"Come on," Andrew said. "Laura's out-of-this-world gorgeous. Her family . . ."

John snorted. "Her mom used to be pretty. I saw some old family photos." John frowned, then said, "They're really nice people."

"Relax! It's just me," Andrew said, clapping John on the back.

"And Him," John said solemnly.

"Stop it," Andrew said, shaking John roughly by the shoulder. "He forgives you. He told me so."

John smiled at him weakly.

"How long did you live with them?"

"A few months."

"Where did you stay?"

"In Luke's old room. That's her oldest brother. He's out of the country."

"Saving the savages?" Andrew said.

John looked at him sharply.

"I'm sorry, man, but that aspect of your faith is just weird."

John sighed. "It's not what you think. Mostly we just dig wells and carry shit. Stuff like that."

"Oh."

"Although I've never actually been abroad myself. Just heard stories."

Andrew was going to ask another question but then stopped.

John seemed uncomfortable, and Andrew wasn't able to recall why he was asking him so many questions in the first place. What did it matter anyway? What had he been trying to figure out?

"To what end—" Andrew began, but then his voice trailed off into a yawn.

"Want some coffee?"

"Fuck no."

They rolled another joint, made short work of the bag of chips, and then rummaged around in the kitchen for more junk food. John made some popcorn, and they sat munching as they watched music videos. All the videos were the same. Hordes of women were grinding up against a singer, who looked arrogant and annoyed with the fawning surge of orgiastic beauty he supposedly inspired.

"So, so exploitative," John said.

"I told you to cut that out," Andrew said, then yawned again.

"I'm speaking from my heart," John said. Then he let out a long, loud belch. Someone in the apartment next door banged on the wall.

"Sorry," John said in the direction of the wall. He picked up the remote, turned down the volume, and muttered something under his breath.

"What did you say?" Andrew asked.

"They're always . . . fucking. Like, so loud, all night. And as soon as anything above a whisper goes on in here, they bang on the walls."

"So let's go give 'em the what for!" Andrew said. All of a sudden he felt terrifically energetic and angry. He rose unsteadily to his feet. John grabbed hold of his wrist and pulled him back down to the couch.

"Let's not," John said.

"We can take 'em!" Andrew said, making a feeble attempt to stand up again.

"No, we can't."

"Surrrrrre, we can." As he spoke Andrew took a handful of one of John's muscular biceps. For a moment they remained in a strange one-armed embrace, John holding on to Andrew's wrist and Andrew holding on to John's shoulder. Then Andrew laughed and lightly shoved John away. "More beer?" he asked as he walked to the kitchen.

"I think we should stick with the whiskey," John said.

"That stuff's too strong for me!" he shouted from the kitchen. Two loud bangs erupted from the wall. "That's it," Andrew said as he marched toward the door, pumping a closed fist into his open palm. He wasn't even sure what he was doing or saying at this point, and he vaguely realized he was making a fool of himself. As he was opening the door and shouting curses, John grabbed him around the waist and threw him on the couch.

"Chill out. I mean it. They're, like, a biker gang over there," John said.

"There's a biker gang fucking all night next door?" Andrew said, and then burst out laughing.

"Shhh," John said, but then he dissolved into laughter as well. They rolled around the couch and floor, hysterical, overturning their beer bottles and popcorn. A cacophony of bangs on the wall accompanied their revelry.

After several unsuccessful attempts at calming down, Andrew announced that he was going to puke. He dashed off to the bathroom and vomited. He stayed and rested against the toilet for a while, dry heaving now and then but not producing much else. John knocked softly on the door.

"You all right?"

"I'm okay."

Andrew stood and gazed at his reflection in John's tiny bathroom mirror. His eyes were watery and red. He touched his finger to his nose, which for some reason felt out of joint. He barely recognized himself. *It's not even me,* he thought. He washed his hands, splashed cold water on his face, and rinsed out his mouth. John had some mouthwash, so he used that, too. When he came out of the bathroom, John was sitting in a folding chair at his tiny kitchen table, also foldable, and staring at an unlit candle. Andrew sat in the chair next to him and picked up the candle. It was smelly and heavy and so large that it bore three wicks. Its scent was sickly sweet. He turned it over in his hands and read the stickered label on the bottom.

"Heaven Scent?"

"It was a gift," John said.

"From Laura?"

John gazed at the ceiling and sighed. "No. Not from Laura."

"Who then?"

"Karen."

Andrew tossed the candle back and forth between his hands. "Did you fuck her or something?"

"Did I *what*?"

"Never mind," Andrew said.

"Why? Did you?" John asked.

"Well . . . yeah," Andrew said.

"Andy—" John said. He put his head in his hands.

"Don't you 'Andy' me," Andrew said. He punched John playfully. John raised his head from his hands and gave him a masterfully blank stare. It reminded him of Laura.

"What's the big deal? I mean, besides the obvious?" Andrew asked.

Somewhere inside his drunken haze, Andrew realized that he was trying to act cool about something he did not feel cool about, and that he was doing this because he hadn't been able to handle his alcohol. John drummed his fingers on the counter and continued to stare at the candle.

"Light it," Andrew said, but then he realized the lighter was in his pocket. He withdrew it, but his hands were trembling.

"Careful," John said. He took the lighter from him and lit the candle himself. They stared at the flames.

"It's Job, right?" Andrew said.

"What?"

Andrew stood up and grabbed the whiskey. He drank straight from the bottle, drank deeply, and then coughed back the acid that crept up his throat. He swayed and sat back down. "Job. The guy who suffers. Who is made to suffer? To prove a point or whatever."

"Yeah," John said.

Andrew coughed, gripped the table, and took a few deep breaths. John sat silent and still, watching him.

"Okay," Andrew said. "Okay."

"Andrew—"

"It's okay."

"Whatever you're going to say—or do—next, you don't have to," John said. "Because, I . . ." John began, and his voice broke into a sob. He covered his face with his hands.

"Shut up. Sorry. I mean, we can do—you can do, one thing. If you want. But only one thing. Okay?" Andrew kept his eyes fixed on the candle as he spoke.

After what seemed like an eternal pause, John said, "Okay."

Andrew closed his eyes and surrendered to a swirling dark of dizzy blackness. *It's like moving through darkness.* Even so, he wished he'd drunk more. He thought about Laura. Or did he? He wasn't sure what he was thinking about anymore. It wasn't even a person. It was a nebulous creation, a mixture of every pretty thing that had ever tortured and soothed him. Marcia's tiny hands and pale soft skin, Sara's legs and hair and earlobes, Karen's angry glistening eyes, and *Laura Laura Laura Laura*

Laura. Floating spasms of beauty in front of him, just out of his reach, just grazing his fingertips. He felt John's huge caressing hand on his thigh, then on his stomach. Andrew flinched and tightened his grip on the table. John's hand paused, then slowly drew up to Andrew's chest and rested over his heart. He heard John lean forward, then felt his lips lightly press on the hollow of his neck. Andrew opened his eyes and pushed back from the table.

"Okay," Andrew said, then stood up. Without another word or glance he walked through the living room and out the door.

As he walked down the hallway, he heard ecstatic moans coming from the neighbor's apartment. He felt unbearably aroused.

33

ANDREW WAS HALFWAY TO HIS house before he realized he'd left his sweatshirt at John's apartment. He cursed as he stumbled to the ground, where he stayed for a few minutes and tried not to puke. Slowly, he stood up. The sidewalk wavered beneath him. He cautiously took a step forward, then another one. He felt a prickling on the back of his neck and looked up. Someone was staring at him from across the street. He wondered why. He took another step, then realized he was walking on his tiptoes. His arms were raised to his sides for balance, as if he were walking on a tightrope.

"I am so wasted," Andrew whispered.

"No shit," said the man across the street. He looked none too sober himself.

"I guess I wasn't whispering then!" Andrew yelled. Andrew

felt extremely clever when he said it. The man snorted. Andrew walked on, trying to appear nonchalant and in control. A police car drove slowly by, and Andrew kept his eyes on the ground and his hands in his pockets, his default physical position. He'd maintained this stance virtually his entire high school career. A defense position, he thought, like a Tai Chi–type thing.

The walk home took an hour; at least it felt as though it did. At some point he stopped and pissed behind some bushes. When he reached his house, he sat on the steps and stared at the stars. If he stared at them long enough, they swam and zoomed before his eyes like a magnificent light show. A magnificent light show. He thought of David and frowned. The door opened behind him.

"Andrew?"

It was Laura.

"What are you doing here?" Andrew said, his heart racing.

"I live here."

Andrew looked up and down the street. He'd walked to Laura's house. For a moment he was so embarrassed, he thought he'd die on the spot. Then a drunken careless confidence took over.

"Look at this munificent light show. Brought to you by our Creator Himself!" Andrew said. He waved both arms toward the sky.

"Shhh. Are you drunk?"

Without looking, Andrew reached behind and pulled her

over to him. She stumbled, but he caught her and gently placed her next to him on the porch steps.

She rubbed her leg and grimaced. "I scraped my shin."

"Watch the lights."

"You are so drunk. And you smell like pot."

"And yet my reflexes are still intact," Andrew said, and then he burped.

"Andrew, go home," Laura hissed.

"I was just hanging out with John," he said.

"Oh?" she said slowly.

"We didn't go fishing. I can tell you that much."

"What did you do?"

"What do you think we did?" He looked over at her. She was wearing some kind of filmy pink nightgown. "You're beautiful."

"Where's John now?"

"And you apparently know what pot smells like."

"Look, Andrew, just go home. We'll talk in the morning, okay?"

"We'll talk now!" Andrew said.

"Shhh. If my parents wake up, we're both dead." She crossed her arms over her chest and shivered.

"Take my sweatshirt."

"You don't have one."

"Are you dating Matt?"

"No."

"But you did?"

"Why are you interested in this?"

"Really, Laura? Really? You have *nooooooo* idea."

Laura frowned and looked away.

"How 'bout John? Oops! Maybe not, eh?"

"Andrew, please," Laura said. She grasped his arm and looked at him intently, her eyes pleading.

"Does everyone know? That's it, isn't it? Everyone actually knows that John is—"

"Stop, stop," she said, putting her hands over his mouth. He kissed her fingers. "Go home," she whispered. "We'll talk tomorrow, okay? I promise." She stood up and kissed his forehead.

Andrew stood up. "The promises of Laura Lettel," he muttered as he walked away.

This time he managed to get to his house. Instead of going inside he made his way to the backyard and collapsed. He thought about Laura in that ridiculous pink nightgown. Who actually dressed like that? It was as though Laura were trying to be a fantasy dream girl. Oh God, what nonsense. What was he thinking? Where was his Bible? In the absence of Marcia, who usually had all the answers, he needed to consult something else, some weighty text. He patted his pockets. He must have left it at John's apartment. In the sweatshirt.

The wet grass was seeping into his clothes and moistening his back. It was cold but oddly soothing. Like a gentle cool kiss from the earth. Like that kid whose heart froze when he ate too much Turkish delight. What was that from again? Some book from his childhood. He'd loved that book. He wondered if he'd forget everything that he loved as he grew up. If as an adult, forty years from now, he'd forget Marcia and Sara. If memories of them would come to him only when he was drunk. The thought made him choke up, and he had to blink back tears that pooled into his eyes. Then he felt like a fool for crying.

The backyard was his brother's domain. Andrew hadn't really spent time here for years. All Brian's sporting equipment was stored in a special shed, built for that purpose. Brian had spent hours and hours out here tossing the ball around or kicking the ball around or bouncing the ball around. Andrew used to watch him. And then he stopped watching him. That was it. No story, no grand showdown. He used to be interested in his older brother, and then he wasn't. Brian had never been interested in him. Or maybe he had. Maybe when he was a baby and Brian was three, Andrew had been a source of fascination or amusement. And then one day he wasn't. They were like two would-be strangers peering at each other in the dark. *Who is that? Oh, it's you.*

"It's me," Andrew said to the stars.

34

WHEN HE WOKE UP, he was very cold and soaked through with dew. His head ached with such force that he thought he might pass out. He rolled over on his side. He dry heaved, spat, and glanced at his watch. It was already seven. He was an hour late for work. Cursing, Andrew shot up, ignoring the pain in his head, and ran into the house.

Brian sat on a kitchen stool drinking coffee and reading the newspaper. "You look like shit," he said.

"Thanks."

"Get laid at least?"

Andrew ignored him. He let Becky out and threw some food in her bowl. He sped down the streets and drummed his steering wheel impatiently at red lights. He'd never let Neal down before. His friends, Becky, but never Neal.

When he reached work, Cory silently pointed him in the direction of Neal's golf cart.

"Neal," Andrew said as he jogged toward the cart. Then he stopped, gasped, and doubled over. He dry heaved. When he stood up, he saw that Neal was watching him with a solemn expression on his face.

"You okay, son?"

"Yes, I'm fine." Andrew felt humiliated.

"Not like you to be late."

Andrew stared at his shoes. "I'm sorry," he said.

"It's all right. First time for everything," Neal said.

"Thank you. Ben's out by the pond?"

"Why don't you stay out of the sun today?"

"Okay."

"You look like you've been partying."

"Oh, I—" Andrew said.

"You're okay, son. Head over to west shed and tell Cheeve I sent you."

"No problem," Andrew said. He looked up and smiled, but Neal had already turned away from him. Andrew followed his gaze. Neal was watching Ben, who was hacking away at some bushes by himself. Andrew shoved his hands in his pockets and took off in the direction of west shed. He felt awful, guilty, and rejected. Work was the one place where he generally kicked ass, or at least didn't suck too badly. And now Neal didn't even want him to work with Ben. He was fucking up all over the place.

West *shed* was a misnomer. Like the shed behind Neal's office, it was a vast warehouse that had always struck Andrew as eerie. When he entered the darkness of the place, he was momentarily blinded. He heard a noise to his left, a soft shuffle, and then a cough.

"Cheeve?" Andrew said. He felt positively frightened.

"Hello?" a voice called.

"It's Andrew."

"Oh. Hey. What are you doing here?" Cheeve stepped forward into the light. He looked perplexed and almost frightened himself.

"Neal sent me."

"Working on some window boxes. You know how to handle a hammer and nail?" Cheeve said.

"Sure do." Andrew straightened up when he spoke.

"Is that right?" Cheeve said.

They worked hard and spoke little. Andrew started to feel better, manlier. *We're just two guys hanging out and hammering shit,* he thought. No weird overtones, no gay subtext, no bullying.

Because I am a bully, he realized. Andrew had teased John, interrogated him, drunk his booze, smoked his pot, ate his food, and threatened his neighbors. He'd also had some bizarre exchange with Laura, the details of which were vague in his memory. Had they kissed? What had he said to her exactly? He hammered harder in an attempt to vent his anger and guilt.

"You all right?" Cheeve asked.

"Aren't window boxes on a corporate building kind of mismatched?" Andrew asked.

"They're not for the main buildings. They're for the sheds. Make 'em look nicer," Cheeve said.

"Weird."

"I know it. Some busybody in corporate didn't like our ugly warehouses, so the window boxes became priority number one."

Andrew didn't know what to say in response, so he just grunted in disapproval. They were too far away to join the others for lunch, so they sat alone on a shaded picnic table by the shed. Cheeve offered him half of his sandwich, but Andrew's stomach was still too queasy to eat anything. Cheeve asked him about his life, what school he was going to attend, and what he wanted to be. Andrew told him that he'd never given it much thought. Privately, he realized that this was because his obsession with Laura had clouded over any ideas about his future. But he told Cheeve that he assumed he'd study English or history, subjects he was good at, and figure out his life at some point along the way. Cheeve nodded as if this were the most sensible thing in the world.

"You've got a good head on your shoulders," Cheeve said.

"You think so?"

"Sure," Cheeve said pleasantly. "You're a good boy, Andrew." He took a big bite of his sandwich. Then words came flying out of Andrew's mouth.

"I'm in love with this girl who is super-religious. So I

infiltrated her youth group and pretended to want Jesus in my life or something, so I could get her to love me. Or get her to make out with me. Or both. Shit, I don't know anymore. Then maybe I had these experiences with God or something. There's this guy, John, who's totally gay, and he likes me and I like him too, but I don't know about the gay stuff. I let him kiss me because I was bored and angry and . . . other things. I don't know. John is part of the religious group and they're pretty conservative, probably like anti-gay and shit. So he's all fucked up, you know what I mean? And also I slept with this other girl in the group. And my friend is in a coma. And my best friend is all wrapped up with taking care of her at the hospital, and something about it just isn't right. My mom doesn't care about me. And, Christ, my fucking brother . . ." Andrew stopped and put his head down.

Cheeve swallowed. "Hmm," he said.

"I'm sorry I told you those things," Andrew said in a small voice. He pressed his face into the picnic table, willing himself to disappear through the slats. "I'm sorry," he said again.

"Stop apologizing."

"Okay. Let's just forget—"

"Sometimes it's easier to spill your guts to someone you don't know that well. That's normal, okay? There's nothin' wrong with that."

"Thanks," Andrew mumbled.

"My wife died slowly. She was in the hospital, dying, for six months."

"I'm so— That's terrible," Andrew said. He picked his head up and placed his hand on top of Cheeve's arm. Cheeve glanced at Andrew's hand and patted it gently.

"I can't help you with the God stuff," Cheeve said.

"I know."

"Or the gay stuff."

"I'm not gay," Andrew said quickly.

"Whatever," Cheeve said.

"No, really—"

"I mean it, whatever, it doesn't matter. And I doubt that bit about your mom not caring about you."

Andrew snorted. "How do you know?"

"Sometimes, in a family like yours, the normal one gets the shaft."

"What do you mean?"

"You know what I mean."

"So you think *I'm* normal."

"Don't be ornery," Cheeve said.

"I'm not—" Andrew began before he stopped himself. Cheeve was right. And Andrew knew exactly what he meant. Instead of dealing with the shit storm of dysfunction that was Brian and their father, his mother had chosen to distance herself from *him*. And she had done this because he was normal, because he was safe. He might snap at his mother every once in a while, but unlike his father, he never yelled or hit. And unlike Brian, he didn't ignore her or treat her thanklessly.

"Okay, I get it," he said.

"What's going on with your friend in the hospital?"

"Maybe she'll wake up; maybe she won't."

"I meant the other one," Cheeve said.

"Marcia? She's really smart. She's going to be a doctor. She's supposed to be getting ready for college, but instead she's practically living at the hospital and taking care of Sara. It's like they're drowning together." As soon as he said it, he realized it was true.

"She sounds like she needs help," Cheeve said.

Andrew plucked at his T-shirt. "What can I do?" he said.

"You know what to do," he said.

Andrew felt like sobbing. The truth was that he *didn't* know what do to. How could anyone expect him to know what to do? At any rate, something was expected of him, whether he could rise to the occasion or not.

"Well, those goddamn window boxes won't build themselves," Cheeve said.

They walked back to the shed.

35

"I'VE GOT TO GO TO New Hampshire," Andrew told his mother.

"That's where Sara is?" she said.

"And Marcia."

"Are they okay?"

"I don't know. But I've got to go help. Will you take care of Becky for me? I'll be gone a few days, I think. I'm sorry."

"It's all right. I can do it. What about work?"

"I fixed it with Neal." Neal had been very understanding, but perhaps just the tiniest bit remote. Andrew was no longer the only summer hire who showed up stone sober. He was ashamed, but he had bigger problems to think about.

He picked up his keys. He'd already showered, packed, and written a list of instructions for his mother regarding Becky. The one thing he hadn't done was call Marcia. He didn't want her to talk him out of coming, something he sensed she might do

"What's going on with Brian's case?" he asked, more out of consideration for her feelings than actual interest.

"It's complicated," she said.

They rarely hugged. But he put his bag down and held her. "Are you okay?" he asked.

"Sometimes," she said, or at least that was what he thought she said. Her voice was muffled in his chest.

"I love you, Mom," he said. "I know you feel bad about everything. It's not your fault." She held him tighter. "If you ever want to leave," he began, and he felt her stiffen in his arms. "I mean, if you ever want to change things, change your situation, I'll help. I'll help you." She patted his back, once, twice, then she let him go.

During his three-hour drive, he thought about Marcia and the night they had become friends. They were eleven. She'd been alienated, friendless; he nearly so.

It'd been all over a game of Kick the Can.

Marcia. Little, weak, weird Marcia. The white girl with the foreign accent. Shy in an arrogant way, awkward, bone pale, the last picked in a pickup game of anything. Marcia in the cafeteria with a hot tray under her nose and a book held open by her elbow. Eating and reading. She could not do a single sit-up or push-up in gym class. Her classmates had giggled at her behind her back, but they'd also left her alone.

Andrew had avoided feeling sorry for her. Already he'd known that pity and sorrow, feelings that were very natural to him, were not to be indulged or exposed. It was unmanly, something he'd understood without anyone having to tell him. He'd known to avoid the painful tug that scratched him raw. The dying baby bird that had fallen out of its nest and landed on the sidewalk in front of his house, the commercials about starving kids in Africa, his mother's face after a fight with his father, and the friendless loner with no father at all.

In the summertime and early autumn all the kids in the neighborhood assembled themselves for a nightly round of Kick the Can. A coffee can was placed in the center of the sidewalk. Then the designated can guard closed their eyes and counted to fifty while everyone else hid. The goal for the can guard was to find where people were hidden and then touch the can while shouting the names of those he had discovered. The goal for everyone else was to kick the can while the guard was away looking for the hidden players. Once the can was kicked, or all the players were discovered, the game was over.

As with all sports, Brian had dominated. He'd hid ingeniously close and sprinted out as soon as the guard had crept away. He was speedy and decisive. His confidence was thrilling. Even then, there'd been something remarkable about his skills, something special. Andrew had been aware of this beauty, this specialness, aware of it and respectful of it. But Brian had not spoken to his brother during the game. He'd had his own set of friends.

One night Andrew had made an outrageous and ill-planned dash to kick the can. He'd been defeated as everyone had watched from their hiding places. After the first round was over, Brian had sneered at him. Andrew had drifted away, kicking rocks in front of him, imaginary cans, thinking thoughts long lost to him now.

Andrew had wandered with his hands shoved into his pockets, his face hidden beneath a baseball cap and a hooded sweatshirt. It had been late September, and the breeze had had just a snap of winter in it.

"Can sticker, can sticker!"

Andrew had heard the shouted taunt that was meant to humiliate the guard. A can sticker was a guard who was a coward because he was too afraid to venture out and find people, lest his can be kicked while he was away.

Marcia had been lying hidden in a bush when he discovered her. Rather, she'd crouched half under a bush and half under the rotted-out porch of an abandoned house. She'd been close enough to see the can and the activities around it, but far enough away so that she'd not actually been participating in the game.

Crouched and quivering, Marcia had sucked furiously on a lollipop and watched the game with a complicated expression on her face that Andrew had never forgotten.

"People were wondering where you were," he'd said.

Marcia had looked up. At first she'd looked scared. Then she'd lowered her eyes only to raise them again slowly. Her expression had said, *Yeah, right.* Andrew had sat down next to her, and for a few minutes they'd watched the game in silence. Then he'd spoken.

"It's okay. Who cares, right?"

He'd nudged her shoulder with his.

"Right?" he'd asked again.

"Right," she'd said.

36

IT WAS AN AMAZING HOSPITAL. It looked and felt like an upscale mall. Cafés, a bank, and even a dry cleaner lined the halls of the entryway. A security guard directed him to neurology. It turned out he was in the wrong building. He navigated to the correct building using various indoor bridges. The hospital reminded him very much of Avella. All this wealth, he mused, all these paintings and soft lights and grandeur. It was still a house of death and sickness, drugs and tubes and sharp metal instruments. He shivered, trying to push down his fear of the place.

When he reached the right floor, Marcia appeared around a corner almost instantly. She looked both surprised and relieved.

"I've been calling you. Something's wrong with your phone," she said.

"That's weird," he said. "What's up?"

She stared at him for some moments. "How did you know to come?" She started to cry.

"Where's Sara? Where is she?" he asked. He felt as if someone had dragged his heart out of his chest and plunged it into ice water.

"Sara had a stroke. Something about the fevers—not being able to find the source of the infection—"

"Marcia?" Lisa, one of Janet's friends from the cheese factory, came toward them. She looked grim.

"Why don't we go sit down?" Lisa said.

"What's going on? Just tell us," Marcia said.

Lisa folded her hands behind her back. *Like a clergyman,* Andrew thought.

"Bavin and Roberts and the guy from Boston just confirmed. Sara is brain-dead."

"But isn't— Isn't that—" Marcia said, wringing her little hands and twisting away from Lisa's now outstretched arms. "What percent? What parts? Dr. Roberts said that the brain is like real estate. And that some parts are valuable and others are practically worthless—"

"All of it, Marcia," Lisa said.

Marcia stared at her. Andrew felt airless, numb, floating. *Stop!*

"What happens next?" he asked.

"It's Janet's decision," Lisa said.

Andrew hid his tears behind a cough and cleared his throat.

"I don't think Sara would have wanted . . ." he began.

"Don't worry," Lisa said. She looked at Andrew, her expression blank. A chill shot through him as he thought of Laura and her endless, endless, emotionless calm. "They're going to pump her full of morphine and take her off the vent. It's just a question of when. Probably soon. There are some papers to sign, and Janet needs to—to compose herself."

"How long does it take? I mean, after they take the vent out?" Andrew asked.

"Hours, sometimes even days," Lisa said.

"And she won't suffer?" he pressed.

"Not with all the morphine," Lisa said.

"Where is Janet?" Marcia said.

"Still with the doctors," Lisa said. She patted Marcia's arm and then turned and walked back down the hall.

Marcia started to shake. Her whole body trembled with alarming velocity, even violence. She was a blur of flesh and clothes. A shimmering Marcia. Like in a cartoon or a movie. She began to sink to the floor. Andrew grabbed her, felt her body go limp, and then picked her up. He carried her to the empty waiting room and laid her down on one of the couches. Her face, like her eyes, looked gray. He stroked her forehead, which felt both hot and cold with sweat. A nurse came in and nudged him aside. She shook Marcia gently.

"Marcia, talk to me. Talk to me, sweetie," the nurse said.

Marcia's eyes blinked rapidly, and Andrew could see the

whites fluttering beneath her lids. The effect was eerie. Then she opened her eyes fully and said, "Sorry."

"You're all right, Marcia. Now, stay lying down for a minute, then sit up very slowly. Then sit for five minutes before you stand up. Better yet, eat something before you stand. Your friend here will help you. Right?" she said, turning toward Andrew. "Stay here until I get back," she said as she hurried out the door.

Andrew got some soda and chocolate from the vending machines. He opened the can and handed it to Marcia. She was sitting up now. She took a few sips and gave it back to him.

"Sorry about that," Marcia said.

"Stop apologizing," he said. "Actually, it was kind of exciting."

"You carried me in here?"

"I did."

"Like a sack of potatoes or like Dracula and Mina?"

"The latter."

"How romantic."

"I thought so."

She leaned back against the couch and stared at the ceiling. Andrew drank some of the soda. The nurse came back in, took Marcia's blood pressure and pulse, and told her not to stand up for a few minutes. Marcia placed her fingertips in the inner corners of her eyes as if to stop the tears. He had done the same thing the night of Sara's accident.

"It's okay to cry," Andrew said.

"I'm worn out from crying."

"Eat some chocolate."

Marcia took the chocolate bar and broke off a piece. Instead of putting it in her mouth, she held it in her fingers as she stared off into space. Then she spoke. "Remember when I went to see *King Lear?*"

"I do," he said. Marcia had once taken a five-hour bus trip to New York City to see some acclaimed stage production of *King Lear* by herself when she was sixteen. She had left at five in the morning, caught the matinee performance, and returned at ten at night. She had told no one of her plans for her little day trip. Not even him and Sara.

"It was amazing. I liked the actress who played the Fool. She wasn't this supersad depressed Fool, like in all the movies. She was mischievous. She was light on her feet and funny and looked abnormally small, almost like a midget. But she had these huge green eyes. She looked made to be watched, you know?"

Andrew nodded. "Go on," he said. Marcia seemed to be going into a kind of trance.

"I was, like, *really* into the play. Enchanted by it. But then I noticed this woman sitting two rows in front of me. She wore a white suit. Her head was bent down, and she was scribbling in the playbill for the entire length of the play, even during the intermission. I couldn't help but glance at her every once in a while. She was handsome, boyish-looking. She had short black hair, a strong face, you know?"

Andrew nodded.

"This woman was completely absorbed in whatever she was writing or drawing on her playbill. When the play ended, everyone stood to applaud. I clapped like crazy for the Fool. She minced up to the edge of the stage and curtsied in this way that was somehow a cross between a little girl playing dress-up and a boy making fun of a girl playing dress-up. The crowd laughed and shouted. It was, like, this frenzied thing. I was so overwhelmed that I had to sit down. And then I felt like someone was watching me. It was the woman in white. She was staring right at me and smiling. This mocking fucking smile. Then she stood up, dropped her playbill in her seat, and left."

"What did you do?"

"I got up too. I pushed my way down the aisle of the crowd. I stepped on feet, elbowed stomachs, and trampled on five-hundred-dollar purses. And all the while, out of the corner of my eye, I could see the Fool on stage, bowing and smiling and winking. I lost track of the woman in white, but when I reached her seat, I saw the playbill lying there. I opened it, turned it over, and looked at every page. There were no drawings and no hidden messages. It was just a plain playbill. Blank. Empty. Nothing."

By the time Marcia finished talking, the chocolate in her fingers had become a gooey mess. It had melted to the point where it had slid from her grasp and plopped on the floor. They stared at it. Then Andrew put his arm around her shoulders. She fell back into his chest and within moments was fast asleep.

She slept for a long time. The nurse came and went, did not

wake Marcia, and did not say anything to Andrew. An hour passed, maybe two, and Andrew's arm felt numb. He was afraid that if he moved, he might wake her up. But the truth was that he enjoyed cradling Marcia as she slept. There were the obvious pleasures of holding a cute girl. But beyond that was something else, something akin to the paternal feeling he sometimes experienced with his dog. Marcia was like that broken little bird that had fallen out of its nest. Very gently, very slowly, he readjusted his position so that he was more comfortable on the couch.

He thought about *King Lear* and wondered why that play meant so much to Marcia. And her experience in the theater with the woman in white and the Fool—what did that mean to her? What was she trying to say to him? Maybe nothing. Maybe it was just a raw moment in her life that she could not make sense of, and for some reason that moment had bearing on what she was going through now. *Sara.*

Sara.

Andrew hadn't thought about Sara. Dying. Already dead. She was just an extension of the machinery keeping her alive. It could not be happening. She would open her eyes and make a joke, point her toes, stretch her arms, grin.

No, he knew there would be no miracles tonight. He knew she was gone. He'd always known.

He cupped Marcia's head in one of his hands and supported her back with the other as he slowly eased himself out from under her. He lay her down on the couch and stood up. She snorted and rolled over. She did not wake.

As he walked toward Sara's room, he felt like he was inside a telescope. Everything near him seemed out of focus; only far ahead of him was the landscape sharp and clear. But the closer he came to her room, the blurrier it got. He reached the room. He stepped inside, keeping his eyes on the floor until the last possible moment, and then he looked up.

Sara was alone. No, *he* was alone. Because whatever was lying there in that bed—

Sara was horribly transformed. Her body was swollen, her face almost unrecognizable. What did that? The stroke? His eyes clouded with tears as he braced himself against the wall for support. He heard rather than felt himself gasping. Or was that the ventilator? Something in this room was lunging for air, barely getting enough, and coming back for more. Something. *Don't faint,* he thought. He found himself kneeling by her bedside—how had he gotten there? It wasn't important. He held her limp hand. Her palm was clammy and her fingers ice-cold and bloated. He ran his eyes up and down her, avoiding her face. Waterlogged. Blue skin, lilac veins. A drowning victim. *Gasp,* went the ventilator.

Andrew traced his fingertips up her arm and onto her shoulder. He looked at her face. Swollen. Ghastly. Still Sara. He kissed her forehead, then her hairline, then her hair.

He stood up and left the room. Janet was just outside the

door, a friend on either side of her. She came toward him like someone crawling up out of a pool of mud to grasp at weeds. He held her. They were silent. No one sobbed. Janet clung to him, and he felt her nails dig into his arms. Deeper and deeper went her ragged nails. He was sure she drew blood, but he willed himself not to flinch. Abruptly, she released him and stepped back. The look on her face was impossible. He lowered his eyes. *I never want to see that look in someone's face ever again. Not ever.* But he reached out his hand anyway, and she took it and squeezed.

Janet walked into the room, followed by Lisa and another friend, her flank of guards. The one who was not Lisa briefly hugged Andrew. He walked back down to the waiting room, where Marcia still slept.

37

"ANDREW? DREW?"

Andrew woke to Marcia gently shaking his shoulder. Startled, he half rose from the waiting room couch, then sat back down. For a moment he wasn't quite sure where he was.

"Did you see her?" he asked.

"Did I see whom?" Marcia said. She sat next to him, her hand still on his shoulder, as if to restrain him.

"Janet's face. Her eyes."

"I know."

"I don't ever want to see someone look like that again," he said. As he spoke he realized that his voice came out thin and whimpering. He cleared his throat. Marcia handed him her coffee. He took a sip and almost gagged.

"Sorry. It's battery acid," she said.

"It's okay," Andrew said. He flexed his shoulders and stood up.

"It's time," she said.

"Okay," Andrew said. He reached down and took her hand. As they walked out of the waiting room Andrew tossed the coffee cup in the trash. "Sorry," he said, "that was yours."

"It's okay. I'm done." Marcia shivered.

"Are you cold?"

Marcia gripped his hand tighter and said, "A little."

"I wish I had my sweatshirt to give you."

"I know you do, Andrew."

They stood outside Sara's door. "Janet is . . . ?" Andrew said.

"She wants us to say good-bye first. Then she'll go in."

"Then we should stay here?"

"No. Her friends will stay. Lisa told me it's too painful for Janet to be with us now. So we'll say good-bye, leave, and contact Lisa later. That's the plan. Okay?"

"Okay, Marcia."

"So, we can go in now."

They stood perfectly still. Then he felt one of Marcia's shaking hands on the small of his back, guiding him forward. She came in behind him, as if to use his body as a human shield from some unknown attack.

They contemplated Sara one last time. The sheets were pulled back; someone must have cleaned her or put a fresh gown on her body. *Or perhaps that was Marcia again,* Andrew thought with a shudder. He forced himself to take Sara in fully, although this was not how he wanted to remember her. Sara didn't look like herself or even like a sad sleeping version of herself. Her face and body were bloated and discolored. Blue and red and yellow. There must be some reason for that, he thought, some medical reason. But he didn't feel like asking Marcia about it, not now and not later. Not ever.

Marcia walked over to the bed and leaned in close to Sara. She whispered, "Sara? Sara? Remember our Spanish class's trip to Costa Rica? Remember the handsome Australian who sat next to you on the plane? The climber? Neither of you said a word but there was . . . *something*. This heat that you felt in the air between you and him. It distracted you from your fear of flying. And remember how you wished you'd said something to him and always regretted it? But somehow enjoyed the silence, too? And later, how you even enjoyed the regret? You didn't say these things, but I knew what you meant. I want to wish you those moments for all eternity. You're not serene. You're not playing a harp on some stupid fluffy clouds. You're feeling anxious and intrigued and . . . excited. All those feelings you had that made you feel so alive and so like yourself. I wish you to forever be in that moment. Flirting. I want that to be your heaven." She moved even closer to Sara. She put her lips right up to Sara's ear and, hesitating just a moment, gently kissed the lobe.

Andrew stared. *I love having my earlobes kissed.* She'd said it to Marcia, too. There was so much he didn't know about Marcia and Sara and their love for each other. So much he didn't know.

He wanted to say something special to Sara. Something meaningful and potent. Marcia took a few steps backward, her gaze fixed on Sara's face. The fingers of the two girls grazed gently apart as she moved away and Andrew stepped forward and knelt down. He could feel Marcia's eyes on him, but he whispered so low that he was sure Marcia couldn't hear him.

"Sara? Listen. Marcia will be okay. And so will I. And so will your mother. You can rest easy. Or not so easy, if that's better. Whatever Marcia said about excitement and regret—" Andrew trailed off and looked into Sara's face. He gently pried open one of her eyelids and examined the large, black, unseeing pupil. Marcia made a slight movement but did nothing. He drew back from Sara and stood up.

"Ready?" he asked.

"I'm ready."

Most of the staff was occupied in another room where lots of machines beeped and whirred, people shouted at one another, and an unconscious person lay quiet and still. Quiet and still like the ocean of Laura's eyes, like her calm smile. He always thought about Laura. She was somehow constantly present in the back of his mind. Even at a moment like this. Thinking about her was a habit he couldn't break. They walked to the elevators.

Marcia looked exhausted. Her eyes were glazed and her

expression was blank, blank, blank. It could not have been less devoid of human emotion. He didn't know what to do next. He didn't know how to help her, or what to feel. Sara was dying. Soon she'd be gone. As the elevator doors closed Marcia said, "Let's go back to my room."

38

THE PLACE WHERE MARCIA AND JANET had been staying was just five minutes from the hospital. It was a regular chain motel that had been purchased for the families of long-term patients. It looked industrial and anonymous and for this reason reminded Andrew of Laura's church. Marcia silently led him to her room.

"Did you stay with Janet?" he asked as she fumbled with her key. They were the first words he'd spoken since they left Sara's bedside.

"At first. Then another room opened up, so I relocated. It was better that way."

They went inside and Marcia turned on the light. Andrew stifled a gasp. The room was a mess. Towels and clothes were strewn all over the floor. The garbage was overflowing with cartons of Chinese food and soda bottles. Books on neurology and traumatic head injuries lay everywhere, open and heavily high-lighted. Andrew picked up one of the books and flipped through its pages. Marcia's tidy, neurotically small handwriting—"the scrawl of Satan," Sara had called it—was in the margins of al-most every page.

"Sorry about the mess," Marcia mumbled. She pulled the covers back from one of the queen-size beds and lay down. Andrew sat on the edge of the bed. Something sharp dug into him. It was a massive textbook. He picked it up. On the cover was a horrifying yet beautiful painting of a brain. It was a multicolored collage of every shade imaginable. It was like a rainbow vomiting a rainbow giving birth to a rainbow. The book was called *The Human Brain: A Symphony*.

This is what Sara's brain must have looked like, he thought. *A gorgeous fucking disaster.*

"Do you think it's over?" he asked.

"Probably not," Marcia said.

Her words made him sick. Sara was dying, *dying*, and here they sat.

"I'm so cold," Marcia said.

Andrew flipped off his shoes and crawled in next to her. He pulled her close. They slept.

When he woke up, they were no longer touching. It was mid-night. The room was dark except for the dim glare of the digital clock. He couldn't even tell if Marcia was awake or asleep. Her breathing sounded ragged.

"Is it over?" he said.

"Maybe," she said.

He heard the shower running and woke up again. It was two in the morning. He drifted in and out of consciousness. The shower stopped, and Marcia emerged wearing a ratty oversize T-shirt. Her hair was sopping wet. She turned off the light in the bathroom. She made her way over to the bed and tripped on something. They groped blindly for each other. Andrew found her arms and dragged her onto the bed.

"Marcia?" he said.

"Don't ask," she said.

She flopped her head on his chest and slept. He stared into the darkness, blinking rapidly.

Though I walk through the valley of the shadow of death I will fear no evil, for thou art with me. Laura dug her toes into the sand. The salty air blew back the amber strands from her face. *Look at me,* he begged. She shook her head. He reached his fingertips to her face, but as soon as he made contact her whole body dissolved under his touch. He pulled his hand away and screamed.

Three a.m. Marcia was on the phone. The lights were bright. He sat up. She put the phone down. Their eyes met. She shut off the light.

"She's gone," Marcia said.

Four a.m. They'd spent the last hour crying.

"We should have sex," Marcia said.

"We should *what*?"

"We should do something life affirming. Celebrate existence. That's what Sara would have wanted."

"Don't be crazy."

"I'm not. Don't you want to?"

"Kind of," he said.

"Well?"

"You don't mean any of this. And I'm in love with Laura."

"You had sex with that other girl."

"That was a mistake. Let's resolve not to be crazy right now."

"Fine," she said, sounding relieved.

Five a.m. They no longer attempted sleep. They sat up in bed, eating old slices of pizza and drinking flat soda.

"It was my fault," Marcia said for what felt like the hundredth time.

"Stop it."

"She wanted to stay in. Rent a movie and chill out. I was

the one who insisted on seeing *Un Chien Andalou*."

"A thousand things could have happened that night. Or any night. Sara was a bad driver."

"She wasn't."

"We need to stop talking about this."

Marcia lay back on the bed. Her hair was still damp. She shivered. Andrew threw the blanket over her. She pulled it up over her head.

"I guess I've always kind of had a crush on Sara," Marcia said. Her voice was muffled beneath the blanket.

"Me too," Andrew said through a mouthful of pizza.

"But I don't think I'm gay."

"It doesn't matter. Sometimes it's more complicated than that."

"I know."

"Want to know something crazy? That guy John and I almost, like, did something. He kind of kissed me. Only I stopped it and just left."

"Whoa."

"I'm such an asshole."

"Don't say that."

"No, really. I provoked him. I invited it. I thought I was being nice or something. And I was drunk."

"Is he okay?"

"I don't know."

"Does his church know about him?"

"I think so. The kids do, anyway."

"That's no good. I think that church is wicked conservative."

"Really?" Andrew recalled the reggae in the soup kitchen and the almost hippie vibe that the youth group sometimes gave off. But that was the youth group.

"Really. I've heard things."

"What things?" Andrew stopped eating and looked at her. She pulled the covers off her head and sat up.

"Ever heard of 'pray away the gay'?"

"What? No shit. That can't be real."

"Of course it's real."

"So they'd just make him pray a lot? I mean, if they found out?" Andrew was thinking of Chip, who seemed extremely shifty. Who else was in charge over there?

"Pray a lot, or worse. Conversion therapy, aversion tactics. That shit gets very dark. Like torture," Marcia said. She picked up his unfinished slice of pizza and nibbled at the crust.

"Fuck," Andrew said. He thought back on all his interactions with John. John's affection and nervousness toward him, his pained expressions, his repressed sobs, his tentative kiss . . . his silhouette against the sun, standing on the mountain cliff and staring down.

"Fuck, fuck, *fuck*," Andrew said. More action was required of him. Confide in an adult? Cheeve, Neal? No one seemed appropriate. What would Sara do?

"What time is it?" Marcia asked, interrupting his thoughts.

"Early. Why do you ask?"

"I should call Kyle."

"Who?"

"Kyle Donovitch. You know him. Sara had been out with him a few times."

"Oh yeah, the jock. Why do you need to call him?"

"Um, let's see, because he was crazy about Sara, he sent flowers, and offered to help Janet in any way he could."

"He did?" Andrew felt hot shame course through his body. He should have offered to help Janet, sent flowers. "Why didn't you tell me about him?"

"It wasn't that important. Also, I thought it would make you uncomfortable. You're so touchy about guys who play football."

Andrew thought back to the days after the accident, when Kyle had followed him around the school. Andrew had ignored him, rebuffing any attempts at communication. Would Matt or John or Laura have been so unkind? Definitely not. Maybe there was something to this whole God business. But then again, both Sara and Marcia would've handled the situation more gracefully than he did. It wasn't about God, or the absence of God. It was about him, his own failure, his own prejudice and lack of compassion. He felt a sudden headache coming on. He closed his eyes and rubbed his temples. So he was judgmental about athletes. There was so much he didn't know about himself.

"You okay?" Marcia said.

"Yeah. Look, I'll start cleaning this place up while you call Kyle."

Andrew found some garbage bags under the bathroom sink and collected all the trash. He tied off the bags and placed them in a neat pile by the door. Marcia had a brief but emotional conversation with Kyle. Andrew tried to be respectful and not listen in. By the time she got off the phone she was sobbing again. Andrew patted her back and handed her some tissues.

He collected all her clothes and books and threw them into her suitcase. He brushed his teeth and splashed cold water on his face. When he came out of the bathroom, Marcia was still in a heap on the bed.

"Come on. There's nothing more we can do here."

Marcia groaned in response.

"Let's go," he said. "Up and at 'em."

39

"I GOT A STORY FOR YOU," Andrew said to the reporter who was sitting on the porch steps when Andrew pulled into his driveway. He'd dropped Marcia off at her house a few minutes earlier. He was exhausted and emotionally spent.

"Do you now?" the reporter said. It was the same sharp-eyed guy from the day before.

"Once upon a time," Andrew said as he got out of his car and walked toward the house, "a nosy reporter had his ass taken to the local jail for—"

"Looks like she's going to drop it."

"What?" Andrew stopped with his key in the door.

"I said," the reporter said slowly, "it looks like they got her to *fuck off.*" He watched Andrew's face.

"She's not going to get anything? Like, a settlement or something?" Andrew asked.

"Why? Do you think she deserves that?"

Andrew quickly opened the door and shut it behind him. He poured himself a glass of water and drank it in two gulps. He greeted Becky, who immediately responded to his frantic mood by placing her front paws on top of his feet—a strange habit of hers from their childhood. It comforted Andrew. It always had.

What had he said to that guy? What was it, exactly? Something about a settlement? Whatever he'd said, it would be printed somewhere.

There was a knock at the door. He decided to answer it. Maybe he could reason with the reporter, ask him not to print what he had said in exchange for some bogus quote about Brian. But when he opened the door, Laura stood gazing up at him, a smile on her face, his sweatshirt in her arms. With the sun against her back she looked dewy and soft and warm. Then his gaze shifted upward, and he saw the reporter walking toward them.

"Hello, dear," the reporter said to Laura.

Laura turned. She looked uncertainly at Andrew and then back at the reporter. She started to say hello when Andrew grabbed her by the arm, pulled her into the house, and shut the door in one swift motion.

"Who was that?" she asked.

"Reporter. A real dickhead," Andrew said. He sat down heavily on one of the counter stools. It creaked beneath him.

"Here's your sweatshirt." She presented it to him and smiled again.

"How did you get it?" he asked, but he already knew the answer.

"John's gone off on a spiritual retreat. He wanted to make sure it was returned to you."

"What about his job?"

"Oh. I don't know. Maybe he has vacation or something?" Laura said as she sat in the stool next to him. "Karen's going to meet him out there."

"Oh."

Was it his imagination, or had Laura looked at him very sharply when she mentioned Karen's name? Laura laid her arm on the counter. Her hand seemed to reach toward him. She gave him one of her Mona Lisa smiles.

"That's nice," Andrew said. Laura's smile widened.

"John said that you and he had a really nice talk. That you inspired in him the possibility of new faith. Pure faith."

Andrew put his head in his hands. "Do you have any way of getting in touch with him?"

"My dad does, for an emergency. I think he does, anyway. I'm not really sure." Their knees were barely touching. "John's been sad. I'm so glad you were able to help him."

Andrew stared at her hand, golden pink against the scratchy white counter. Her fingertips drummed slowly. *Drum. Drum. Drum.* It was a tune of impatience. What did she want? It was hard to tell with her. He grasped her hand in both of his and brought it to his lips. He kissed each knuckle gently. Then he turned her hand over and kissed the center of her palm. He placed her hand back on the counter. She was radiant, perfect, still, expressionless. As he looked at her, Andrew felt the usual violent urge to grab her and hold her. Becky walked up to him and nudged him.

"I have to take Becky out," he said.

"Let's go for a walk then."

The reporter was still parked in Andrew's driveway.

"Come on," he said as he pulled her toward the living room and opened one of the windows.

After he climbed out, Becky scrambled through and landed deftly in his arms. Then Laura carefully eased her legs astride the ledge. She looked down at him, and he reached up to help her. He held her briefly around the waist as she lowered herself down into the backyard. They giggled. Then he took her hand in his and Becky's leash in the other. They snuck around the side of the house and dashed down the street. They stopped at the next block, panting and laughing as they looked back at the reporter, still waiting outside and clueless that they were gone.

"He's here about your brother?"

"He said it's over. I don't know if I believe him."

"Ask your parents."

Andrew ignored this. They went to the outskirts of their neighborhood at the edge of the park. Andrew took Laura's hand, and they walked into the woods just as the last streetlamp flickered and came on.

"You're not very close with your family, are you?" she said.

"No."

"That's too bad."

"I guess," he said.

"Family is everything."

"Hmm."

"John said that you felt God's presence on the mountaintop, and it frightened you." Laura squeezed his hand. "You don't have to be frightened."

"All right," he said. Andrew barely knew what he was saying. He felt instinctively that Laura would allow him to kiss her, and this was the only thing that concerned him now. He also knew that he could not sustain the charade under which conditions he was permitted that kiss. This was it. This warm soft air, this early-evening sun, this compliant and blissfully ignorant and blissfully beautiful Laura, was a gift. *John's gift,* Andrew thought with a twinge of guilt but also with amusement. Pure faith, new faith, indeed.

Then again, in a way, it did feel pure. The air was warm, and the wind was cool and gentle. They went off the trail and into the grass. Years ago, some wandering hippie had sprinkled Kentucky blue grass seeds all over the park. Most of it didn't survive the Vermont climate. But there were some hidden patches of it that, while not quite flourishing, mixed in with the native grass and looked astounding. Here and there were soft carpets of greenish, bluish, lavender beauty that shimmered in the breeze and barely gave under the weight of your body.

They reached a small field that held a tiny shelter. He tied Becky's leash to one of the shelter's pillars. She curled up in a fading patch of sun and closed her eyes. He watched her for a moment.

Andrew walked slowly back toward Laura. It occurred to him that they had not spoken for quite some time. He felt like he was inside a silent movie: the quiet was alive, more present in the air than anything else. Every cell in his body felt suspended, sepia toned, balanced between dimensions of sensation. It was as if he were experiencing a perfect memory. Stunned by the state he was in, all he could do was move toward her and toward her and toward her. And she, Laura, was poised and still. Waiting. He stopped when he was just a few inches from her.

"You can kiss me if you want," she said.

For a moment he was so startled by her words that he seemed to snap out of a fog. But he pulled her up to him and kissed her anyway. Her lips were warm. Her body was warm. She opened her mouth, and he kissed her deeply. He felt like he was breathing her in or like they shared the same lungs. She tasted very sweet and clean, like flowery soap. He pulled her body closer and kissed her more forcefully. He was aroused but knew there was nothing doing there. He could kiss her all he wanted. That was it. They kissed and kissed and kissed. It grew cooler as their bodies grew warmer. They lay down in the grass, and Andrew spent what felt like hours sucking on her neck and the maddening hollows of her collarbone. But when he tried to touch her breasts, his hands were promptly redirected.

"Sorry."

"It's all right," she said.

She was panting when she spoke, and Andrew felt like he might go crazy. As with Karen, the taste of her was what amazed him the most. Laura didn't taste musty and piney and hot. She was sweet, like sugary candy. Eventually their kissing slowed. They had been lying on their sides. Andrew tried to crawl on top of her, but Laura playfully pushed his chest so that he lay on his back.

"I love you," he said.

There was a long pause. Andrew held his breath.

"I've got to head home," she said.

"Okay."

"I'm going to evening service."

"Okay."

"Want to come?"

"Yes."

"Really?" she said. Andrew was surprised by the tone of her voice. She sounded ironic, sarcastic even. She drew out the word *really* as if it had ten syllables.

Andrew heard Becky yawn, stand up, and stretch. His groin ached, but the pain in his chest was even worse.

"You know why I'm here," Andrew said finally. "Why are you here?"

Laura stood up. "Let's go," she said.

Andrew got Becky, and they walked back out of the woods and into their neighborhood. They no longer held hands. Andrew felt weak, as if all his organs were leaking some precious force that had kept them going. The sidewalks seemed to rear up to meet him.

"You know," Laura said, "at the very least, you really ought to try with your brother."

"At the very least? What does that mean?"

Laura sniffed.

"I don't give a shit about my brother."

"That's not right."

They were standing outside her house now, gazing angrily at each other. Or at least Andrew was angry. Laura looked indifferent.

"God gave you a family, Andrew. They're your responsibility." She turned and walked up the steps. Andrew had to clench his jaw to keep from crying out. But then he didn't know what he'd say, either. *Don't go? Screw you?* Her hand was on the doorknob. She was opening the door.

"Why did you give me that note?"

She stopped and turned halfway around. "What?"

"That day you gave me the note. We'd barely spoken before that. Was it because of Sara? Did you think I would be, like, easy to convert or something? Or did you actually care about me? Or Sara, for that matter? She's gone, you know." His voice choked as he spoke. He'd pushed Sara's death out of his mind, and telling Laura was like experiencing it all over again.

Laura closed her eyes and said a quick prayer. Then she came down the steps.

"I'm sorry about Sara. Truly. And to answer your question, I called you because my group believes in helping those in need."

"Me, in need? Seriously? I'm not poor. I'm not oppressed, I'm not—"

"*Spiritual* need, Andrew. My group—"

"Stop talking about your fucking group. You guys hover around tragedy like a bunch of vultures, hoping to get vulnerable people into your church. People like John."

"You don't know anything about John," she snapped.

"*You* don't know anything about John."

"Well, you don't know anything about me," she said.

"I—"

"Seriously, Andrew. What do you know about me? About my life, my family, my feelings, my God?"

She's right, Andrew thought. He was shocked at his own ignorance. He'd spent three years following her around, and he didn't even know the name of her faith. He'd never asked her about her family, never really asked her about herself. He'd just brooded and lurked and stared and stalked.

"You were always hanging around. In school, I mean. I would see you everywhere," Laura said.

Andrew blushed. Well, what had he expected?

"All the guys hang around you," he said. "You know that, don't you?"

"You were different," she said.

Even though he was angry with her, and himself, Andrew felt immensely gratified by her words. He was different. That was something. "Am I still different?"

"What do you mean?"

"Would you give me another chance?"

A long, long moment passed between them. *Time slowing down,* he thought. He held his breath. Laura looked at the ground and then very slightly shook her head. A curtain of her honey-colored hair fell over her face. He gently touched a loose strand with the tip of his finger. She either didn't notice or pretended not to notice. He could've asked her why she kissed him, or had allowed him to kiss her, but he already knew the answer. He'd done the same thing to John, probably for the same reasons.

"Fine," he said.

She turned around and walked back up the steps.

"Laura."

She stopped.

"Listen to me. I have to get in touch with John," he said. "Can I have that number?"

She looked surprised. "It's for emergencies."

"I need it," he said.

"I think it's in my dad's study, but I'm not sure." Her voice was completely calm. Calm and a little snotty.

"I'll wait."

He stared at the stars. He'd had her and lost her again. Maybe he could reason with her? Try some other approach? He felt neutered. *I should be more forceful,* he thought. *I ought to man up and take control.* He made involuntary fists with his hands, but within moments they were loose and by his sides. It just wasn't in him; it wasn't meant to be. Becky licked his dangling fingers. After a few minutes another of Laura's pig-faced siblings, a small boy this time, emerged from the house.

"That's for you," the boy said, handing Andrew a slip of paper.

He looked down at the paper on which a phone number was neatly written. He turned the paper over. There was nothing else.

40

WHEN ANDREW GOT HOME, he fed Becky and poured himself a glass of water. His mouth was dry after all the kissing. He felt, all at once, elated, deflated, and numb. All the fantasies he'd ever had about Laura seemed to be imploding in his brain. His girlfriend, his wife, his sexual conquest? What had he been thinking? He'd never had a chance, not with any of it. It was time to focus on someone he could actually do something about.

He nibbled on a piece of bread and stared at the phone number. He picked up the phone, started to dial, and then abruptly hung up. He paced the kitchen, weighing options that he couldn't coherently express, even to himself. He looked at Becky, who met his hard gaze with her own soft stare. He grabbed the phone and dialed the number again. It rang for almost a minute before a man with a familiar voice picked up. Where had he heard that voice before?

"I need to get in touch with John. It's an emergency," Andrew said.

"What's the emergency?"

"It's personal."

"He's halfway up to the cabin by now."

"You don't have walkie-talkies or something?"

"Reception doesn't reach. What was your name again?" The voice was growing stern and authoritative, paternal in an asshole kind of way. *Who is this creep?* Andrew thought. *And what does he know about John?*

"Okay, it's not a life-threatening emergency. When will I be able to reach him?"

"You can only reach him if it's an emergency. How did you get this number?"

"Chip?"

"Excuse me?"

"This is Chip, isn't it?"

There was a long silence followed by a deep sigh. Andrew knew he was right. It was Chip on the other line, the shifty balding youth pastor with the wavering faith.

"You're the new kid, right?" Chip said.

Andrew had never understood the phrase "It makes my blood boil" until this moment. He was nobody's goddamn new kid.

"My name is Andrew. John is my friend. I need to speak to

him, or at the very least I need a message relayed to him. *Now.*"

"That's not how this program works, friend."

Program? Andrew thought, and he felt an awful quiver of fear in his gut. He also felt uneasy for Karen. *Karen's going to meet him out there,* Laura had said. What for? Andrew fought to control his voice.

"I'm not your friend. Get a message to John or . . . or I'll tell your boss that you've got some kind of fucked-up relationship with the youth study group."

"What did you say to me? You little—"

"I'm not going to argue with you about this." Andrew's voice shook. "Tell John I called. Tell him I said—I said that everything is okay with him. That it's totally okay. Tell him I'm his friend. That I'm sorry about the other night. That it was all my fault. And tell him he's okay, just as he is."

"Fine," Chip said.

"John is going to get that message," Andrew said. "Tonight," he added.

"All right!" Chip said. Then he hung up.

Andrew stared at the phone for a few minutes.

"What was that about, faggot? Your boyfriend?"

Andrew turned to the sound of Brian's voice. As in a horror movie, he emerged from the shadows. His walk was unsteady and his eyes were bloodshot.

"You're wasted," Andrew said.

"Who's John?" Brian said.

"My friend."

"I thought you only hung out with girls, momo."

"What do you want?"

"Nothing, man, nothing," Brian said. His words slurred. "She dropped it."

"I heard."

"No case. No case at all. And her lawyer? Sheesh . . ." Brian's voice trailed off into a very wet burp. Andrew felt his own stomach lurch.

"Where are Mom and Dad?"

"Fuck should I know? Out celebrating?"

"Or working overtime to pay your legal fees," Andrew muttered.

"You want to know what happened that night?"

Andrew thought for a moment. "No," he said.

"I haven't told anyone. Not supposed to. Not even the lawyer knows everything. He was all like, 'The less I know, the better.'"

"I don't want to—" Andrew began.

"Shut up and let me talk. I know you think, everyone fucking thinks, that I could do something like that. I'm telling you, bro: it didn't happen. I was playing beer pong for, like, six hours. Strip beer pong, but not with her. I mean, she could've been with these two guys, and one of them is kind of a dick, but I don't know."

"You don't know what happened? You literally can't recall that night? What you did and . . . what you didn't do?"

Brian nodded. At first it seemed like he was nodding yes, then no, then yes again. Andrew looked away.

"My girlfriend dumped me," he finally said.

"So you'll get another one."

"Fuck you!"

"Fuck me? Fuck me?" Andrew shouted. "Are you kidding me?"

"I know what you think of me! I know!" Brian started to weep.

Andrew's own eyes were wet. "I don't know what you want from me, Bri. You're a mess."

Neither of them said anything for a few moments. Andrew listened as Brian tried to calm down and stop crying.

"I got rough with this girl once in high school," Brian said.

"Cynthia?"

"Yeah. How did you know?"

Andrew thought back to the myriad of Brian's girlfriends. Pretty girls who came by the house, tried and failed to please their mother, and eventually drifted and morphed into other pretty girls. Some of them chatted vaguely with Andrew. Cynthia had always been nice to Becky. "She liked dogs," Andrew said.

"What?"

"Nothing. Never mind."

"Cyn got all skinny and shit after we broke up."

"I remember."

"Maybe I deserve this," Brian said.

Andrew bristled. "Deserve what, exactly? So people are suspicious of you. Treat you badly? Like you're a loser or something? How many people have *you* treated like that?"

"Don't be an asshole. You don't understand."

"I never will."

"Look, I'm sorry I wasn't a better brother to you."

"Whatever."

"And I'm sorry about Dad."

Andrew said nothing.

"I should've done something about that."

"It only happened a few times."

Brian looked at his feet. "The other night was the worst," he said.

"What are you talking about?"

"When Dad slugged you?"

Andrew swallowed and licked his dry lips. "I thought that was you," he said.

"I know." Brian leaned against the wall and slid down. "I know what you all think of me," he said. He closed his eyes. Saliva bubbled onto his mouth. His grip loosened on the beer can he'd been clutching.

Andrew watched Brian for a long time. His huge strong body was slumped over and still. He looked like a sleeping giant, which in a way he was. Andrew went to him and took the beer can out of his hand. He hesitated a moment, then tilted his neck and drained what was left. He placed his hand gently on Brian's forehead.

Then he closed his eyes and prayed for his brother.

41

SUMMER WAS OVER. JANET HAD taken Sara's ashes and buried them in her garden. It had been a simple ceremony. Andrew had recited the Lord's Prayer, which Janet had seemed to appreciate. When they'd left the house, he'd run back inside and given her his Bible. She'd been touched, perhaps even a little amused. She'd given him her old smile, her wry Janet smile.

He and Matt occasionally hung out. They never discussed Laura or Karen, or even Jesus for that matter. John had not returned Andrew's many phone calls, although Andrew had managed to get out of Matt that John had packed up and left town to do some hiking in Colorado. "He's on his own journey now," Matt said. Andrew hoped that that was a good thing.

He and Matt went bowling with Marcia, went out for pizza, saw a movie every now and then. They went on a disastrous fishing trip in which Matt ended up in the ER with a hook in his pinky. It had been more funny than scary. "You know what?" Matt had said to him after a tetanus shot, pain medication, and minor surgery. "You're my first secular friend." Andrew had laughed.

He told the story to Marcia a few days later.

"So you're an atheist again? Welcome back to the fold."

"I don't know what I am," Andrew said. "Maybe agnostic."

"Is that why you prayed at Janet's house? For Sara?"

"For Janet," he said. "I think—I think religion is for the living."

"Whatever," she said.

His car crept up the mountain to Avella. It was midnight, but Neal's security guard friend waved them through. Becky woofed hello. She'd become the unofficial mascot of the maintenance and security branches at Avella. Neal and Ben were going to take her in during Andrew's first year at college, when he was required to live in the dorms and couldn't have a dog.

"You sure you want to do this?" Marcia said.

"Why not?" he said.

They parked the car by Neal's office and walked across the perfectly mown lawn.

"It's beautiful," Marcia said.

"I know."

"Like the stately gardens of some nineteenth-century baron. Maybe we shouldn't be here."

"It's fine, Mar," he said.

They reached the pond. It was more like a miniature lake. They had put the finishing touches on it only the week before. It wasn't deep, but you could definitely submerge yourself. Andrew tied Becky to a bike rack. He and Marcia slipped off their clothes. Both had bathing suits on. Marcia's one-piece was the same one she'd been wearing for three summers. It was threadbare, and the straps dug into her back. She shivered. They stepped in.

"Holy mother of God, it's cold," Marcia said. They pumped their arms and legs in an attempt to warm up.

"I envy Brian right now: he's always hot," Andrew said, his teeth chattering. Brian had left for preseason training shortly after the charges were dropped. The not-really-speaking routine had resumed between them, but something small had changed. The aggression between them had dulled, and Brian seemed more subdued in general. Andrew didn't like to think about Brian too much; he was still a strong dark shadow, a furnace, a force of nature that could go in many directions. Andrew was still frightened of him, and for him.

"Then he must never be comfortable," Marcia said.

"Maybe not," Andrew said.

They swam around each other. The water rippled and softly lapped his body. The water started to feel warmer, or at least less uncomfortable.

"Do you have it?" Andrew said.

Marcia opened her palm. She held a tiny golden box, a relic

of her time in Korea. Inside the box was a bit of Sara's ashes. He covered her hand with his and closed his eyes. From memory he recited Psalm 23.

"That's nice," Marcia said when he finished. "Something you learned from your born-again girlfriend?"

"It's from the Psalms. And they're not born-again."

"Was she ever your girlfriend?"

"Out of my league. She's a different species. She's on a different plane of existence."

"I can relate."

"I know you can."

"Well, I think—"

"Marcia," he interrupted. He knew she was nervous, babbling, stalling for time. He reached out with his free hand. Marcia reached back. They were silent. Quiet tears rolled down Marcia's face. His, too, he realized, as he felt the hot wetness gather in his collarbones.

They lowered their hands together and released the little golden box.

"Bye, Sara," Marcia said. Her voice was a whisper, a ripple on the water.

The only light came from the stars and moon. It grew dim and bright, dim and bright, as the clouds shifted in the night sky. They were still and silent, lost in their separate thoughts. Marcia shivered. Then she giggled; she actually giggled. It was the first time he'd heard her laugh since Sara had died.

"What?" he said, smiling at her.

"Nothing, it's stupid," she said.

"Tell me."

She looked at him slyly, a little like Sara.

"I was just thinking about you and those Christian kids. I mean, at least you got some action this summer."

"Care to round out my triumph?"

"Oh, go to hell, Drew," she said, and they laughed together.

Acknowledgments

I would like to gratefully acknowledge the following people:

My agent, Esmond Harmsworth. Thank you for your graceful advice and guidance.

All the wonderful people at Viking Children's. Kenneth Wright (I can never thank you enough. But here goes, thank you for giving me a chance, understanding my book, and setting me off in the right direction). My brilliant editors: the incisive Regina Hayes and the indispensable Alexander Ulyett. Thanks also to cover designer Maggie Olson, interior designer Jim Hoover, copy editor Kaitlin Severini, production editors Janet Pascal and Abigail Powers, and my publicist Bridget Hartzler.

All my teachers, especially Diane Les Becquets (for so many things, the least of which is aligning the stars), Richard Adams Carey, Merle Drown, Craig Childs, Ellen Schmidt, William Vesterman, Kerrin McCadden, John Bate, and Judith Chalmer.

Walead Esmail, for your lovely poem.

Jomo Omari Edwards, Lisa Chan, Sam J. Miller, Robert Greene, and Rebecca Mahoney. Thank you for reading my book (or listening to me read my book) in its many, many iterations, and for offering great criticism and insight.

Laura Vogel, Amanda Dunham, and Jamie Ann Brassill, for your excellent babysitting skills. Without you ladies this novel would have never been finished!

Jenevieve Johnson of the Jenny Wren Café. Thank you for your sandwiches, hospitality, and fascism-destroying brownies.

Sierra and Brandy, for Springfield. Love you ladies.

Peggy and Steve, thanks for being such wonderful people.

Extra special thanks to Lisa Chan, for more things than I can list.

Kevin, you're the best big brother in the world. As of this writing I owe you the Buddha card.

My parents, Roger and Chandrakala, my first and finest teachers.

Steve and Autumn, loves of my life.

PRATIMA CRANSE

was born and raised in Vermont. She now lives in New Hampshire with her husband, daughter, and their two magnificent cats. When she's not writing, Pratima enjoys jogging very slowly (some might call it shuffling) and spending time with her family.